# A CIRCLE OF MOONLIGHT

# CURTIS EDMONDS

**Scary Hippopotamus Books**
**Trenton, NJ**
**http://www.scaryhippopotamus.com**

# ALSO BY THIS AUTHOR

## A Circle of Firelight

## Wreathed

## Rain on Your Wedding Day

For herein may be seen noble chivalry, courtesy, humanity, friendliness, hardiness, love, friendship, cowardice, murder, hate, virtue, and sin. Do after the good and leave the evil, and it shall bring you to good fame and renown. And for to pass the time this book shall be pleasant to read in, but for to give faith and belief that all is true that is contained herein, ye be at your liberty: but all is written for our doctrine, and for to beware that we fall not to vice nor sin, but to exercise and follow virtue, by which we may come and attain to good fame and renown in this life, and after this short and transitory life to come unto everlasting bliss in heaven; the which He grant us that reigneth in heaven, the blessed Trinity. Amen.

— William Caxton, Preface to *Le Morte d'Arthur*, by Sir Thomas Malory (1485)

FOR MY FATHER

# If Only In My Dreams

**Ashlyn | Christmas Eve | West Orange, New Jersey**

"I suppose I shouldn't ask you about your holiday," Dr. Lindbergh says.

I lean forward in my wheelchair and give the doctor my best glare. I can't think of a withering reply, which is just as well. Four months after my brain injury, I still struggle with my speech; I worry that whatever I say might not come out right. I know the glare will work.

Lindbergh rolls his eyes behind his thick glasses. "Ashlyn, come on. You know I am not the one keeping you from being home for Christmas."

I have not been home since August, when my car was pancaked by a glazier's van in New Brunswick. After a month-long hospital stay, I transferred to the rehabilitation hospital in East Orange. I was supposed to make my first trip home today—but my younger sister Penny came down with a serious respiratory infection in early December. Penny has cystic fibrosis, a debilitating lung disease, and what would be a couple of days in bed for most people means three weeks in Children's Hospital of Philadelphia for her. This infection was so bad that they installed a catheter in her chest, the better to deliver antibiotics.

The doctors did their job; my parents brought Penny home earlier this week. Another infection might be more serious, or even kill her. As I am somewhere where I might encounter all sorts of exotic germs, my parents asked me to stay at the rehab hospital and not come home for Christmas.

My mother drove up this morning and gave me my presents; my dad and my brothers are coming up the day after Christmas to hang out. I'm not going to see Penny at all, except through FaceTime. She was in the back seat when I had my accident; she had a mild concussion but that was it. My mother arranged for Penny and me to take the same therapeutic riding class six weeks ago, but I haven't seen her since.

It is not Dr. Lindbergh's fault that I will not go home today, and I know it's not fair to blame him for that. But it is completely fair for me to be unhappy with him for keeping me from walking, which is totally his fault.

"Want to walk," I say. I have both aphasia and apraxia as a result of the brain injury; despite four months of speech therapy I still sound like a cranky toddler at times. "Ready to start."

"Ashlyn, we've been over this," he explains. "You need three things to be able to walk. First is balance; if you don't have that you'll fall over. Second is support. Your legs should be strong enough to keep you upright. Third is the actual motion of walking. All three of these things work together—they reinforce each other."

I make the circular motion with my hand that means *yeah, yeah, go on.*

"You have done well in PT. Your leg muscles are much stronger. But the brain injury may have affected your sense of balance, and that in turn influences how well you can perform the motion of walking. Until we know for sure how well you can balance, we can't risk having you walk independently. There's a good chance you might fall, and that would set back your recovery."

"Don't want to f-fall," I say.

"Of course not. The best way to make sure you don't fall is to give you something to lean on— parallel bars, or crutches, or a walker. All of that, though, is contraindicated by the wrist injury. The wrist hasn't healed to the point where I am comfortable with you putting any weight on it. Until that happens, I don't see you walking anytime soon."

I intensify my glare at Dr. Lindbergh. He is not a bad doctor. He is young, with an untidy mop of curly, red hair, and thick glasses with thin gold frames. There's half a hospital-cafeteria sandwich on his desk, and what I think is a glob of Thousand Island dressing on the front of his white lab coat.

"Want to try," I say. I had set a goal for myself; I wanted to be able to walk by Christmas, at least a few steps. I am not there yet; I am still in my wheelchair. But I feel strong enough to try, and I am frustrated that Lindbergh doesn't agree.

"Look, Ashlyn," he says. "You've been working hard to build your load-bearing capacity, and you're almost there. Your left wrist, though, still isn't at a hundred percent. We've had this conversation; you'll need permanent screw to stabilize the wrist bones. That's causing some of the pain; the loose bone fragments are causing the rest of it. A surgeon can go in and clean them all out."

"Walking is more important," I say, tripping over the sibilant in *is*. I would omit the verb, but I am tired of sounding like Ashlyn Revere, Unfrozen Cavewoman.

"I understand that. I respect that. Additional surgery will set back your rehab, no doubt about it. Having said that, your left wrist isn't getting any better, and you're overworking the right wrist to compensate—and that wrist had prior damage of its own."

"I know." I had jammed my right wrist months before the car crash, when I had tried to punch a hole in a cinder-block wall after losing a field hockey game. Not my finest moment.

"What worries me is that once we give you a walker, you could lean on it hard enough to cause pain in those wrists, and that could lead to a fall. The wrist surgery will set you back two or three weeks. A fall with broken bones will set you back two or three months. It's not a risk I want to see you take."

Dr. Lindbergh is right, and I know he's right, and that makes it worse. It would be easier if he were wrong. It would also be easier if I didn't feel the nagging soreness in my wrist, like mismatched gears grinding against each other.

Lindbergh runs his stubby fingers through his hair. "There is one other option, though. I think we can get you on a treadmill, if we put you in an upper-body harness and attach that to a lift."

I turn down my withering glare a notch, and try to visualize how it would work.

"We use the lift to support your body weight, then we maneuver you onto a treadmill. With me so far? You can walk as much as you can manage, however slow or fast as you like. With the harness holding you up, you can't fall. As you build up muscle strength, we reduce the tension on the lift. Before too much longer, you ought to be able to use the treadmill independently. Then you'd be ready to walk normally."

"When? Now?"

"Not right now. Too many people off for the holiday. Soon, maybe? Day after tomorrow? What do you think? Will that make your holiday season brighter?"

No, it won't. I will still be alone, without my family—outside brief visits and FaceTime calls. I will still be injured, scarred, and vulnerable. I will still be struggling with my speech, and my memory loss, and my fine motor skills. I will only be one step closer to what I want, which is to have my independence back.

As long as that's a step I can take on my own, I'm all for it.

"Deal," I say to Dr. Lindbergh, and stretch out my hand for a fist-bump.

"Deal," he says. "Merry Christmas to you, Ashlyn."

"M-m-merry Christmas, Doctor."

## JENNIFER | CHRISTMAS MORNING | RESIDENCE INN, HENDERSON, NEVADA

It is six in the morning in Nevada, but my body clock is still set on Chapel Hill time. I knew when I got up that I would not be able to go back to sleep, so I came downstairs to catch up on homework and check out the breakfast spread in the hotel lobby. It has not disappointed so far. I am sipping cranberry juice and clearing croissant crumbs off my copy of *Biochemistry and Nutrition for Nurses.*

"How are you so tall?" a small voice asks.

I look up from my textbook and see a little girl, maybe four years old, in a soft wooly coat. Her mother—or I assume that's who she is—is sitting in the back of the lobby, typing impatiently on a laptop, without so much as a glance at her daughter.

"I drank all my juice when I was your age," I tell her. "My mother is a dietician—do you know what that is? She helps people learn what they should eat, and she always served us healthy food. That helped me grow tall." Six feet, one and a quarter inches, to be exact.

"I don't like the purple juice. I like the orange better."

"That's good for you, too, as long as you don't drink too much of it. Are you having a good Christmas?"

"We're leaving to see my Nana here in a minute. Mommy says that Santa Claus brought all the toys there this year."

"Well, I hope you get something nice in your stocking," I say. "What's your name?"

"Angelica. What's yours?"

"My name is Jennifer. Jennifer Lamb. Nice to meet you, Angelica."

"Shouldn't you be with your parents?" the child asks.

*You ought to be with yours,* I think. Her mother is still typing away. "They're back home, in North Carolina. They will see me on television, though. I'm playing in a basketball game later today."

Angelica's mother closes her laptop with a decisive *crack* and walks over to collect her. "Sorry if my daughter was bothering you," she says.

"She's fine," I say. "Don't worry. I need something to distract me from all this reading."

Angelica's mother is tall, with sharp features and artfully teased hair. "Did I hear you say you play basketball?"

"You did. University of North Carolina. Pre-season tournament; we're playing Marquette at two-thirty."

"That's great. I played backup point guard in school. Arizona State. We made it to the Sweet Sixteen my junior year. It was an awesome experience."

"We went out early last year," I say. "Beat Rice in the first round, lost to Gonzaga."

"Well, good luck to you, then," she says. "Come on Angelica. Let's go see Nana."

After they leave, I get up from the table, stretch, and then walk over to the counter to get another croissant.

Even though it's a chilly morning, the hotel has the air conditioner turned up to teeth-chattering levels. I consider running up to the room to get a jacket, but I decide to pour myself some hot tea instead.

I am halfway through the third chapter of the biochemistry textbook when I look up to see Coach Morgan sliding into the chair opposite me.

"Good morning," she says. She is uncharacteristically sloppy in a tattered pale-blue sweatshirt, and is cradling a paper cup of coffee. "Getting in some classwork, I see."

"Trying to get a head start for next semester," I explain.

She nods approvingly. "I thought I would get up early and walk a few miles on the treadmill, but I decided I needed coffee first. I saw you here, by yourself, and I thought I would say hello."

"Hello."

Coach fiddles with the brown cardboard sleeve on her cup. "I have to tell you something, Jennifer, and I figure now is as good a time as any."

"What is it, Coach?"

I flash through the last month or so of practice, mentally reviewing my performance. *What have I been doing wrong?*

"This is important. You're my rock on this team, Jennifer. You are the one player I can count on. You're the most dependable player I've ever coached. I am so proud of what you have accomplished. I trust you out there, and believe me when I tell you that I wouldn't trade having you on the team for anyone else in the conference."

"Thank you, Coach."

"Which it's why it's hard for me to tell you that I'm starting Unique at power forward today."

If she had slapped me in the face, it wouldn't have hurt any less.

"You've worked so hard, Jennifer. You deserve every opportunity I can give you, but I have to think about the team, too. Unique—well, you've gone against her in practice. You know what she can do with the ball in her hand. She had a rocky freshman year, but all she's done in practice is light it up, and we need points however we can get them."

I want to say something, anything, but when she puts it all together, it's obvious. Unique Templeton is an inch smaller and about fifteen pounds lighter than I am, but that makes her a half-step quicker. She has a soft fall-away jump shot that she can drain from anywhere on the court. I'm a better defender, no question, but Unique is a legitimate scoring threat.

I never thought she was good enough to take my job, but now she has.

Coach tilts her head to the left. I know she is waiting for me to say something, trying to anticipate which way I will jump. If I am going to shout—if I am going to cry—she would rather it happen here, in this deserted early-morning hotel lobby. Not in front of the team, because the team comes first.

*You're my rock*, she said. Rocks don't whine. Rocks don't complain. Rocks endure.

"What Unique will need," I say, "more than anything else, is a good working relationship with Monica. Monica has a hard time finding the happy medium on the court. If she has the hot hand, she gets overconfident and starts taking risks. If she goes cold, she gets tentative and slow. I know how to help her find the right rhythm; if Unique can do that, she'll be golden."

"What would keep Unique from being able to do that?" Her voice is soft, almost collegial.

"It's about expectations. If you expect Unique to score, and score big, she will put less emphasis on being a good teammate and working with Monica. It won't work unless they feed off each other, both trying to get the ball to the open teammate. If they're competing against each other for the ball, you're setting them both up to fail. They need to learn to be unselfish."

"I know. That's how you've played your entire career, unselfishly. I am asking you to do that one more time, Jennifer. For the team."

I bite back my tears, because rocks don't cry. "My parents are watching today," I say. "The whole family will be coming over for Christmas, and they'll have the TV on, expecting to see me play. I don't think I'm being selfish, telling you that."

Coach nods a fraction, and comes close to smiling. "I understand, Six. Don't worry. You're still a part of this team. You'll get your fair share of minutes. You've earned that, maybe more than you know. If you'll excuse me, it's time for me to get up on that treadmill."

"Okay, Coach."

"Thank you, Jennifer. Thank you for understanding. I hope we can make it work."

"We'll see," I say, and that's all I can say. Maybe she wants me to say thank you, maybe she wants me to slobber all over myself in self-pity. I can't do either.

I am a rock. Rocks don't react. Rocks don't feel pain.

But rocks can crumble.

If you hit them hard enough, rocks can break.

**PENNY | CHRISTMAS DAY | MONTGOMERY, NEW JERSEY**

"Jason, you can't take that deal," I say.

"You can't tell me what to do, Penny," he says.

"Yeah, you can't tell him what to do," his twin brother Ray chimes in.

"You be quiet. Ray wants Park Place. All he's offering is Connecticut Avenue."

"I need Connecticut Avenue," Jason says.

"He needs Park Place, and he has, maybe fifteen hundred dollars over there, and he can use that to blow us both out of the water if we land on those properties."

My brothers are now old enough to get the rules of Monopoly, but not old enough to evaluate a good deal or a bad deal. Unless I am wrong about that. Ray is the competitive one. Jason is the smart one, the one who is devious—or he would be if he weren't as easy to read as a Dan Brown potboiler.

"Wait a second," I say. "You're letting him win."

"No, I'm not," Jason says.

"Penny, let him do what he wants to do," Ray says.

"Okay. Maybe you don't want Ray to win. Maybe you don't care who wins. Maybe you're bored, and you want us to keep playing so you can sneak off and play *Fortnite*."

Jason makes a face at me. "You are officially my least-favorite sister right now."

"Call Ashlyn and tell her. I'm sure she'll be thrilled to hear that."

"I already talked to her. She says she wishes she could come home."

"I wish that too," I say, and I do. I've been home from the hospital four days, and it feels like I was gone for a month—but Ashlyn's been gone longer than that. She and I were in a car wreck last summer; a glazier's van somehow flew into the air and crash-landed on top of my mother's old Volvo. I got off with some cuts, scrapes, and a low-grade concussion. Ashlyn got a broken wrist, a broken leg, and a broken skull—and she almost died in the operating room when a jagged piece of rib bone came an inch from poking her in the heart. After that, she almost died when she had surgery to remove the pressure from a blood clot on her brain. She has been stuck in a rehab hospital ever since, busy trying to learn how to walk and talk again, while I have been sitting around the house waiting for word from my pulmonologist about my lung transplant.

Because of my most recent hospitalization, I have a shiny new piece of medical equipment lodged in my actual body; a catheter that delivers my antibiotic regimen straight into my bloodstream without having to swallow a million actual pills. This is not quite an improvement, but it helped me get home in time to spend Christmas Day with my family.

Except for Ashlyn.

I can either be sad for her or happy for me, and given that choice, I'll take happy.

"Okay. You kids put Monopoly away. I'll go warm up the PlayStation. Deal?" I say.

"That means I win, right?" Ray asks.

"It means you get to hear me laugh at your weak *Fortnite* skills. Hurry up."

My father is sound asleep in his recliner, the remote control in his hand. I try to sneak it out carefully, like Indiana Jones trying to winkle a golden idol from a hidden altar. I do not succeed, and his eyes open halfway. "Yes?"

"We wanted to play *Fortnite* on the PlayStation. Sorry to wake you up."

"I wasn't asleep."

"You were snoring. How did the Jets do?"

"They were down three touchdowns at halftime. I switched to ESPN."

I look at the screen; it's showing a women's basketball game.

"North Carolina playing Marquette. I think."

"Then you won't mind us switching to a video game."

"Not very Christmas-y, is it? Violent video games?"

I snort at this. "You watched *Die Hard* last night, that's as violent."

"It's a Christmas movie."

"Be that as it may. You can go back to sleep; they'll be..."

I stop, because I can't see my dad in his recliner, it's all a blur.

"What is it, Penny? Are you okay?"

I am not okay, not one bit okay, and I have no idea why. I start coughing—no big surprise there, but it *hurts* for some reason. I have a high pain threshold and this hurts worse than anything I've ever felt. I fall to one knee in the deep pile carpet.

"You're turning blue." He doesn't sound sleepy anymore.

I stop myself from coughing and suck in air. There is a deep pain in my chest, like an icepick to the heart. All I can see is the beige blur of the carpet.

"My name is Dennis Revere. I'm calling for my daughter." There is an edge of panic in his voice that worries me almost more than the pain. "She was fine a second ago, and now she looks like maybe she's having a heart attack."

*Heart attack?* I have not lived seventeen years with cystic fibrosis to die of a heart attack. I don't know what's wrong with me but your heart stops in a heart attack; mine is pounding a mile a minute, each beat sending hot spikes of pain through my system.

"She's still breathing—she has trouble breathing, she has cystic fibrosis—but she hasn't stopped. Something's definitely wrong."

I am down on all fours now, panting with effort, my fingers clenching and unclenching in the deep pile of the carpet. I will not die today. I will not ruin Christmas Present and all the Christmas Futures by dying. I am determined to stay alive, although I have no idea how to do that other than to keep breathing. I cough some more, thick fluid dripping from my mouth.

"What happened?" my mother asks, on the fringe of my consciousness.

"No idea. I'm on with 9-1-1. Call Dr. Morton."

I am still breathing, with deep, shuddering sobs. The pain has a metallic edge to it, hard and bitter, and it is not subsiding one little bit.

"Morton says have her sit up, see if that helps."

*That's brilliant.* Sit up, that's the best he can come up with? If this doesn't kill me, I am writing a strongly worded letter to the Pennsylvania medical authorities.

My parents lift me up off all fours and deposit me on the couch. I can feel the pain subside slightly. My breathing is slow and ragged, but I am moving air in and out. Dad hands me an oxygen mask, and the cool air takes the edge off my panic.

"I guess this means we're not playing *Fortnite*," Ray says.

"Go upstairs, you two," Mom says, at the border of my consciousness. "Change into something warm.

Hurry. Morton thinks it's an air embolism, from the central line. Dangerous but treatable. We need to leave right away for the hospital."

"Tell... Morton... he can... go to..."

"Penny. Language. We're going to the hospital. It will all be okay. You understand? You're all right. Hold out a while longer."

"Sorry," I say. "Ruining. Christmas."

"It's okay, sweetheart. Just keep breathing. That's all I'm asking right now."

# Recovery

**Ashlyn | December 26 | West Orange, New Jersey**

"Sorry we're running so late," my dad says. "I had to bring these two hooligans, and they wouldn't come until I promised to get them donuts."

"Apple fritters," Ray says.

"With chocolate milk," Jason replies.

"So now they're all hyped up on sugar. I need to find a park somewhere on the way home so they can run around before it seriously starts snowing."

I am pleased to see my younger brothers, but I am not sure why Dad felt he had to bring them here. I would say something, but my mouth is full of McDonald's sausage biscuit.

"Are you sleeping all right?" Dad asks.

"Fine," I say. The one thing I have gained from the brain injury is the ability—usually—to go to sleep when my head hits the pillow. That, and the lucid dreams that I've had about my own private fantasy world, the Realm of Summervale, ever since the accident. I haven't told anyone about Summervale, except for Penny—who rescued me in the middle of the direst of the dreams, right after my brain surgery. I mean, how do you explain your dreams to your parents?

"That's why I didn't call last night; I didn't want to wake you up and worry you. Penny is in the hospital again, down in Philly. Not CHOP this time, the actual Penn hospital."

I say something that sounds like *infection?* around the mouthful of biscuit.

"Not quite. You remember; the infection last time was so bad that they put in a catheter to help direct the antibiotics where they needed to go. They didn't install the catheter correctly, though, and that led to an air bubble getting into her system. Last night, it got lodged in her heart."

"Okay?" I ask.

"We think so. Your mother called Dr. Morton, and he thought it was an embolism, and he was right. The treatment for that is to put her in a hyperbaric chamber overnight, to let the bubble dissolve. We drove her down to Penn; couldn't wait for the ambulance. They should be letting her out any minute now."

"S-scary," I say.

He resettles his glasses back on the bridge of his nose. "We were lucky. The bubble stayed in her heart and didn't go to her brain. Scared us both halfway to death. As bad as I feel that you had a lousy holiday, believe me, we all had a worse one."

I unwrap my second biscuit. "How long?" I ask.

"How long will she be in the hospital? They'll keep her tonight for observation, I think, and then home tomorrow, but she'll definitely be okay. They wouldn't let her take her phone or her Kindle into the chamber, and she was furious. At least she has her priorities straight."

I reach out and take his hand. This isn't fair for him, isn't fair for Mom, to deal with two daughters with medical issues. It isn't anyone's fault that we are—genetics in Penny's case, a moment of carelessness by another driver in mine—but it has hurt them, and I don't have any way to keep it from hurting them other than getting better.

"Dr. Lindbergh says they will try you on the treadmill soon."

"First s-steps," I say. "I can't wait."

The treadmill is fun for about five minutes, until it turns into work. I make a note to bring my iPad for the next session so I can have something to read. I have sort of an unpaid internship with a publishing company, so it's a good use of my time. The treadmill is set on the lowest speed level, without any incline, but that doesn't bother me. Dr. Lindbergh doesn't want me to push it, so I won't, at least not yet. For now, it's enough to be upright and doing something that feels close to walking, feeling the familiar rhythm of my feet once again, enjoying the trickle of sweat down my back. It's not where I want to be, but it's the next step in the process and I can deal with it.

"I think we have proof of concept," Dr. Lindbergh says. "How are you tolerating the harness? Is it chafing you at all?"

"A little," I say, although it's not bothering me that much. I would put up with a lot worse.

"Okay, that's what, twenty minutes? Can you give me five more?"

"Easy," I say. The trickle of sweat is more like a rivulet. "Can I get a..." I know the word is *towel*, but I can't say it, even though it doesn't have any sibilants or anything. This is apraxia at work; I know what a towel is, I should be able to physically say the word, but I can't make it come out right. Dr. Lindbergh stares at me before he realizes what I am trying to say, and then hands me a towel.

"I know you don't want to hear this," he says, "but this is... well, it's inspiring, is what it is. This is the sort of thing you go to medical school to do. To help people recover."

"Not there yet," I pant.

"You're headed in the right direction, though. I'm proud of you."

The treadmill slows to a stop, and I wait so the Hoyer lift can be repositioned to drop me back in my wheelchair. My ankles are sore, and it's a positive relief to have the harness come off.

Nneka, my LPN escort, has been waiting on the side, playing with her phone. "All right," she says. "Hot shower? Quick lunch? Occupational therapy? Makes for a full day, then."

"Let's go," I say. *One step closer.*

### JENNIFER | DECEMBER 26 | MCCARRAN INTERNATIONAL AIRPORT, LAS VEGAS, NEVADA

"Mind if I sit here?"

"Go ahead," I say. It doesn't matter who sits next to me on the airplane, because I am not a talkative flyer. My plan is to turn on the white noise setting on my soundproof earphones and sleep all the way back home to North Carolina. Coach Morgan set a 1AM curfew after we dropped eighty points on Marquette, and I made the most of it. Monica and Joy and I took a cab over to the Bellagio. We had a huge buffet dinner and hit the slots; I won $300 in the first couple of minutes, and cashed out to spend the rest of the night playing blackjack with house money. I had enough left to treat everyone to gelato. We got in before curfew, but I am tired, and not very good company.

"Thanks." Adele Andersson settles in next to me. She is an assistant trainer; maybe four-eleven, with fair Swedish skin and a long pale blond ponytail. I don't know her well at all, although I have seen her around campus, riding her bike—I have the impression she's a triathlete, something like that. Come to think of it, Adele has been working with Unique all summer on her conditioning, while I was in Asheville, changing bedpans at Mission Hospital for my nursing internship.

She sits down, and fishes something out of her carry-on. "Here," she says, handing me a pale-blue bottle of sports drink.

"Thanks," I reply.

"You need to stay hydrated, the better to recover from all this air travel and high altitude." I can hear a slight a trace of an accent when she says this; she's obviously worked hard to lose it. One reason I'm staying in North Carolina; I don't want to change how I talk.

"I know. I mean, I appreciate it." I am trying not to be rude, but more than that I am trying to forestall the conversation I have had with six other people in the last 24 hours about why I am not starting anymore. What's done is done and I don't want to talk about it—don't want anyone's pity, least of all my own.

"This is your senior year, correct? Nursing degree?" Adele asks.

"That's right." I fiddle with my earbuds in what I hope is an obvious way.

"I am not trying to pry, Jennifer. The Coach asked me to talk to you about what you have planned after graduation."

"I'm going back to Asheville. Mission Hospital. Once I pass my exam to be a nurse, I'll be able to start right away. My mom has worked there for twenty years, and I interned there over the summer. Since I know everyone there, it'll be easy to get started."

"You're not thinking about graduate school, then?" Adele asks.

"I'm thinking about it. Not right away. I need to pass my exams for RN first, then save up to get my master's. No rush."

"I am working on my master's as well, in athletic training. I graduate in May, like you. Then my student visa is up, and I will return home to Sweden. That means there is an opening for an assistant trainer for next basketball season. It comes with a full scholarship to graduate school. Coach thinks it could be ideal for you."

I open the bottle and take a sip. I don't much like the blue flavor, but there's nothing to be gained by complaining about it.

"I've been on a scholarship for four years, but it still costs money to go to school. Grad school would add too much debt." That, and my younger brother will be starting at UNC-Asheville in the fall; grad school would put too big a strain on my family's finances.

"You should think about it, though," Adele presses. "You'd get a stipend, for one thing, and you'd still get to travel with the team."

"I appreciate the offer," I say. "It's not right for me now."

"Give it some thought," she says, smiling. "It's a great opportunity."

"I get that, but going from playing basketball at North Carolina to being an assistant trainer? I don't... it feels like a step backwards, doesn't it? Like giving up the part of yourself that's competitive."

Adele's expression hardens. "I never thought so," she says.

I have just stepped in it—I'm not sure *how* I've stepped in it, but I have, and it's time to backtrack. "That's not what I meant."

"It is what you meant."

I have definitely stepped in it, and deep. I am already sorry, but since I have no idea how I managed to talk myself into this mess, I can't talk my way out.

"You have only competed at the college level in America. Talk to me when you've competed at the international level."

"I was not trying..."

"I am an Olympic medalist. Did you know that? Short-track speed skating. I won the bronze in the thousand meters, and a silver in the 3000-meter relay."

"I didn't know." I lower my eyes down to my lap, where my fingers are playing with my earbuds.

"I trained for years for a gold medal, up every morning for skating practice at four o'clock, like clockwork. I missed out. By half a second. Nothing left to do but train harder for the next Olympics. Then two months after I got home, my Achilles tendon snapped while I was boarding a bus."

"That's terrible. I had no..."

"I went from being a world-class athlete to being on crutches. I had good trainers to work with. I made it back to the ice. Still didn't matter. I couldn't get the speed back, no matter how hard I tried."

"I can't imagine what that's like," I say.

"I learned a lot, though. About myself. About training. So I went back to school, and finished my degree. I learned English well enough to study here. I know I'll never be an Olympian again, but I don't think I took a step backwards."

"I was talking about me, not you. I wasn't trying to be critical."

"I became a trainer because I wanted to see other women succeed to the best of their athletic ability. Maybe you don't want that, and that's fine, but it's not a step backwards—and if you think it is a step backwards, then you know, you may be right. It's not for you."

"I am so sorry. Listen..."

"I would rather not. I made the offer, you turned it down, and that was all I was supposed to do. If you will excuse me, I think we will both be better off if I find another seat. Enjoy your flight."

Adele unbuckles from her seat, picks up her bag, and finds a more congenial place to spend the rest of the trip home. I down the rest of the vile-tasting blue drink. *You have permanently alienated the person who tapes your ankles*, I think.

I have one last weary thought before I turn my headphones on: at least I feel terrible about something stupid I have done rather than something that has happened to me. There's not much comfort I can take from that, but every little bit counts.

**PENNY | DECEMBER 26 | PENN HOSPITAL, PHILADELPHIA, PENNSYLVANIA**

"How's my favorite patient?"

Morton smiles at me, the toad, his bright green eyes alight with mischief.

"Don't you *favorite patient* me, you quack."

"It's a great pleasure to see you well," he says. Morton was cut out by God to be an undertaker; how he became a doctor is a mystery to me.

"Easy for you to say. You didn't spend ten hours in a torture chamber."

"It's a hyperbaric chamber, and it saved your life. Show a modicum of gratitude."

"I wouldn't need to show a modicum of gratitude if the butterfingers nurse who put in the central line hadn't let that air bubble into my actual beating heart."

Morton blows out his breath. "Yes. That was unfortunate. Even when we take the best precautions, fate conspires against us. However, the reverse is also true. It was fate that directed that bubble into your right ventricle while you were awake, and while I was enjoying the holiday with my family and available to take your mother's call. Otherwise, things might not have worked out so well for you."

"What do you mean, *so well*?" From my perspective, everything has worked out pretty awful so far.

"So well in terms of the transplant committee, which has moved you up to the top three nationwide. The other two patients are in Minneapolis and Seattle, which means you're the top contender for a new set of lungs on the East Coast."

"I'll believe it when it happens," I say.

"Well, all I can tell you is to keep your phone close by. As you do. At any moment, you might hear a ping, and that will be me, telling you that your new lungs are ready for you."

My phone pings.

"That's not me," Morton says.

"I know, I know." I pick up my phone, and watch the brief video. "Cool."

"Don't let me keep you from your social media addiction," Morton says.

"Wait, you'll want to see this," I say, and show him the video.

"Who is Nneka Okafor?" he asks.

"She is my informant. Watch the video."

Morton blinks. "This is your sister? She's walking already? That's remarkable. I had no idea she was doing that well."

"Considering that you were measuring her for a body bag not that long ago, I would say she's doing extremely well."

Morton hands me back my phone. "I never once wanted your sister to die," he says. "My concern was entirely for your well-being; she would have been the ideal lung donor for you, if she had perished. Fortunately for her, she did not."

"Fortunately for you, you didn't try to make me take her lungs."

"Perhaps you will have better luck soon. I do have a question for you."

"I am busy resting comfortably. I am not here to be a research participant, or to do your paperwork."

"Heaven forfend. I was curious as to whether or not you might be hungry."

"You don't know me at all, do you."

"I am only bothering to ask because, at the moment, your mother is somewhat indisposed."

"Meaning?"

"Your mother was awake the entire time you were in the chamber, worried to death. I called in a colleague to consult, and he recommended a sedative. A rather, shall we say, generous dose of sedative. She is in the next room, getting some well-deserved rest."

"Is your colleague prescribing anything else?" I figure it never hurts to ask.

"Not for you, Little Miss Junior Drug Addict. I, however, find myself *in loco parentis* for the moment. If you are hungry, and our humble hospital fare is not to your liking, I could perhaps be persuaded to supplement your diet."

"Excellent. Write this down. Reading Terminal Market. Roast pork sandwich, from DiNic's. Two slices of pizza, extra cheese. And Beiler's donuts."

"I am not driving across town to Reading Terminal Market. Non-negotiable. I was thinking WaWa."

"There's a Beiler's not three blocks from here. Dozen donuts, six glazed, six crullers."

"WaWa."

I hate Morton so much. "Fine. Two buffalo chicken hoagies. Chips—Zapps, not Herr's, Cajun spice. Two bottles of Coke Zero. Tastykakes, of course. Butterscotch Krimpets if they have them, if not, whatever they do have. And a pretzel with cream cheese filling."

"You realize that when you get your new lungs, you'll have to stop eating like a stevedore."

"*Carpe diem*, doctor," I say. If he can quote Latin to me, I can do it to him. "You're burning daylight."

# A Little Swordplay

**Ashlyn | February 14 | The Realm of Summervale**

The river in my dream runs clear and sparkling now, where once it had been brown and turbulent. It slips by softly now, with goldfish dancing in the swift current. But the river is still deep and dangerous, and there is only one way across.

I have crossed this river once, and that was half a year ago. In the weeks before my accident, I had a recurring dream about battling an unknown guardian for the right to make it to the other side. After the accident, when I was lying in a barbiturate-induced coma, I was able to cross the river, and explore the Eastern Marches of Summervale—my dream kingdom, influenced by the fantasy novels I read growing up.

Like many rivers, this one is a border—in this case, between the Eastern Marches and the Western Marches of Summervale. I am the Marshal of the Western Marches, but as I am the single long-term human resident, I suppose I can give myself any title that I wish. The Eastern Marches are another matter. Some miles beyond the river lies the city of New York— not that one, the one in Summervale, which is slightly different from the one I know in waking life, and is ruled indifferently by a Dark Lord.

I have no interest today in challenging the Dark Lord, after suffering a crushing defeat at his hands in our last battle. I have been busy governing my lands, wandering the back roads, and becoming familiar with the shifting landscape. I have concluded that the

Western Marches are restful, beautiful, and dull. It is time to expand my horizons.

I make my way down the dusty river road to the limestone bridge, with its cracked paving stone. A guardian once more waits for me at the center of the bridge. This time, the guardian is different—someone both unfamiliar and recognizable, menacing and welcoming. She has a long black mane of hair which whips around her slender shoulders in a phantom breeze and is idly leaning against a two-handed sword, bright silver, almost as long as she is tall.

"I am Lady Ashlyn Revere," I say, "Marshal of the Western Marches, and I wish to cross."

"Took you long enough," the guardian says, with a voice that sounds like a cellophane wrapper crackling in a quiet theater.

"I have had a long journey," I reply.

"Yeah, yeah, yeah," she says. "Look, don't bore me with the whole long litany, there, Lady Ashlyn." There is a hint of a sneer when she says my name. "You tried taking down the Dark Lord, you and that ragtag army of yours, and he beat you like a steel drum. Well, I got news for you, whatever it is you're selling, I ain't buying. You stay on your side and I stay on my side. You know? The Dark Side."

"I am somewhat familiar with the Dark Side," I say.

"You familiar with A.J. Valentine?" she asks. "Because if I recollect correctly, you had him squished."

"At the time, he was trying to kidnap me. My recommendation is that you do not try that."

"If you're making ready for another assault against New York, my recommendation is that you do not try that. A lot of people paid dearly when you did, particularly one T.J. Valentine."

"I paid dearly for that as well." T.J. joined my ranks and fought bravely, and died when the Dark Lord set a ferocious metallic bull into the battle.

"Well, that worked out for me, seeing how the Dark Lord made me Warden of the Eastern Marches afterwards. C.J. Valentine's the name. I would say 'at your service,' but I don't want you getting any weird ideas."

"No danger of that," I say.

C.J. cocks her head to the left and arches a thin, precise brow. "How're you feeling?" she asks, not unkindly. "I hear you've had a rough time, out there."

"I'm getting better," I say, and it's mostly true.

"Okay then. Tell you what. I've got my instructions, and they're to keep you occupied until the Dark Lord sends over an army of orcs or whatever it is to kidnap you and take you back to New York. Maybe, though, let's suppose that I ignore those instructions. Follow me?"

"Not sure." My hand drifts to the hilt of my sword.

"You're getting the gist of it, I can tell. Suppose we dispense with the formalities, and maybe get in a little swordplay? I gotta tell you, I've been waiting here a powerful long time, and I'm so bored I might chew my left foot off if something doesn't happen soon."

"Is that a challenge?" I ask.

"Not even. More like an offer for some sparring practice. It's been ages since Lady Heartbreak here has had a proper workout." She twirls the tip of the sword a little, to indicate that's what its name is. "I figure you're wanting a chance to test your mettle, too. Not much happening in the West right now."

"You're right about that," I say. "Rules?"

"Nobody tries to hurt each other on purpose. I will thank you kindly to keep that wand of yours sheathed."

"Fair enough," I say. I would love to use my new wand in combat, but it would be an unfair advantage in sparring. "Are you ready?"

"Born ready," C.J. says. She takes a cautious step back, both hands on her upraised sword. I unsheathe my blade and manifest the small circular shield I favor. I make a few tentative lunges in her direction, and she parries them deftly.

C.J. springs forward, sword held high, as though to split my skull. I bring up my shield and block the heavy blow while trying an experimental slash at her ankles. I miss, as C.J. steps to my left. With a backhanded twist, she smashes the flat of her sword against the side of my knee, and steps back as I howl in pain.

"You gotta learn to be more careful, there, Lady Ashlyn."

I shake off the hurt and embarrassment and make another cautionary lunge in C.J.'s direction. She sidesteps away from my sword and makes a twirling leap, again to my left, and whacks my shoulder with the flat of Lady Heartbreak. I stumble for a moment, then I take a step back to steady myself.

"Do my ears detect the jingle of chain mail?" C.J. asks. "You're better prepared than I thought."

I make a clumsy backhanded slash in her general direction, more to keep her away from my left side than anything else. She jumps back, and I press my momentary advantage, forcing her to bring her sword up to parry my determined attack.

"That's better," she says. "Dunno who trained you, but he taught you something. Too bad it ain't enough."

She makes a quick step toward me, and I hold my shield up, bracing for another of those wild leaps to my left side. If she tries it again, I will smash her in the face with the shield this time and see if she has any other smart remarks to make. Instead, she feints left, and jumps to my right. I'm already moving towards my left, so I make a turn to face her. We circle each other like we're in a revolving door.

I take a cautious step backwards, in the direction of the Eastern Marches. "No you don't," C.J. says. "Naughty, naughty, trying to sneak past me that way."

"My goodness, whatever would the Dark Lord think if I was able to get past his Warden that easily?"

"Dunno what he'd do to me, but I can guess what he'd do to you. Nothin' good. Besides, we're running late as it is."

"What do you mean by that?"

C.J. takes a quick glance at her wrist; she is wearing, for some unaccountable reason, a vintage Casio wristwatch—the same kind my dad wears. "Six fifty-two. You wake up in three minutes, right? Shower, breakfast, physical therapy. That's the routine, yeah?"

"Something like that."

"Well, there you go. Lady Ashlyn, it was a pleasure sparring with you. Come back some other time, maybe I won't go easy on you."

"That's what you were doing all this time? Going easy on me?"

"Well, whatcha think I was doing? I mean, c'mon, Lady Ashlyn." There's a definite sneer in her voice now. "It ain't like you're all that accomplished with the sword, now. And the one good sword you had, you lost, you remember that, right? Of course, I'm going easy on you."

"My recommendation is you do not try that. *Ventas servitas,*" I intone, as I draw my wand from its holster. The single unicorn hair, embedded in a tight spiral, gleams in the sunlight. I direct a hearty gust of wind at C.J.'s direction. The sudden blast knocks her against the side of the bridge, and she topples over. I disperse the wind and look down to see a sodden C.J. make her way to the eastern bank.

"You are gonna get it next time," C.J. says. "That ain't fair."

"Life isn't fair," I reply. "Catch you later."

# HI, I'M ASHLYN REVERE

**ASHLYN | MARCH 1 | WEST ORANGE, NEW JERSEY**

"Boy."

Nneka scans the half-empty hospital cafeteria. "Where?"

I waggle my fingers in the boy's general direction. It's a wasted effort; he's not paying the slightest bit of attention to me or anyone else.

"Ooooh," says Nneka. "Good eye, Ashlyn. Cute. Very cute."

I suppose that he is cute, in his way. Bushy black hair, thick eyebrows with dark eyes lurking underneath them. College-age, or maybe a year or two older, about the same as me. He is gnawing abstractedly on a stale hospital bagel, but that's not why I pointed him out.

"I know him."

"From where?" Nneka asks.

I pinch three fingers together, hold them up to my temple, and make the explosive gesture that means *I don't know*, because I don't know. I recognize his face, but I can't remember anything else about him and it's not coming to me. Speech therapy is helping me talk, and physical therapy is helping me walk, but nothing can touch the random gaps in my memory. Especially since I never know they're even there until I run across them. I know I have seen this boy before, but the neurons in my brain that store what his name is and where I met him aren't connected anymore.

"Do you know if he likes Nigerian girls?" Nneka asks.

I think she is kidding. Then I think about it some more, and I realize that she isn't. A lot of the nurses

38

engage in some low-level flirting with patients; Nneka makes something of a science of it.

"I know him," I say.

"Well, *I* don't know him. Maybe you should introduce us."

No time like the present. I put down my English muffin with peanut butter (I need all the protein I can get) and hit the joystick on my wheelchair. I back it into the table behind me, but I don't knock anything over so it's all to the good. I maneuver over to where the boy is sitting.

"I know you," I say.

He looks at me, and I recognize the half-surprised, half-pitying look that I often get when people see me for the first time. I know what I look like. They shaved my head for the surgery after the accident, and it is still growing in. You can see the pink line of the skull fracture through what ash-blonde hair I have now, that and the round dent from the burr hole procedure. My face is still scarred from the shallow cuts from the window glass; I am waiting to have the plastic surgery until after I can walk again. I don't mind the way the boy looks at me, but I won't pretend that his pity doesn't sting.

"I'm sorry," he says, "but I don't think we've met."

Nneka has her hospital-issue tablet out. "Hello. I think your name is Ben. Ben Shepherd, isn't that right? You're a new patient."

"Yes, that's right," the boy says guardedly. "Pleasure to meet both of you."

I pull up the name Ben Shepherd in the fractured remains of my mental data bank and can't come up with anything. I know a Cissy Shepherd; she was on my field hockey team at North Carolina, and she has a brother. A twin brother, I think. He goes to Duke, and I think I met him at a mixer. This boy is wearing a dark blue shirt. He seems nice, but he could still have gone to Duke. Obviously, I haven't seen him here if he's new. Could he be Cissy's brother?

Worth a shot.

"I know your sssssss..." and that's all I can get out. Seven months of speech therapy and I can't say a simple thing like *sister*. Great. "I know Cissssss..." and that doesn't work either. Too many sibilants. I am getting better at speech therapy, but sibilants are proving elusive.

"I'm sorry," Ben says. "I don't understand."

I try again. "You en see," I say, pointing to myself, and then point at him. "Duke."

He looks puzzled. "I go to Duke," he says. "Or I went to Duke. This is my last semester; I'm finishing up with online classes."

"You en see," I repeat, since I can't say *University of North Carolina* yet. "Hockey. Sissssss-ter." He is compellingly handsome and I'm making a mess of it.

"Your sister or my sister? My sister is still at North Carolina."

"Right," I say. "You en see. Me, too."

He looks at me, searchingly, and then I see the spark of realization in his dark eyes. "You're Ashlyn Revere," he says.

"That's me," I say. I make a mental note to myself to ask my speech therapist to help me say, *Hi, I'm Ashlyn Revere*, so I can avoid awkward situations like this in the future.

"We met one time, in Durham, for Cissy's and my birthday. You were on the field hockey team with her, right? You were in a car accident."

I point to my nose, which means *Bingo.*

"My God. I didn't recognize you. I'm so sorry. I know Cissy told me about, um, the accident when it happened. I was so sorry to hear about it. I didn't know you'd be here, though. I mean, I never thought I'd be here, either."

I had not considered the question of what Ben is doing here. If he's not visiting me, then I can't imagine he is in our cafeteria for the food. "Why?" I ask.

Ben is sitting in a manual wheelchair—I hadn't noticed, mostly because it's normal for people here to be in wheelchairs. He rolls back far enough so that I can see the bottom of his legs. One foot is gone.

"Oh, no! How?"

"Cancer," he says, with a note of pain that sounds distressingly familiar. "I was playing pick-up ball over the Christmas break over at the YMCA in Hillsborough. All of a sudden, my leg collapsed out from under me. I thought I had torn my Achilles tendon—I was right about that, but not in the way I'd thought. I had a cancerous growth in the bone of my left heel; it had become brittle and when the bone broke it took the tendon with it."

"Did they not try to save your poor foot?" Nneka asks.

"They did indeed. I was at Memorial Sloan Kettering over in Basking Ridge for the last two months. Surgery, then radiation, then more surgery. They got the cancer, but then there was an infection, so it ended up being safer to amputate."

"How awful," I say, and I wish I could say more than that.

Ben smiles. "Thanks, but I know it's not as awful as what happened to... well, a lot of other people around here, I guess. All I need is a new foot, then I'll be learning to walk again."

"Walk," I say. "Me, too."

"That's our goal, then. We'll walk out of here together. If you don't mind walking with someone from Duke, that is."

I reach my hand across the table, and he shakes it. "Deal," I say.

"Well, this is all very nice," Nneka interrupts with a sly smile at Ben, "but it's time for Ashlyn to go to therapy. Mr. Shepherd, you'll let me know if you need anything? Anything at all."

I spend the rest of the afternoon doing occupational therapy (dealing cards, in case I ever decide to get a job dealing blackjack table in Atlantic City) and speech therapy. I get frustrated in speech therapy; I can't think of the word *paint* for some reason. Emily the therapist is able to get me to calm down enough to keep trying.

"The aphasia and the apraxia run on different tracks," she says. "Or more accurately, two different regions on the left side of the brain. We're making progress on the apraxia, bit by bit. For some reason that nobody understands, though, the aphasia tends to get better all at once—sometime within the first thirty weeks after the injury. Doesn't always happen, but when it does, it's dramatic."

"Huh," I say.

"The problem is that you can't make it happen, you can't force it. All you can do is try to make progress until you get to that point."

This is frustrating, but there's nothing for it but to keep trying, until Nneka picks me up and guides me to the gym.

"Back on the treadmill again," she says.

"Walk," I say, steering the wheelchair out of the way of a passing orderly.

"The sooner you walk out of here the better, so you don't go poaching all the cute boys out from under me."

"Not dating," I say. Not yet, anyway. Walking is the goal right now, although it's a transitional goal. It is— shall we say—the first step towards everything else that I want, which includes dating. Eventually. I'm willing to put that on hold.

"That young man from breakfast may have a different idea," Nneka says. "He likes you."

I give Nneka my most derisive snort.

"Do not sell yourself short there, girl. You never know."

# LAST TIME FOR EVERYTHING

## JENNIFER | MARCH 4 | GREENSBORO COLISEUM, NORTH CAROLINA

We are holding hands in the tunnel, Monica Criswell and Joy Moody and me. The three seniors. We are praying together, as we've been doing all year.

"We ask for your protection, dear Lord, as we take the court today. We ask that our effort be a witness to Your glory. We ask that you watch over us as we play, and as we leave this place, and as we go our separate ways after graduation. And we ask this in the name of Your beloved Son, Jesus Christ of Nazareth. In His name we pray. Amen."

"Amen," I echo.

"This is it," Joy says. "Last game together."

"Don't say that," Monica says. "Don't sell us short yet."

"All we can do is play the way we know we can play," I say. "Let the committee take care of the rest."

In half an hour, we will tip off against Duke in the semifinals of the Atlantic Coast women's basketball tournament. Duke is the number-two seed and will undoubtedly make the March Madness tournament— they would be the overall top seed if not for Notre Dame, which was undefeated in conference play and has already beaten Virginia in the other semifinal.

To be brutally honest, we have no business being in the semifinals of this tournament. We have played poorly all year; it will take a miracle to get us into March Madness, even as a low seed. We have been lucky this week, catching an injury-ravaged Georgia

Tech team in the first round, and getting off a buzzer-beater against Wake Forest. We play Duke next, and we've lost to them twice in conference play. Our luck will not hold out.

This looks like the last game of a lost season. Monica has been inconsistent, and Joy has been battling a high ankle sprain all year. The bright spot in the lineup has been Unique—she's third in the conference in shooting percentage. I am happy for the team's sake that she is doing well, but my playing time has diminished and it gnaws at me more than I care to admit. I've started one game this year—Senior Night, our last home game, against Boston College. I don't even know if I'll get on the floor today, for what in all likelihood will be my last game as a competitive athlete.

We walk out of the tunnel together, onto the floor of the arena, and begin the shootaround.

The airhorn sounds for the timeout, and we gather around Coach Morgan on the hardwood. I have been a spectator for this one, because Unique Templeton is having the game of her life. She's twelve-for-eighteen for three-pointers so far, close to the college record. We were up on Duke at halftime, 38-24, but the Blue Devils have been whittling away at our lead. After a 10-2 run by Duke, we are up 64-60, with three minutes left to go.

"Six," says Coach, meaning me. "I need you in there. You're on Buckley; don't let her touch the ball. They might beat us today, but I will be damned if she's the one to do it. The rest of you—the key is patience, you understand me? The clock is on our side. We play our game, we take the open shot, we deny them anything easy, we can win this thing. You with me?"

The pep talk is brief; after that, we get to specifics—or as specific as we can, with the Duke band blaring "Seven Nation Army" behind us. My job is simple. I am shadowing Carissa Buckley, *Sports Illustrated* cover girl, daughter of Senator Paul Buckley, academic All-American, who has been publicly agonizing over whether to choose the WNBA or Yale Law School. Four years of conditioning, practices, and sacrifice would all be worth it if I could wipe that self-satisfied smirk off her face.

If these are the last three minutes of my collegiate career, I am making them count.

I put my warmup jacket neatly on my folding chair and step onto the court, nerves and adrenaline mounting in a familiar heated buzz. I get a good look around as we wait for the TV commercials to end; a seething mass of blue-clad partisans in the lower bowl, topped by a ring of empty green seats. It's like taking a long dive into a familiar pool, expecting the shock of the cold water, but knowing it will be fine in a moment. Joy takes the ball from the backcourt, and finds Monica on the perimeter. She has an open shot but doesn't take it, not with twenty seconds still on the shot clock. I jog over to the top of the key and set a pick; I get on Carissa's blind side and she crashes into me with a satisfying *smack*. Monica gets free and drains a pull-up jumper. I follow Carissa down the court, and deflect a long pass away from her, sending the ball out of bounds.

The Duke point guard takes the inbound pass. Six points down and running out of time, she drives the lane but finds nothing. She looks for Carissa and sends a bounce pass in her direction. I dive for it, slapping the ball towards Monica, who scoops it off the floor and takes it down the court for the easy layup. We're up eight now, which improves the odds significantly. Now they'll start shooting threes, now they'll have to foul. If we can make our free throws, we can put the game out of reach.

The Duke point guard feints a drive and throws it out to their shooting guard on the perimeter, who launches an arcing three that barely glances against the backboard on its way into the basket. I follow Carissa back down the court. Joy takes her time bringing the ball up, draining time off the clock. She makes an errant pass, and Duke makes the steal and takes it down the court for two. Coach calls a thirty-second time-out and lectures us about ball security, and we troop back onto the arena floor.

This time, Joy is careful and conservative, and we get twenty seconds off the clock before Monica throws up a jump shot that clangs off the backboard. Carissa and I both go after the rebound; I grab it, but I don't pull my hands away fast enough and she gets her hands on the ball as well. Duke has the possession arrow, so I give the ball back to the referee and follow Carissa to the opposite baseline.

We trade off the next two possessions; Duke missing a three from the top of the key, and Joy missing a medium-range shot. Twenty seconds left, Duke still down by three, and their point guard is looking for Carissa. I take a half-step back, to give her a little encouragement, and the ball comes sailing in her direction. Carissa tenses for the shot, and I time my leap, feeling the welcome pain as my fingers brush against the ball, interrupting its flight. Monica snatches the ball before it goes out of bounds, takes the hard foul, and makes one of the two free throws on the other end. Ten seconds left.

The Duke point guard heaves up a three; it clangs off to the right but the Duke center is there and gets the easy tip-in. Joy takes the inbound pass, but is swarmed by the Duke backcourt; she is by far our best free-throw shooter, and they want to avoid fouling her if they can. Joy tries making a long pass to Monica, but it's tipped and lands right in front of me. I dive on the ball, and Carissa Buckley falls on top of me. I hear the whistle blow for the foul call. Six seconds left.

Monica and Joy help me to my feet, and I take my place at the free-throw line. If I can make both shots, we'll be up four; they'd have to make two shots with six seconds left, which they should not be able to do. If we win, it means we get one more game—against the top team in the country, yes, but they have nothing to play for. We win the tournament, we're definitely in the NCAAs, and anything can happen in March Madness. Can't it?

I make sure my feet are on the right side of the foul line. I bounce the ball, once, twice. My career free-throw percentage is, what, seventy percent. *I can do this.*

The first shot looks perfect, centered, but it hits the backboard and the front of the rim and caroms off. The Duke fans in the stands cheer ironically. The referee tracks down the rebound and passes it back to me. I try to steady myself. This may be the last shot I ever get to take. If I make it, we'll be up three; the best that Duke can do is tie.

I spot Coach Gordon on the bench, who is waving at me frantically. She is pointing towards the right, where

Rowena, our center, is lined up. I understand; she wants me to miss the free throw on purpose, to direct it so Rowena can grab the rebound, or tip it in.

I shake my head. I see you, but I am not throwing away my shot.

Coach points her finger emphatically at Rowena.

*I am a rock.*

I toss up the ball, spinning it off to the right, and start running backwards to play defense. Rowena jumps up for the rebound, but the ball goes off her fingertips and lands squarely in the hands of the Duke shooting guard. She throws it cross-court, on a high arc, to Carissa Buckley, their best shooter. Three seconds left. I get in position, between Carissa and the basket. Whatever happens, she is not getting around me. I try to read her face, but I don't see anything in her cold eyes. She could go right, she could go left, or she could back up and take the three for the win. Out of the corner of my eye, I see the Duke point guard running, waving her arm, ready for a pass she'll never get. Two seconds left. If I know Carissa, she won't resist taking that last shot, draining the game-winning three. Seven tenths of a second, and I commit myself. I don't want to spend the last second of my last game as a spectator. I leap into the air as the shot comes off the hands of the golden child, the cover girl, the Senator's daughter. I feel the telltale *thump* of the ball against my fingertips.

I don't turn around. I don't have to. The North Carolina fans in the stands raise their arms, jumping and dancing. Carissa Buckley is staring at me, a snarl on her face, like I am a dead mouse in her cereal bowl. I point my finger at her and give her a quick Dikembe Mutombo finger-wag. North Carolina 67, Duke 65.

Monica and Joy corral me, and we start jumping together. We have one more game as teammates, maybe more than that if we can win the tournament. I turn and look towards the Duke bench, and catch sight of Carissa Buckley, her face a mask of disappointment and rage.

I know I shouldn't smile at this, that I shouldn't take any pride in her failure, that I shouldn't stake my happiness on her pain. I do it anyway. She will play in the tournament, and then choose between law school in New Haven or the WNBA, or wherever she decides she wants to go—a glittering future of possibilities. I am headed back home to Asheville, whether that's sooner or later. She will have her moments, but this one is all mine.

# Nothing But the Wheel

**Penny | March 6 | Montgomery, New Jersey**

"Wake up, Penny. We're leaving in five minutes."

I shake my head, blind in the dark, and cough. The alarm clock says three-twenty. "Is the house on fire?" I ask.

"No. Hurry and get your shoes on."

I take a moment to comprehend this. My mother hoards sleep, treasures it. Four children, one in a rehab hospital, one (yours truly) with a chronic disease, two rowdy eight-year-old twin boys. She doesn't wake up at three-twenty in the morning without a good reason.

Like the house being on fire.

Which it isn't.

I take a deep breath, cough again, and grab my phone to use it as a lamp to find my shoes. There's a text from Dr. Morton: *Got you some lungs.*

My stomach lurches and my hands begin to shake.

"Here we go," I breathe to myself.

I rush downstairs, still in my pajamas, because Mom said *get your shoes on* and not *get dressed*. There is a difference, and the difference is time. Every minute counts now. I have a suitcase already packed in the van; clothes aren't important. I head out to the garage, getting in the shotgun seat as my mother is turning the engine over on her Toyota Sienna. The garage door lifts, and we pull out of the development.

Mother is normally talkative early in the morning, but this is early even for her and I can tell she is not in the mood for chitchat. This is fine. I don't need her to tell me anything.

This is what I know: someone has died or is about to. That is a fact. People die every day, but they are not usually the right people. The right person is five-foot-eleven, like me. That's an average man or a tall woman. Ideally young and in good health, which mean that they were in an accident that was bad enough to kill them but to leave their lungs intact. And they have to have signed their organ donor card; that's the key.

I don't need to know or want to know who it is. That was the problem last year, when they thought Ashlyn might die. Morton wanted me to get her lungs—even though she's a couple of inches taller, her lungs are a better genetic fit. That was the last thing I wanted—to have my sister die, and to owe her for every breath in my lungs for the rest of my life and never be able to say thank you. She pulled through the surgery, though, which made me happy, but left me waiting for some other stranger to die.

We reach the stoplight on 206 and turn south. That tells me less than I would like to know. Morton has a pair of lungs for me, but he didn't say where those lungs were. We live in Central Jersey, about halfway between New York and Philadelphia. If we had turned north, we might be headed to New York—and New York has a large population and New York Presbyterian does a lot of transplants. We're headed south, though, towards Philadelphia. This likely means that we're going back to the Penn Hospital complex, my second home. That's the ideal set of circumstances—it's a familiar location, with familiar doctors. Morton is annoying and pompous, but he's saved my life three different times at least. I don't like him but I trust him.

Is it necessary to get up this early to drive down to Philadelphia, though? I try to do the mental math, which is not my strong suit. Would they want to start prepping me for transplant surgery this early in the morning? Don't think so, which tells me that maybe we're driving to the Philadelphia airport. That could mean Cincinnati—I was there for a clinical trial when I was twelve. It could mean Atlanta—there's a transplant center there. Or maybe Houston. I look over at Mother, whose gaze is locked onto the road. The light ahead turns yellow, and she hits the gas, which is unlike her, but every minute counts.

She would have told me to get dressed if we were getting on a plane. Unless it's a private plane. They have those—Angel Flights, they're called, when you get someone's corporate plane to take you to get a transplant. That would be cool. Flying in a Gulfstream in my pajamas. I decide it's as interesting an option as anything else, enough so that I doze off a bit. I wake up to find myself alone in the van, in the parking lot of the Lawrenceville WaWa. I am startled until I realize that Mom is inside getting coffee. I dig my phone out of the pocket and do a quick Google News search for "Philadelphia murder."

### *FATAL BEATING IN CENTER CITY*
### *Record Murder Pace Continues*

*Another violent episode in what could be Philadelphia's worst year for murders continues as a man in his late 20's was assaulted in an alley near the Betsy Ross House on Arch Street. The victim was taken to Thomas Jefferson University Hospital, where he was pronounced dead shortly after midnight due to a massive brain contusion. No arrests have been made and police have not released a description of any suspects. The victim has not yet been identified.*

Well, that in and of itself doesn't mean anything. I mean, who knows. Just because somebody was beaten to death in a Philadelphia alley doesn't mean that I automatically get his lungs. It could be someone else dying of something else entirely—a buggy accident in Lancaster or a brain aneurysm in Cherry Hill. I will never know, and I am comfortable with that. I am in no position to be picky, either.

"Thought you were asleep," my mother says. She puts her extra-large coffee with cream and sugar in the cupholder and climbs into the minivan. "Thought I could grab some coffee before you woke up."

"Did you get me anything?" I ask.

"I got you a Sprite," she says, pulling a bottle out of a plastic bag. "No breakfast for you before surgery."

I am starving. I would arm-wrestle a brown bear for a Tastykake right now, but I will be a good patient for once.

"Okay then. No worries."

"Easy for you to say. You know where we're headed, right?"

"Not New York." I say.

She starts the car and backs out of the parking lot. "If we were, I would have gone to the Starbucks in Hillsborough. Too bad."

"So that means Philadelphia. Or so I'm guessing. Maybe the airport, but I am thinking we're going back to Penn."

"You are correct. Dr. Morton called; he has a match for you. They'll prep you for surgery as soon as we can make it down there. Your father will take the boys to school and go up to the hospital to tell Ashlyn. He'll drop the boys off at Aunt Stephanie's after school, and then he'll drive down."

"I understand." I wish Dad was here, but I know that both parents can't leave the house at a moment's notice.

"Are you ready?" Mom asks.

"I want the waiting to be over. I know it's a dangerous surgery, and I know that you guys are stressing over this, but I am tired of waiting around for a transplant. I want to get it done and over with so maybe I can go to college and be normal for once."

"I don't care if you're normal. I don't want to lose you. I almost lost you and Ashlyn last year, and that nearly killed me. Same when you had that embolism; I was a nervous wreck the whole time."

"You're not going to lose me," Mom." I glance over, and her hands are gripping the wheel tightly. "Morton is a jerk, but he knows what he's doing."

"I wish I could be that sure. But if I lose you, then what? Who do I have left to hold on to?"

"You'll lose me if I don't get the transplant, you know."

"I know. I'm prepared for that. I have been prepared for that for seventeen years now, ever since we found out you had this wretched disease. I know it can kill you, but I also know we had time. I've been counting every second. I don't want today to be the last day." Her voice starts to shake and I fight a rising painful lump in my throat. I do not tell her that I would risk my life a thousand times for my future, my independence. I do not want to say anything that I can't take back, not today.

We are crossing the toll bridge over the Delaware, the one that runs next to the old bridge that says TRENTON MAKES, THE WORLD TAKES. My phone chimes with an incoming call and I answer.

"Tell your mother she can drive you back home," Morton says, disappointment threading through his voice.

"Wait, what?"

"I'm sorry, favorite patient. This isn't a good match. We'll hope for better luck next time."

"Who is getting the lungs?" *It had better not be anyone I know*, I think.

"Nobody. They're unusable. None of the organs are; I have colleagues calling other potential organ recipients as I speak to cancel transplants. The risk is too high."

"The risk of what? Tell me what the risk is; if it's reasonable, I'll take it."

"Penny?" my mother asks. "What's he saying? Is the surgery off?"

"Not if I can help it. Tell me what the problem is, Morton."

"I can't. Medical privacy."

"Medical privacy be damned."

"Penny. Language," Mom says.

"Whoever this was, he's dead. Or she's dead. She doesn't have any medical privacy to speak of, and I don't even know who they are to begin with, so don't play the privacy card. Tell me why."

56

"The donor had an underlying medical condition that made transplant surgery inadvisable. Believe me, I'm as disappointed as you are."

"Underlying medical condition? Cancer? What?"

"Tell your mother I'm sorry about getting her up so early." *Click.*

"Is the surgery off?" Mom asks.

"Yes," I say. I try to keep the disappointment out of my voice, but I can't control the frustration. *Damn it to hell.*

"Oh, Penny," she says. "I am so sorry. Did he say why?"

"Something about an underlying medical condition. Which could be anything. Doesn't matter; the organs are unusable. He apologized for waking us up this early."

Mom takes the first exit she can, takes Route 1 back the other way, and heads across the Delaware in silence. I open my Sprite to have something to do, something to put in my mouth to keep me from talking. We drive on in the iron dark, my mother holding onto nothing but the steering wheel.

# A Temporary Thing

### ASHLYN | MARCH 12 | WEST ORANGE, NEW JERSEY

"I've got to hand it to you, Ashlyn, there are some bold choices here."

"I know," I say. "Courage pays dividends."

"You've got Georgia Tech beating Oklahoma State."

"Tougher conference."

"Sure, I guess," Ben says. "But Murray State beating Vanderbilt? No way that's a stronger conference."

"Good feeling," I say. I am not about to admit that I have not watched one minute of either Vanderbilt or Murray State basketball this year, but I bet Ben hasn't either. Sometimes you have to go for the unlikely upset.

"You have Cornell beating Temple, and then beating Wisconsin in the second round. Come on. There's no way. At least you have Duke winning it all."

"It's their year," I say. North Carolina, somehow, missed the men's tournament for the first time in eight years. The UNC women's team is moving on, though, after beating Duke in a big upset in the semifinals of the Atlantic Coast tournament. I may have brought this up to Ben two or three times

"Well, I hope so, too, but I think Kansas is too good. We'll see."

We are sitting together in the hospital cafeteria. Ben has a turkey sandwich and the vile syrupy canned pears; I have the barbecue chicken wrap and Doritos. Nneka is making her way back to the table; she has the Cobb salad and an extra glass of iced tea for me.

"I hope that the two of you are not still talking about sporting events," she says.

"Of course," I say. "It's March."

"Not a fan, then?" Ben asks.

"My father is. He follows the Nigerian team in the World Cup."

"The Super Eagles," Ben says.

"You've heard of them! Then you know. They lose. They lose, every four years, and my father is always so disappointed."

"Well, that's the way sports go, you know. There can only be one champion."

"This is what bothers me. There are over a hundred countries in this world, and only one, as you say, can be a champion. What happens to the other ninety-nine? Must they all go home disappointed? How terrible is that?"

"It's good preparation for the disappointments in life," Ben says.

Nneka cocks her head, the soft curls of her hair bouncing, and considers this. "Yes. Perhaps you are right. How are you progressing, then? Is your new foot almost ready?"

"Not yet," Ben says. "There are a lot of options, and it's not clear which one will work best. To complicate things, I need two different feet—one for everyday, and one for competition. The competition one—the carbon-fiber blade—is easy, but the everyday one is trickier."

"Competition?" I ask.

"My track coach was an assistant for the Paralympic track team, and he thinks I have an outside shot of making the team for the javelin throw."

"More sports talk," Nneka grumbles.

"That would be amazing," I say, slower than I would like. I don't think I can wrap my mouth around a long word like *Paralympics*.

"You ought to look into it, Ashlyn. Won't be long before you're walking again, and you were a college athlete. You could work your way on the team, too."

I take a bite of my wrap. "Walk first. One thing at a time."

"I hear you. They're going to have the tournament games on in the common area; I'll set up a little spread for tomorrow night. I hope you can stop by."

"Maybe," I say. "A lot to do. Reading book for work." I am still sounding like Unfrozen Cavewoman, even when I try to talk in complete sentences.

"I know. Well, I have a lot to do—they've got me doing cardio on the handcycle. You?"

"More s-speech therapy."

"She is doing very well with that," Nneka interjects. "She has not used her sign language in weeks."

I consider this for a moment. I haven't noticed whether I've stopped doing the sign language or not. It's certainly possible; I'll mention that in speech therapy.

"Well. Anyway. Good luck, and I hope I see you tomorrow night."

"Bye," I say.

"I told you so," Nneka says. "He likes you. Which is a good thing for him, because if he liked me, I would turn him down. I don't need all that sports talk in my life."

"S-something in common," I say.

"Relationships have been built on less," she says. "You're going to his party?"

"Don't think so," I say. It's not that I don't like Ben, or basketball, but watching sports on TV is not the easiest thing for me to follow anymore. I think my concentration is getting a bit better, but it's been forever since I've watched something longer than a TikTok video.

"You understand, this is a temporary thing, right? Once he gets his new foot, he's not going to darken the door of this place again. Strike fast, Ashlyn. Win his heart."

"Walk first," I explain.

"You don't want to walk; you want to walk down the aisle. Maybe he does, too. Catch him now before he changes his mind."

I take the last bite of my wrap. Nneka has a point there; walking isn't going to help me that much if I don't have someone to walk with. Is that Ben? Is it anybody? Does he like me because I'm here? Because we're both scarred, both hurt, both recovering? Does that matter?

All I know is if I ever want to say my wedding vows without sounding like an extra in a zombie movie, I had better get working on my speech therapy.

# WHAT'LL YOU HAVE

### JENNIFER| MARCH 19 | THE VARSITY, ATLANTA, GEORGIA

"You shouldn't worry about those free throws," Unique says.

I take a big bite of chili dog and try my best to ignore her. I was okay walking over here from the team hotel, even though I am not a big fan of The Varsity, the overgrown hot dog stand across the highway from the Georgia Tech campus. We're playing in the NCAA tournament, matched against Louisiana State at the Georgia Tech arena tomorrow, and I am trying to be a good teammate to Unique. I have not said a harsh word to her about taking my spot in the starting lineup. I have practiced alongside her, pointing out the weak spots in her game. I was supportive when she went three-of-fifteen from the field against Notre Dame, but I will be God-damned if I will sit here and listen to her critique me for my free-throw shooting.

"These things go in cycles. You know that. Sometimes you have the hot hand, sometimes you don't. At least it didn't cost us anything."

My missed free throws didn't cost us anything because Unique had the hot hand against Colorado State. We were up fifteen points by the time I got into our first-round tournament game. We were able to sneak into March Madness based on our win over Duke in Greensboro—we're the 10 seed, and we drew Colorado State as the 6 seed. I got to play the last five minutes, and missed three free throws in that time. We still won, we still advanced to play LSU tomorrow in the next round. I am still annoyed that I missed three straight free throws, and I don't need Unique reminding me of that.

"You don't have to talk to me if you don't want to," Unique says. "I get it. You have a lot going on, and I'm not your favorite person right now. Trying to be helpful."

I don't need her condescending to me any more than I need her critiquing me. I take another bite of my chili dog.

"I asked you to come here," Unique says, "because I thought you might like it. It's my favorite place in Atlanta. I used to work here when I was in high school."

"You're from Atlanta?" I ask. I hadn't given it any thought one way or another.

"Not too far from here," she says. "I got recruited hard by Georgia State. I liked Georgia Tech, but they got picky about my SAT score. I'm glad I chose North Carolina. And I'm honored to be your teammate, even if you don't think so."

"Unique, look. I appreciate your trying. And I'm glad I got to be your teammate, too. I wish things had turned out different this year, you know? This isn't how I pictured my senior season. It's not your fault, and I'm glad you got the opportunity to play, but it was at my expense, and you can't expect me to feel good about that." *Or missing those free throws*, I don't say.

"I know," she says. "If we were ever on the floor at the same time, that would have been something."

"I suppose. What are you drinking?" It looks like sludge, and is an unhealthy shade of orange.

"This?" Unique hands me her cup. "Want to try some? It's an F.O. That means frosted orange. Soft serve and orange soda."

"No thanks. Sounds too sweet."

"Suit yourself. Seriously, though. I think Coach made a mistake putting me at power forward. I've been able to make it work on offense, but I always feel like I'm not pulling my weight out there on defense. Tomorrow, I'm on Courtney Wheeler, and she's a monster."

Courtney Wheeler from LSU is six-seven, two hundred and forty pounds, and is relentless. First-team all-SEC the last three years. I've been watching video of her all morning, and I have no idea how we'll defend against her. Unique is right; she will be at a considerable disadvantage in that matchup.

"Wait a minute. You said if we were both on the court at the same time."

"Sure," Unique says.

"Well, what if we were? What if we put a double-team on Wheeler?"

Unique takes a sip of her drink. "Won't work. You'd be leaving someone open in their backcourt."

"Is that a problem, though? They don't have anyone back there who is even an average shooter. They've been living and dying all year on getting the ball into the low post and Wheeler taking the high-percentage shot. If we lock down Wheeler, we're taking a risk, sure, but they have to beat us with their weakness, not their strength."

"You're putting one of our other starters on the bench that way," Unique says. "It won't be easy."

"I'll talk to Coach in the morning, before practice. She might go along with it, or she might have a better idea. It's worth a shot."

## Jennifer | March 20 | Alexander Memorial Coliseum, Atlanta, Georgia

It's the second half of our second-round game against Louisiana State. We're up seven with eight minutes to play. Unique and I are double-teaming Wheeler, and it's worked well so far. Wheeler got into foul trouble early in the first half, so she's watched a good deal of the game from the bench. She's playing with four fouls now, and that's making her tentative—which is not her game at all. Monica and Joy have held down the fort in the backcourt, and Unique's three-point shooting has given us the lead.

Joy takes the point and is starting to slow the game down. She passes to Monica, who doesn't have the shot, and passes it back. I drift over to the top of the key, looking to set a pick. Joy ducks left, feints right, and pulls up the mid-range jumper. It goes long, and I set up for the offensive board. It comes off the glass a little high, and I tense to make the leap I'll need to snag the rebound.

I feel a shockwave course through my body as Courtney Wheeler, all six-foot-seven, two hundred forty pounds of her, crashes into me as I leave my feet. I hear the whistle in the second and a half before my body impacts the hardwood, with all my weight landing on my right elbow.

White and red flashes explode behind my eyelids as my elbow hits the ground and I skid on the court. I try to sit up, cradling my arm. The pain isn't as bad as I thought it would be. In fact, it doesn't feel much like anything.

Adele the trainer hustles over, carrying a first-aid kit and an anxious expression. "Is it broken?" she asks.

"No," I say. Or I don't think it is. The elbow pad has taken most of the shock.

"Try and move it for me."

I manage to flex the elbow, but all I can feel is a painful tingling sensation up and down my arm. "I hit my funny bone," I say.

"Your what?"

"Sorry. It's an English expression. I think I hit the ulnar nerve the wrong way, my arm is all numb and tingly."

"Not serious, then. Can you make it to the bench?"

I give her my left arm, and she helps me to my feet. I can hear a smattering of applause in the crowd.

"Wait," I say. "I get to shoot two."

"Not now you're not," Adele says.

"What's going on?" Coach Morgan asks, as we make our way to the bench. "Are you all right?"

"My arm's numb," I say. "I think I can still make the free throws, though."

"No chance," Coach says. "Have a seat, you're done for the rest of the game. Good work, Six."

"I want to make those last two free throws, Coach." I don't want to walk off the floor like this.

"Not if your arm isn't working right, Jennifer. Look, you'll have at least one more game after this one. Sit down, take it easy, we got this."

I find an empty chair at courtside, and Adele the assistant trainer hands me a towel and some sports drink—the awful blue stuff again. Coach sends out the backup point guard to the line, and she sinks the two free throws I was supposed to make. We're up nine now, and if we can hold on, we're on our way to New York to play whoever wins the Michigan-UCLA game in Hartford later tonight. I look down the bench, in time to see Courtney Wheeler trudge off the court into the locker room; knocking me over has earned her a fifth foul. Her season is done, and I'm moving on for one more game—in Madison Square Garden, the greatest basketball arena in the world. One last chance to show what I can do, to make my mark—that, and to get my touch back at the free-throw line.

# F ACE T IME

## A SHLYN | M ARCH 21 | W EST  O RANGE, N EW  J ERSEY

My editor pitched the book I am reading for my (still unpaid) publishing internship as *Aladdin* meets *Pirates of the Caribbean*, but it's reading more like *Twilight* fan-fiction set in the Arabian Gulf. The plucky female protagonist is agonizing, for what feels like the twelfth time, over her feelings for the bad-boy corsair who has kidnapped her. I find myself hoping that their next encounter with a Greek trireme proves fatal for all aboard.

I'm ready to turn off my tablet and call it a night anyway. I had occupational therapy in the morning—I have graduated from dealing cards to sorting marbles—followed by lunch with Ben, followed by speech therapy (those God-damned sibilants are still causing me trouble) and a satisfying workout on the rowing machine in physical therapy. Then Ben and I watched the Elite Eight game in his room—Duke beat Baylor by seven, which is good for my bracket but bad for my disposition. There are however bright sides even in the most depressing outcome; the Duke team's success is helping to lift Ben's spirits, which rise and fall with news about his new foot. He had thought that they had a prosthesis that would work well for him, but he was having trouble balancing when he walked on it, and it ended up giving him back spasms.

Tomorrow will be a better day. They're going to try letting me walk on the treadmill without the harness for a while. By that I mean they're going to put the harness on, and if I do well walking, they'll take it off for the last few minutes. It's not quite walking on my own, but it's the next best thing and at this point I am willing to take anything that looks like progress. Dr. Lindbergh is still telling me my wrists are too fragile for me to use a walker, so I'm still using the wheelchair, until the day comes when I can donate it to someone else who needs it.

I turn off the Kindle app and prepare to plug my iPad in to charge when the FaceTime app chimes; it's Penny calling. No surprise that she's up this late; Penny keeps vampire hours when she's allowed to.

"What's up, sis," she says. She is in her room, having been thwarted in her ongoing efforts to colonize mine. For some reason, she has painted her walls a shocking bright yellow, with floral chalk patterns that make it look as though she's sitting inside a Vera Bradley handbag.

"Okay," I say. "You've been decorating."

"You like it? Chalkboard paint. Makes it a lot easier to change the patterns. I figure if you're in prison, they ought to let you decorate your cell, you know what I mean?"

"Prison?" I ask.

"Or the next best thing. They haven't let me out since the false alarm. Afraid I'll get infected and won't get a transplant, but then whenever I talk about getting a transplant, they get all choked up and weepy."

"They're s-s-scared," I say. "You need transplant, but... chancy." *Risky*, that's what I wanted to say.

"It's a chance that I'm willing to take, and it's my life. Or what's left of it. You're looking much better, though. Color in your cheeks."

"Walk tomorrow. Almost."

"I know. Nneka's been sending me the videos. Will they take the harness off? It looks uncomfortable."

"Not too bad, but I want it off. Tomorrow."

"Of course, my question is, who was that you were talking to on the next treadmill?"

"Nobody," I lie. It was Ben, of course, trying out his new foot.

"Nobody. You were having quite the chat, though. Does this nobody have a name?"

"B-Ben," I say. I need to practice that. *Ben. Ben. Ben.*

"Ben. He looks like a Ben. Tall, dark, and handsome. Probably means he's aloof and arrogant, though."

"He is not," I reply.

"Well, then, he must be a great big snugglepuppy. Is that it? Has my big sister found herself a snugglepuppy?"

"Stop," I say, not missing a beat over the sibilant.

"See, now I want to know more. Is he a snugglepuppy? Are you snuggling up together, watching basketball?"

"Teasing."

Penny adopts a look of mock-horror. "Teasing? Excuse me? Have you never once read the Little Sister Handbook? I'm not just allowed to tease you about boyfriends. I'm required to. It's my civil right."

"He is *not* my boyfriend."

Penny stares at me, her eyes twinkling, because she knows, and she knows that I know, and I will get Nneka for telling Penny about Ben if it's the last thing I do on this earth.

"Not dating. I'm in hospital. He's in hospital. Lost a foot. We're friends. That's all."

"That was like, almost a paragraph there. Mostly complete sentences. Your speech therapy is going great. It almost sounded like my big sister was yelling at me."

I hope my occupational therapy will help me strangle you when I get the chance. "Stop teasing. S-serious."

"I am serious. I'm glad I get the chance to tease you about this. Anyway. Spill. Tell your little sister. Is he warm and cozy to snuggle up next to?"

I have not gotten close enough to Ben to tell. I can't possibly admit this, so I use the weapon at hand. "Let's s-say we're not five feet apart."

Penny's face gets pink. "Oh, you did not go there. Unbelievable. Worst movie ever, did you know that?"

"S-sorry," I lie.

"If I was going to have a boyfriend—and let me point out that, despite being totally cute and available, I don't have a boyfriend now, and you do, *which is completely unfair*. The last, very last person I would pick would be, you know, someone else with cystic fibrosis. Aside from the fact that such a boyfriend would substantially increase my risk of infection with horrible diseases, every single boy I have ever talked to with CF is boring and stupid and pointless. No thank you."

"Good to know," I say.

"Of course, in the only movie they will ever make about CF, this sappy, stupid girl falls for this other guy with CF, in a whole universe filled with cute guys who don't harbor lung infections, she picks this idiot, you know, because she's shallow and desperate. I mean, seriously."

I let loose a theatrical yawn. I have pulled Penny's string out far enough. "Need to s-sleep. Big day tomorrow."

"Big date with Ben tomorrow? Going to watch some more basketball?"

"Maybe," I say. In fact, we will—the women's tournament is on, North Carolina playing Michigan; I invited him to watch it in my room for a change.

"Okay, then. Good luck with the treadmill tomorrow. Tell Nneka to send me the video."

"Goodnight," I say.

"Good night, big sis. Love you."

"Love you."

"Have fun snuggling with Mr. Snugglepuppy."

I switch off the connection, put the iPad on the charger, and am asleep almost before I turn off the light.

## ASHLYN | MARCH 21 | THE REALM OF SUMMERVALE

"I understand congratulations are in order," Nicholas says.

"What are you talking about?" I ask.

We are surveying the perimeter of my castle, which is a work in progress. It looks like something Mad King Ludwig would have put together, if Mad King Ludwig had a phone with the Minecraft app. I resist the temptation to reduce it to rubble and start over.

"I understand that you are starting to heal from your unfortunate accident," Nicholas says. He is a glossy black Talking Rabbit, with a cultured accent. He is also the symbol of my impending death, although I have sort of come to terms with that. He was my first guide to Summervale, and is now my top assistant as I navigate the political waters of the Western Marches.

"Pretty much," I respond. "They have me on a treadmill; I'm improving on endurance, working on speed."

"That is excellent news indeed, Lady Ashlyn. I am encouraged to hear it."

"Still a lot of work to be done, though."

"As you have here as well. The Duchess of Frost is requesting your presence at the Seasonal Carnival next week."

"Give her my regrets, and I'll try to make the next one."

"Very well. The Talking Beavers would like you to speak at the dedication of their new college of engineering."

"No, but tell them I will be there for graduation. Anything else?"

"Given your penchant for delay, I hesitate to tell you."

"All I'm saying is less diplomacy and politics, and more sorcery and swordplay."

"If you ignore diplomacy and politics, you may get more sorcery and swordplay than you want."

"Fair enough," I reply, trying to hold back a yawn. "What else do you have?"

"There are issues with the foundation of the castle. The dwarves would like a brief word."

"Well, I suppose. If it's brief."

"T'will be brief enough, Lady Ashlyn," a voice says to my right, and I look to see two filthy dwarves make their way out of the earth.

"I prefer not to be ambushed on the grounds of my own castle," I say. "Show some manners, friend dwarf."

"Beggin' your pardon, ma'am, but this is an issue of fundamental concern," the red dwarf says. He is the taller of the two, by half an inch, if that. His ears are pointed, and his round helmet might once have been green.

"If we can dispense with the droll jokes, thank you."

"Very well, Lady Ashlyn." This is the black dwarf, with bushy whiskers well-powdered with coal dust. "My name is Holland; this is Lincoln."

"The pleasure is mine," Lincoln says.

"We have something of an issue in the dungeons, Your Worship. We were digging a small annex down there, under the moat—nice and cool down there, perfect place for a wine cellar, if you don't mind me saying so."

"It is not as though I drink anything here, so I don't see the need," I explain.

"No, Your Worship, but you might be doing some entertaining," Lincoln explains. "Anyway, we were doing a little digging, as we do, and we struck a nice vein or two, yes we did."

"A vein of what?" I ask.

"Coal," Holland says.

"Copper," Lincoln says.

"Can't be both," I say.

"Well, begging Your Worship's pardon, it is both," Lincoln says.

"This 'Your Worship' business is giving me a pain, you guys. How could it be both?"

"Coal to the left, copper to the right," Holland says. "Can't dig both at the same time."

"This interests me why?" I ask.

"Depends on what you want," Lincoln says. "Coal heats the castle, coal drives the forge."

"Copper is useful and beautiful," Holland says. "New pots and pans for the kitchen, new cladding for the roof. Perhaps a bracelet to adorn your neck."

"We cannot agree," Lincoln says. "Both are useful, both can be mined, but we must choose one resource to develop first. We have come to ask for your aid."

"So that's it? All I have to do is make a choice?" I ask.

"Yes, your... yes, Lady Ashlyn," Lincoln says. "As you must make a choice to pursue Sir Ben's advances."

"Okay, okay. Wait one second. What did you say?"

"Holland here would like to see you end up with the Shepherd boy," Lincoln says. "Me, I think you should spend more time on working out and growing stronger."

"She needs love to grow," Holland says. "Love will help her give love in return. Something that you'll never understand, Lincoln, not with your nose in the coal mines your whole life."

"Okay," I interject. "You guys are way out of line."

"Coal keeps the fires burning around here," Lincoln retorts. "Lady Ashlyn has the rest of her life to burn with passion. She needs strength and independence."

The red dwarf shrugs at this. "There's more to life than strength and independence. There is love, and beauty. She needs that, too."

I look over at Nicholas, who is munching on a dandelion and trying his best to look inconspicuous. "Did you put them up to this?" I ask.

"Heaven forfend, Lady Ashlyn. I do think that Lincoln, in his way, is making a good point. What exactly are your intentions with Sir Ben?"

"I intend to eat lunch with him tomorrow," I say. "Afterwards, we're going to watch a basketball game together."

"Basketball?" Holland asks.

"It is a sporting contest," Nicholas says. "Broadcast over a glass screen. I believe Lady Ashlyn is a supporter of the Tar Heels."

"Tar's no good," Lincoln says. "Won't burn like coal. Which is it, Lady Ashlyn? Your alarm will be on any time now."

"Copper," I say. "Love and beauty."

# Face Arms Speech Time

**Jennifer | March 27 | Madison Square Garden, New York**

We are losing. It's no shame to lose to a better team, and Michigan is a better team—they're the Big Ten champions, number-two seed in the East Region. They are beating us every way they can. That means this is the last game of my college basketball career, here in the Sweet Sixteen, in Madison Square Garden. Assuming that I ever get to play. I'm on the bench the whole first half. Unique has been battling, but she can't keep us in the game by herself, and the Michigan backcourt is too talented. It's 70-55, six minutes left, when Coach turns to me and tells me I'm going in the game.

"Bring us home, Six," she says. "You've had a great career, now go out there and finish it. Make us all proud."

I head out on the floor. The great arena is half-empty; it was filled by UConn fans for the first game, but they're all headed home now. (I learned this week that Madison Square Garden sits right on top of a large train station—it makes sense, because there aren't any parking lots anywhere around. Growing up in North Carolina, I never realized that.) But even with a smaller crowd, I feel an electric surge of emotion. It was a thrill to walk onto on Michael Jordan's old home court in Chapel Hill, or to walk into Cameron Indoor for the first time. The Garden is a different experience altogether—this has been the center of basketball in the world for decades, and today I get to add my story to that long line of heroes.

I take the inbounds pass from Monica and pass it to Joy, who dribbles her way up the court. I settle down in the corner, and the Michigan back-up power forward moves over to guard me. Joy drives down the lane, dishes to Monica on the wing, and her jump shot goes in, clean and true. Michigan takes the ball back down the court, and their point guard steps back and shoots an arcing three-point try that finds the net. Back down the court again, and I savor the moment. The blur of the fans in the stands, the bright maize of the Michigan uniforms, my feet solid against the floorboards, the wild rhythm of my heartbeat.

Joy tries her own three-point shot from the top of the key; I maneuver past the Michigan forward and get into position for the rebound. It bounces my way, and I line myself up for the high-percentage shot. The blocky Wolverine center swats at my arm, and the referee blows the whistle for the foul. The ball hits the backboard and bounces off the hoop. We're in the bonus, so I shoot two.

I take my place at the top of the key. Monica and Joy are on my left, Rowena on my right, and they're all clapping for me, cheering me on. Two free throws, maybe the last shots of my college career. Then I can go home, back to Asheville, where I will tell people for the rest of my career about the Sweet Sixteen game I played in Madison Square Garden.

I don't want to miss, don't want to leave the game with that bad taste in my mouth. I cradle the ball in both hands, next to my body, and then raise it high and send it on its way.

The ball lands with a thud at Rowena's feet and skitters out of bounds. She looks at me, a note of alarm on her face. I stand there, at the free-throw line, embarrassed and lost. *What happened?* I've missed plenty of free throws, but never that badly.

Adele the trainer races out onto the court as the whistle blows for a time out I didn't know we were calling. "Are you okay?" she asks.

"I'm okay," I say.

Adele cocks her head, as though she's looking at me for the first time. "Jennifer," she says. "Can you smile for me?"

I don't know why she is asking this. There's a time out, but everyone seems to be milling around, watching me, instead of going to the bench. The game is on TV, maybe that's why. I give her as wide a smile as I can.

"Lift your arms for me." She raises her arms, shoulder high.

This triggers a small note of panic in the back of my brain. This is a test. FAST. I know this from nursing school. Face, you ask someone to smile. Arm, you ask them to lift their arms. You do that when you think someone has had a stroke, but I'm not having a stroke. She's wrong. I lift my arms.

"Can you tell me what the score is?"

FAST. Face, Arms, and now Speech. I look up at the scoreboard, but I can't make out the flashing lights. I am not having a stroke, here, in the middle of a basketball game. I'm not. It's not possible, not here, not now. "I can't see the scoreboard," I say, and then I hear myself, and it's unrecognizable. I glance to the right, and my arm is hanging loose by my side.

"We need an ambulance," Adele shouts, and it's all I can hear in the entirety of Madison Square Garden.

Face. Arms. Speech. That leaves T, which stands for

## ASHLYN | MARCH 27 | WEST ORANGE, NEW JERSEY

Ben and I sit in shocked silence as the North Carolina player at the free-throw line collapses to the floor of the Garden. What must be blood is pooling around her head. A squad of EMTs converge on her, and two more begin pushing a stretcher her way. The ESPN broadcast blinks back to the studio.

"A disturbing scene in New York, as North Carolina forward Jennifer Lamb seems to have an unexplained injury. While this game is in time out, we'll take you to the Baylor-Louisville game in Phoenix, tipping off now. We'll keep you informed of this developing story as we have more information."

"What happened?" I ask.

"Looked like a stroke, with all that blood," Ben says. "Might be an aneurysm in her brain let go. They'll tell us at some point."

We are sitting close together, me in my wheelchair, him in my guest chair. I lean closer to him, and he puts his arm around me.

# Independent Streak

**Penny | March 27 | Montgomery, New Jersey**

I am on my bed, lying on my back, watching an old *Three's Company* rerun off YouTube. I've moved past the Suzanne Somers episodes and am considering abandoning the project and switching my Seventies-era binge-watching over to *Mork and Mindy*.

"If these people had cell phones, all of this would have been avoided," I say to myself, not for the first time.

My FaceTime chimes, and it's Morton. There is one reason Morton would be calling now.

"How's my favorite patient?" he asks. He is at home, in a room that's decorated in Japanese fans for some reason. It strikes me that I am a bit clueless about Morton's home life, and this seems unfair.

"Not that interested in false alarms, thank you very much," I say.

Morton sighs. "You realize that these things are largely out of my control, correct? We can agree on that."

"I am not blaming you personally. The universe is screwing with me. I get that. You are its unholy tool."

"Well, this unholy tool may have good news for you. I just got off the phone with your mother; she's making the arrangements. If you hurry you can make it to New York and check in early enough that your parents can get a decent night's sleep."

"Not Philadelphia?" I ask.

"Not Philadelphia. New York Presbyterian. I'll meet you there in the morning."

I chuck my iPad and its charger into my go-bag. I grab my green hoodie—green for good luck—out of the closet and kick off my Keds and put on my sturdy boots. It doesn't matter, of course—three hours from now I'll be back in those ridiculous angel robes, surrounded by beeping monitors and getting poked by needles. Unless this is another stupid false alarm.

I go downstairs, where my dad is washing dishes, which he never does.

"What have you been eating?" I ask.

"If you think I am telling you about my secret ice cream stash, you're sadly mistaken. Are you ready to go?"

"It's not a secret. You keep Ben & Jerry pints in an old Tyson chicken tenderloin bag in the back of the freezer."

"How long have you known this?" he asks.

"The question is not how long I have known this; the question is about what it will take from you to keep me from telling the boys."

"Not too worried about them. They want vanilla, not Cherry Garcia. Besides, you can't eat anything from now until the surgery starts. Clear liquids only. And you didn't answer my question. Are you ready to go?"

"Physically? Yes. Everything's packed, and if I forget anything, I can get it in New York. Mentally? I don't want to go through another letdown like last time, but if the doctors are ready to go, then so am I."

"Spiritually?"

"I am scared. I know you are both a lot more scared than I am, and I get that, but I'm still scared. Still willing to take the risk despite being scared."

"Okay. Here's the plan; we're all going together. Your mother is upstairs getting your brothers packed away; we'll leave as soon as she gets them ready. We'll drop them off at your aunt's house on the way, so you'll have some time with them in the car."

"Gotcha."

"I'll call Ashlyn on the way and let her know. I was supposed to go in tomorrow and watch her walk on the treadmill, so she'll be disappointed, but she'll be happy for you, I know. We'll be with you, every step."

"I know."

"I love you," my father says. "Always have, always will."

I give him the biggest, strongest hug I can manage.

"Take it easy on your mother. You know how hard this is for her to accept."

"I'll be sensitive," I say.

"That's hard for you. I get that. Do your best."

"One more thing. Plain bagels are fine, but if they have sesame or poppyseed, that's what I want. When they let me eat again, that is. Unless there's a good donut place, which there might be."

"Consider it done."

My brothers tumble their way down the stairs, arguing—I think—over some obscure bit of Harry Potter trivia. I never read those books, because Ashlyn went through a phase where she could not shut up about them. Maybe they're good. Maybe I'll have time to read them afterwards.

"Mommy says you're getting a lung transplant."

"That's where they yank your lungs out of your body and give you somebody else's, right?"

"Right," I say.

"Does that mean you're going to be part-zombie from now on? Cool."

"I never thought about it quite like that," I say. "But if I am a part-zombie, you guys are safe."

"Why?"

"Because zombies eat *brains*."

## PENNY | MARCH 27 | NEWARK, NEW JERSEY

"We're not taking this exit?" I ask.

We have ridden in silence since dropping off the boys, listening to the adult-contemporary station on Sirius together, no one wanting to say anything. I believe my father is asleep, but I'm not sure. Silence works for me, anyway. I have my emotions, Mom has hers, and they don't correspond at the moment. Easier not to say anything.

"We would exit there to take the Holland Tunnel, but Waze says the Lincoln is better right now," she explains. "The faster we get there, the faster they can check you in and start running the tests."

"Did Morton tell you anything about the donor?" I ask.

"They were having trouble getting permission from the next of kin. It's a touchy situation; he didn't elaborate. The donor is brain-dead—some sort of sudden aneurysm. The lungs are fine. Heart and liver, too; they're preparing for multiple transplants."

I decide not to check my phone for anything about the donor's identity; someone's random brain aneurysm won't be newsworthy.

"Have you talked to your sister lately?" Mom asks.

Finally, a safe subject. "Yes. She has apparently acquired a love interest."

"You're not serious."

"She's serious," my father says, stirring from what I had thought was deep slumber. "I haven't met the fellow yet, but he appears to be an actual person, and not a figment of Penny's overactive imagination." I decide to ignore this.

"When you say love interest," Mom asks. "Is this a serious relationship? Is it reciprocated on his part?"

"No way to tell at the moment. Doesn't appear to be incredibly serious, but I'm still doing my due diligence." This last earns a snort from my father.

"Do you have details that you're willing to share?" Mom asks.

"The data is sketchy and incomplete so far, but here's what I have. Name is Ben Shepherd. Hillsborough High School graduate. Student at Duke, according to LinkedIn. Finance major; internship last summer at Capital One in New York. Facebook says he's in the hospital because of a cancerous growth in his heel, which led to a foot amputation, which is why he needs rehab. Apparently, he likes Ashlyn and is very friendly with her, but the relationship hasn't moved the needle yet."

"How did you find that out?" Mom asks.

"The Nneka Broadcasting Network," Dad says. "I'm surprised you aren't on her mailing list."

"Nneka's trying to encourage Ashlyn to make a move, but she's stubborn."

Mom sighs. "I read somewhere that extreme independence is often related to traumatic experiences. I mean, your sister has always had that independent streak. I hope she doesn't turn someone away because she's been through so much."

I ask myself if that's meant to be directed towards me as well.

"I think Ashlyn appreciates all the help she's getting," I say.

"I know she does, but that still doesn't stop her from pushing people away."

Okay, this is really directed towards me now.

"I think there's a difference between wanting to do things yourself and pushing other people away. You can love other people, be grateful for them, and still want to live your own life. Make your own decisions. They're not mutually exclusive things."

Mom takes a long swig from her latte, which must have long since grown cold in its cupholder. She sets it down, carefully, and doesn't speak until we've passed the toll gate for the Lincoln Tunnel.

# A Million Miles

### Adele | March 27 | New York Presbyterian Hospital, New York City

Adele Andersson is trapped, no two ways about it. There is one available power outlet on this ward, and the charger that she has borrowed—begged, not to put too fine a point on it—has a short cord. She has—again, not to put too fine a point on it—stolen an uncomfortable metal chair from an adjoining room, and has been stuck to it as though she was stapled there.

She went to the hospital with Jennifer Lamb. She was the first one to get to her, the first one to realize that she was dying. Not that there was anything she could have done about it. She is a trainer; she can handle sprains and strains and bumps and bruises. Treating a stroke is not something that she knows how to do—and who expects young, highly trained amateur athletes to have strokes in the middle of competition?

She did what she could do, which was to hold Jennifer Lamb's limp hand as she was lifted onto the gurney, as she was threaded through the tunnels of Madison Square Garden, as she was loaded onto an ambulance. Nobody told her to go, but she—and apparently everyone else—thought it was her duty.

Now she is here, sitting in a hallway, somewhere in the vast maze of New York Presbyterian, with Jennifer Lamb's body in the room behind her. Adele has always felt distant from Jennifer; now that distance might as well be a million miles. Adele was never prepared to deal with a sudden hemorrhagic stroke—although no one at the hospital seems to be, not with a stroke of this severity. She is even less prepared to be the liaison between the University of North Carolina and the hospital establishment. She has spent the last two hours giving updates to a succession of ever more senior UNC staffers—the coach, the sports information director, the athletic director, the football coach (for whatever reason), the provost, and most recently, the university president.

They want to know if Jennifer Lamb is dead. This is not an easy question to answer. On one hand, *of course she is dead.* There is no way that anyone survives that, losing that much blood at once. Adele has not seen the ESPN feed—she's one of the few people who has not—but anyone who has seen it *knows.* Knowing by itself, though, is not enough. It is not enough for Jennifer Lamb to be dead for all practical purposes; to satisfy the yawning, gaping mouth of the news cycle, she has to be legally dead, undeniably dead. As of right this second, she is not. The left side of her brain is destroyed. This is what the doctors have told Adele, and this is what she has dutifully relayed to the UNC establishment.

The heart and lungs are controlled by the brain stem, and they are still working. Jennifer Lamb could, in theory, live on like this for a few more hours, until the rest of her remaining brain cells figure things out and shut down her vital processes. But she will not—if *she* is the operative word anymore. Jennifer Lamb is not a person any longer, but a collection of spare parts.

All anyone wants to know, over at the team hotel or down in Chapel Hill, is *when,* which is not happening anytime soon. Adele has said this repeatedly over the past few hours. The doctors will not say that Jennifer

Lamb is actually, legally dead until the people who are coming in for transplantation surgery make it in from the far corners of the tri-state area. Some of them are already here—both cornea patients, one of the two kidney patients. The other kidney patient is on the Metro North, coming down from Connecticut. The lungs are going to someone driving in from New Jersey. The holdup is the liver patient, who is attending a concert at Lincoln Center, and has their phone turned off.

Adele is explaining all of this to the sports information director—or trying to, as the sports information director is trying to communicate with his own onslaught of people asking him questions. "When will we know for sure?"

"When the doctors say for sure. They are only keeping her alive for the transplant surgery. Once that starts, then they will say."

"It could be at two o'clock in the morning, then? Great."

"Is it possible that someone else from the team can be here?" Adele asks.

"The team is taking it very hard. So is the coach. I don't know who we can get."

"I am an assistant trainer. A student assistant trainer." *Who would like to get back to her hotel room and take a shower.* "Here by myself, talking nonstop to the entire university administration."

"Which we appreciate. Honestly. Look, I'll try to get an assistant coach to relieve you, somebody like that. Hang in there. Call me once you know something." *Click.*

Adele rubs her eyes and waits for the next call to come in. She checks her texts, and there are eight or ten new ones. At the top is the one from Coach Morgan. *I am sending Paul Sloan over to the hospital to take over for you. He should be there in twenty minutes.*

"Thank God," Adele mumbles. Paul Sloan is the lead assistant coach and is better suited for the death watch. Even better, she has his cell number and texts him her location so that he can find her within the maze of the hospital complex. The phone rings again, this time from a number in New York.

"Hello?"

"Miss Andersson? My name is Sylvia Blix; I am with the Swedish Consulate here in New York. I understand you are still at the hospital; I wanted to see if I could be of any assistance?"

"Assistance? How do you mean?"

"Well, when one of our citizens is in New York, and trending on Twitter, we tend to take an interest."

"Trending on Twitter?"

"Of course. You were on national television, you know, caring for the unfortunate basketball player. It did not take long for people to identify you as an Olympic athlete."

*"Förbannat!"*

"Indeed. I have already had several press inquiries about you, which is why I am reaching out. I am sure you don't want to talk to anyone now, but in the morning, if you are available, I can arrange for a quick interview."

"No comment," Adele says. "Not today, not tomorrow."

"As you wish. You have my number; please do call if you need anything."

"Oh. Well. *Tack så mycket.*"

"*Varsågod*. Sleep well. If you change your mind, call me."

Adele slumps back into her chair. The phone is ringing again, the university chancellor's number. She considers throwing the phone against the wall, and not for the first time.

## PENNY | MARCH 28 | NEW YORK PRESBYTERIAN HOSPITAL, NEW YORK CITY

We arrived at the hospital around eleven, after an interminable wait in the Lincoln Tunnel—which, contrary to Waze, was packed with traffic. We were greeted at the front desk by Katie, my transplant coordinator. Katie is tall and blonde, with a complexion so perfect that I would not be able to tell you how old she is except for an unfortunate crease in her forehead. I have the impression that she used to be perky but got over it. Because this is a new hospital for me, there is no end of paperwork before I can check in. The parental units are adept at handling it, so after an hour or so I get up and stretch.

"Can I go get a Sprite?" I ask.

My dad hands me a five-dollar bill. "Get me a Coke Zero, too. Hurry back."

It is somewhere around midnight, and the hospital corridors are bright and quiet. I find a vending machine without too much trouble, but I am vexed to find that it's a Pepsi machine. I get a Sierra Mist and a diet Pepsi for my dad, for which I will catch seven levels of hell, but it's not my fault.

I walk back to the little office where they are doing the paperwork, and I stop for a second, out of breath, and start coughing. I manage to hold on to the bottles, but I have to cough so long and so loud that I crouch down, putting my wrists on my knees.

"Are you all right?" someone asks.

She is a short person, wearing a pale-blue polo shirt with what looks like smeared, dried blood on her right shoulder. Her face is red and puffy, and she has an accent I can't place. Her voice is hard, but not unkind.

"I'm fine," I say, wiping a rogue glob of mucus away with my sleeve. "Sorry. Cystic fibrosis."

"Oh," she says. It's always chancy telling strangers you have CF; either they've never heard of it, or they think you're mentally backwards, or else their neighbor's niece has it and they won't quit asking you questions.

"Well, not for much longer. I drove in from Jersey. Lung transplant."

She blinks at me for a moment, looking stricken. I get the impression I have said something wrong, something deeply offensive, but I have no idea what it could have been. She closes her eyes for a moment, as though I had smacked her with the back of my hand.

Her phone is ringing, but she doesn't answer it. "You are... very lucky, you know."

"I wouldn't say that."

"You are, even though you don't realize it. I can't say I knew her that well. We... weren't friendly, but she was a strong person, an excellent athlete. A real competitor. If you get her lungs, then you're getting a true gift. Make the most of it."

I start coughing again, louder this time, and she takes me by the elbow. "Do you need help?" she asks, taking the bottles of soda away from me.

"Are you a nurse?"

"Athletic trainer. You should sit down."

I point towards the room where my parents are sitting, and she steers me to my chair, hands me and my dad our bottles, and leaves without a word.

"Who was that?" Mom asks.

"I have no idea," I say.

"Whoever she is, she doesn't know the difference between Coke Zero and swill," Dad says.

"I think you should try to sleep," Mom says.

It is two o'clock in the morning, and we are waiting on the tests to come back to confirm that the transplant can continue. The surgery is scheduled for seven o'clock, but prep for that starts an hour earlier, and it doesn't seem worthwhile for me to get any sleep now when I'll be asleep for the surgery and for hours after.

"It's the city that never sleeps," I explain. "I'm not tired."

"We are," my dad says. "We'll sleep better knowing that you're asleep."

"I know this is stressful for you guys," I say, "but I never sleep well in hospitals anyway." Too much going on, and then there are the sirens outside.

"At least try," Mom says, her forehead creasing in concern as she smooths my hair.

*Don't worry*, I want to say. I know what this is about. She is worried. I don't think there's anything to worry about; either I live through the surgery or I don't. Nothing to worry about either way. Worry won't help anything or hurt anything. She is going to worry anyway, and I can't stop that, and I can't tell her not to. Anything I say will be wrong.

"I'll stay up with her," Dad says. "You go get some sleep."

Mom gives me a kiss, says "I love you," and nervously tucks a corner of the blanket under me. She walks away, close to tears, staggering a little on her way out the door. My dad follows her out the door, trying to catch her elbow.

"I'll be right back," he says. "Don't forget Parental Lecture 36."

"Which one is that?"

"It's a new one. It says you're not allowed to die on us."

I lie back and stare at the ceiling tiles, waiting patiently for morning.

"You're taking all this very calmly," Katie, the tall blonde transplant coordinator says.

"I guess." It is morning; I am not sure what we are waiting on at this point.

"Have you been here before?"

"Here? No. Morristown Memorial when I was little. CHOP down in Philly more recently. Cincinnati Children's for an experimental study that didn't pan out. Robert Wood Johnson last year when I had a concussion."

"You're a true hospital veteran, then." She has a blank look on her face that I don't quite know how to interpret.

"I suppose. All I know is the food is always the same. Not that I get to eat anything today. And they all smell the same."

"Tell me about it," she says.

There is an edge to that statement, and I get the distinct impression that there's something there, something that isn't ordinary medical-profession burnout. Thousand-yard stare, or that's what they'd call it in a war novel. "What about you?" I ask. "You sound like a veteran yourself."

"Acute lymphoblastic leukemia. Levine Children's Hospital in Charlotte, but they couldn't do anything. I made four different trips to St. Jude's before I was eleven."

I hold out my fist. "Respect," I say, and she bumps it.

"The one thing that I always wanted from people was honesty. When you're a kid, and you're sick, people think it's okay to lie to you, as though that made it better. It never does."

"Always call them out when they do that, and they'll stop," I say.

"Truth. You know there aren't any guarantees, right?"

"Doesn't bother me. There's one guarantee when you have CF, that it will kill you sooner or later."

"Lung transplants can kill you, too. There's a real risk of rejection. If you get past that, then infection. *Staph aureus. B. cepacia. Aspergillus.* Maybe osteoporosis."

"I've seen the numbers," I say. "Once I get past that first month—if I don't die—I can count on twenty more years. Maybe more, if the treatments keep getting better."

"It's important to be positive," Katie says. "The numbers do improve after that first month, but that first month is incredibly tough, and we can't control all the variables. You're getting a great pair of lungs. You're in a world-class transplant hospital. Even so, there's only so much we can do. That means you're going to have to come out swinging. Are you ready?"

"Of course," I say.

The little crease on her face deepens. "No, you're not. You think you are. Anyone who's spent a lot of time in the hospital thinks that they're ready for anything medical science can throw at them. Transplant surgery takes a lot out of you. I mean, literally, it takes your organs out of you, right? It's a lot more difficult than any other medical procedure you'll ever have. Nobody's ready for this."

"I'm as ready as I can be," I say. "There's literally no alternative. Otherwise, I wouldn't be here. I know it's risky, but nothing is as risky as having CF for the rest of your life."

Katie's face goes blank, and I suspect I've hit a sore spot. An obvious sore spot, now that I think of it. As a hospital kid, I learned early not to make close friends with the bald kids in pediatric oncology, because you never knew if they would make it, and lots didn't. She survived, which means she doesn't need to hear me talking about risk.

"Why did you do it?" I ask at length.

"Do what?"

"Come back here. To health care. You escaped. You got out. Why would you come back?"

"Why wouldn't I?" Katie asks.

"I mean, I'm not. I wouldn't. If I make it out of here, I'm not looking at anything health care. Architecture. Urban design. Not this."

"This is important, too. Helping people is important. I had so many people help me, and I knew I needed to give something back."

"All right. Well. Like I said, respect."

"Okay then," Katie says. "I'll go get your parents; I think they're almost ready. Then we'll start heading towards the operating room."

# ALL OF THE WAY

## ASHLYN | MARCH 28 | WEST ORANGE, NEW JERSEY

"They started the first incision about a half-hour ago," my dad says. "They don't know how long it's going to take. Anywhere from three to five hours; it depends on how much her current lungs are sticking to her ribs."

I did not need that particular mental image, but it does help clarify things. "How's Mom?" I ask.

"I will deny this if you ever mention it to your mother, but she's a mess. She has been dreading this, ever since Penny went to the top of the transplant list. It's too much all at once, what with you in the hospital, too. This is not your fault, of course, you're doing your best to get out of there, but it doesn't help with the stress."

There is a nonzero chance that my sister will die today. She has been at the brink of death more times than I can count, but the odds are greater today than they ever had been. I can't do anything to help her, but even if I was in New York with her, it wouldn't matter. There would be nothing I could do except to comfort my parents, wait, and hope for the best.

"Wiss-sh I was there," I say.

"I know, sweetheart. You have your own battle to fight. Are they still going to let you walk on your own today?"

"For a little bit."

"Tell Nneka to send me the video. Or should I ask your friend? Ben, is that right?"

"That's right," I say. If Penny pulls through this, I am going to get her if it's the last thing I ever do.

"He sounds nice," Dad says, but I don't reply. I am absolutely not ready to discuss how I feel about Ben or how I don't feel about Ben with anybody, and that goes quadruple for my parents. How can I, when I'm not sure about how I feel? He is kind, and smart, and likes basketball, and is pleasant to be around. Does that make him a friend? Maybe a good friend? In this environment, yes, and I am not looking for much more than that. He is handsome, and we have a lot in common, not least the shared experience of rehab.

At that moment, Ben's head pops in the door, as though I had summoned him. "Oh, sorry," he says. "Didn't know you were on the phone."

"Tell Mom it will all work out," I say. "I'm thinking good thoughts."

"I'll do that," Dad says. "Walk tall for me today, sweetheart. Bye."

"Bye."

Ben sticks his head back in the door. "Didn't mean to interrupt."

"It's okay. My dad called. Penny getting lung transplant today."

"Wow," he says. "That's serious surgery. Hope it's successful."

"Yeah."

"Are you ready for breakfast?" he asks. "I thought we could go together. Maybe I can give you a push."

I look over at him, closely, and he's not using his crutches. He's wearing a new foot, which is metallic and angular, and makes him look like a cyborg in a cheap sci-fi novel.

"You like it? It's titanium, which makes it a good bit lighter. Balance is pretty good so far. I am walking slow on it, trying to break it in."

"Glad you are up and about," I say. "Not being lazy anymore."

"Compared to you, everybody is lazy. You ready to walk today?"

"You know it."

"Okay, then. Let's go. Breakfast is the most important meal of the day, after all."

"Are you ready?" Dr. Lindbergh asks.

"You bet," I say. I have been walking for about forty-five minutes now, suspended from the Hoyer lift. I've gone a little farther and a little faster over the last few weeks, and they've put progressively less tension on the Hoyer. I have no doubt that I can walk independently, but that is not the same thing as safely.

"You got this, Ashlyn," Nneka says. She has my phone and is getting ready to start the video for my parents.

I slow to a stop—which does not take that long—and Lindbergh unhooks the harness. I am standing on the treadmill, independently. I grab hold of the rails, gently, trying not to tense up. Lindbergh starts up the machine, one and a half miles an hour, zero incline.

I slide back on the treadmill, and move my left foot forward to stop myself from falling off. Then my right, slowly and deliberately, trying to put my weight on my feet and not on my wrists.

"You're doing great, Ashlyn. Keep it up," Dr. Lindbergh says. "Let me know if you're getting tired."

I am breathing hard, but I am not tired. I am working on keeping a rhythm, not slipping, not tripping over my feet. I take another deep breath. *I am doing this for Penny*, I tell myself, breathing hard for her when she can't. It's sympathetic magic, I know, but it works. I walk, and I keep walking, step by step.

"Good work," Dr. Lindbergh says. "I know you don't want to hear this, Ashlyn, but seeing you walk like this is inspiring. I mean, this is why you do rehab medicine, moments like this."

"Getting started," I say. I'm not going to stop, not until I get all of the way back.

I hear a clatter over to my left, where Nneka has apparently dropped my phone. "Sorry," she says. "It started ringing… I think it's your father, if you want to talk to him."

"It's about time to stop anyway," Lindbergh says.

I don't want to get off, I don't want to stop walking, now that I've started, but this is either good news or the worst news, and I need to know. I let Lindbergh turn off the treadmill and gingerly step off the back of it, making my way to my wheelchair. I sink down onto the cushion, and Nneka hands me my phone.

"How is she?" I ask.

"She pulled through," he says. "Surgery was quicker than we thought it would be, even though it felt like a hundred years. Her heart started beating again, no problem. Pulse-ox is looking good. They have her on a ventilator, which is pretty standard. She's resting quietly in the ICU."

"Good," I say. "Good. You okay?"

"We're doing much better now, thanks. They have us in, I guess you'd call it a hotel, across the street, but it's for families. We're comfortable enough, I guess. We're waiting to see if her immune system rejects the lungs.

Ought not to be an issue, they're supposed to be a great set of lungs, but you never know. You doing okay?"

"Walked," I say. "Nneka is s-sending the video."

"Look forward to seeing it. You have occupational therapy, and then PT, is that right?"

"Right."

"Okay. We're going to try to get a little rest. It's like when the twins were born, you sleep when they sleep. Remember?"

All I remember about that was that there was a lot of crying, most of it from the babies. "Rest up. You"—there's a word I want to say here, but I can't think of what it is. "You need it."

"We do at that. Talk to you later, Ashlyn. Congratulations on the walk."

"Deserve," I say.

"Yes?" Nneka asks. "What is it that you deserve?"

I am over at physical therapy, on the rowing machine. Back and forth, back and forth. For whatever reason, I remembered the word that I wanted to tell my dad—that he and Mom deserved rest. Which they do, it's that the word "deserve" managed to fall out of my brain, and now it fell back in. Of course, because it popped into my head, and I am a giant idiot, I had to say it, and now I have to explain it to Nneka. *Gah.*

"Never mind," I say. "Hard to explain."

"You do deserve," Nneka says. "You are deserving. You have worked hard to be able to walk and to talk.

You deserve good things. Like friendship and companionship, and maybe love."

I step up the pace of my rowing. My dad has a kayak and takes it out every once in a while, on the Raritan River, or the quieter waters of the Delaware and Raritan Canal. Maybe I can go with him next time. It is weird that I can row better than I can walk. Maybe I should check to see if I can still swim. Maybe Nneka will shut her trap so I can concentrate on rowing and physical therapy and getting better and stronger and walking out of here.

"He likes you. You are spending a good bit of time together. He will not be here much longer. Tell him how you feel before he gets away."

No such luck. I do not want to talk about Ben. I do not want to explore how I feel about him. I recognize that I am pretty thoroughly fouled up right now, from an emotional standpoint. I have a single-minded commitment to recovery that even I recognize is borderline unhealthy. I am dealing with pain and disfigurement on a daily basis. I have a sister in the hospital whom I'm worried about. I am having recurrent dreams set in my very own medieval fantasy construct. None of this is suited for any kind of serious relationship, but I *like* Ben. I like spending time with him. He is almost startlingly handsome, cool blue eyes in a strong, calm face. Like me, he's scarred, and dealing with pain and isolation. It's perfectly reasonable for me to be attracted to him. I am not sure why he feels attracted to me—if he does—but I think Nneka is right, and he does. That's the important part.

She's right that I should do something soon. He has his new foot now, if it works for him, and he can walk without pain, he can finish the rest of his rehab from home. He could even go back to Duke for the end of the spring semester and graduation. He's not staying here on my account, no matter how badly I want him to. I am never going to know what it feels like when he touches me, the pressure of his lips against mine...

I feel a huge shock of pain in my lower left leg, and let out an undignified yelp. It's a muscle cramp, I recognize that right away, but it's incredibly painful and my feet are strapped into the footrests, and I can't move. My yelp catches Gretel's attention, and she comes over to help Nneka get me out of the machine. Another wave of pain washes over me, and I let out a deep grunt.

"What leg is it?" Gretel asks.

"Left," I gasp.

Gretel and Nneka lift me out of the machine and roll me over on my stomach. I land in a heap, banging my left wrist as they flip me over. Gretel starts kneading my calf muscle, which hurts but not as much as the cramp.

"Relax," Nneka tells me. "It will all be over in a minute."

It's a long minute. Gretel gives my calf a long, deep stroke, and it relieves a lot of the pain. She keeps rubbing it, and the pain gradually declines.

"Nneka, can you get her a Powerade from the cafeteria?" Gretel asks.

"Of course."

"Is that better?" Gretel asks. "Do you think you can get up?"

"In a minute," I say.

"Take your time. You are done for the day. Get rehydrated, come back tomorrow."

I would normally argue about this so that I could keep going, but that cramp hurt and I don't want to damage the muscle. Gretel is right; it's time to call it a day. I push myself up, and I feel a twinge of pain in my left wrist—it's nothing so bad as the cramp, but it hurts and I can't get up.

"What is wrong, Ashlyn?" Gretel asks.

"Wrist." I say. "Banged it."

Gretel doesn't say another word. She gets up, finds my wheelchair, pushes it over next to me, and picks me up roughly around my waist, the way you would lift a rolled-up carpet. She levers me up to my feet, and I fall back in the wheelchair as Nneka returns with a blue bottle of Gatorade. I hate the blue flavor.

"Nneka, take her to Dr. Lindbergh so he can look at that wrist. Ashlyn, rest, rehydrate, and we'll try again tomorrow."

I hold the drink with my left hand, and feel a little relief from the cold bottle. I manage to open it with my right, and then take a deep swig. It tastes abominable, and I remind myself that I need to have a long talk with Nneka about something, but for the moment, I can't remember what.

# You Had Me At Hello

### Penny | New York City | Five Years In The Future

It is a bright day in late April in the New York City of my dreams. I am standing next to a tall blonde girl, who is about my age, or what my age is going to be in five years. We are waiting in line in front of a taco truck.

"Have you seen him yet?" the girl asks. She has an arch Texas accent, and her long hair is pulled back in a French braid.

"Who?" I ask.

"For God's sake, Penny," the girl says. "Try and pay attention."

"I am paying attention," I say. "They have chorizo tacos, and I'm trying to decide if that's a good idea or whether it's a distraction to keep me from getting the chicken tacos."

"This is not about tacos. You know that. These tacos aren't any good anyway, not compared to what you get in Fort Worth. We're only here because that cute guy comes here on Tuesdays."

"Got it," I say. I look around, trying to get my bearings. The street sign says that it's Lafayette Street, and there's a Duane Reade across the street, because this is New York. I am wearing a deep-purple NYU sweatshirt. *That means I'm in college now. That means I survived the transplant. I'm here, in the future, standing in line for tacos.*

Except that I'm not. I'm in the hospital, and having a dream. Still. Better than nothing.

"Look around and see where he is, okay? Don't make it obvious. It needs to be a chance meeting, that's how it works."

The girl—I decide her name is Lisa—is not someone who needs a meet-cute to attract attention. She's wearing aviator glasses, a short jacket and tight jeans and bright-pink cowboy boots. If the cute guy doesn't notice her, it's not from lack of trying. Or else he has chronic astigmatism. *Or a steady boyfriend*, I think, but I decide not to point that possibility out to Lisa.

"If you're showing up every Tuesday to a taco truck in the hopes of running into him," I say, "that's not so much romantic as it is, you know, stalking."

"God, Penny, nobody is asking your opinion here."

"If you like him, it is okay to walk up to him and ask him out. The worst that happens is that he says no."

"Right, then I text Eric, and we go out for pizza. I know. Eric is cute, but Eric's ambition is to own a Greek diner in Jersey, and no thank you."

"What's wrong with Jersey?" I ask.

"Nothing. And everything. And... there he is, he's getting in line behind us."

"So go talk to him."

"Have you not been listening to anything I have been saying? It has to be spontaneous."

"Fine. Then I will go and spontaneously tell him that you think he's cute."

"What? No. Penny, stop."

I give Lisa my best devilish grin and head to the back of the line.

Lisa is not blind. The cute guy is amazingly cute. Dark hair with a hint of a wave on top. A kind face, but with a firm jawline. Strong shoulders under his charcoal-pinstripe suit jacket. Not too tall; maybe five-eleven. Dark eyes that are looking right at me, sparkling in amusement. "Hello," he says.

"My friend thinks you're cute," I say.

"Your friend? The blonde over there in the cowboy boots, the one with that mortified look on her face?"

"That would be her."

"That's very interesting. I assumed that you both liked tacos."

"Yes. I mean, I like tacos. Lisa—that's my friend's name—she's from Texas. She likes tacos, too. That's not why we eat here, though."

"Your name is?"

"Penny. I'm an architecture student at NYU—we both are." I don't know why I am saying this; I have never thought about studying architecture at NYU, or anywhere else. It makes sense in the context of the dream, so I'm rolling with it.

"I see," the cute guy says. "So why did you come over and say hello, and why is she standing there looking like she wants the earth to swallow her?"

"I think she's being shy," I say, although she doesn't seem shy. "As I think I said, she thinks you're cute."

"How considerate of her. What can I do for you?"

"Um. Well. Like I said, Lisa over there, she thinks you're cute. And I wanted to pass that message along."

"I see. One thing you might not have considered, though, Penny, is you might not be the only one who comes to this same taco truck every week hoping to meet someone."

The cute guy looks at me then, and it may be a trick of the light, but there's something else there behind the amusement. Something that's close to longing. I can feel my knees start to buckle under me, the blood running to my face. I open my mouth, and then close it.

"Maybe we can continue this discussion over dinner tonight. Unless you're worried about making your friend over there upset."

"You mean, more upset than she already is," Lisa says, with a bag of tacos in her hand. Her face is red, verging on purple. "Penny, what is your problem?"

"Specifically?"

Lisa glares at me, with a stare calculated to turn a lesser mortal to stone.

"If you must know," I say, "the issue isn't me. It's you. It's that you don't exist, neither of you."

The cute guy looks amused at this; Lisa does not. "You're not making any sense," she says.

"I'm sorry to break it to both of you. Right this minute, I'm in a hospital bed uptown, recovering from lung transplant surgery, and I'm unconscious. This is all a dream. That means that you're not real, and you're not real, and unfortunately for all of us, these delicious tacos aren't real."

"You have officially lost it, Penny," Lisa says. She takes the bag full of non-existent tacos and flounces back towards the NYU campus, her cowboy boots stomping the springtime puddles.

"She seems nice," the cute guy says.

"Well, no one likes being told that they don't exist."

"I suppose not. So where does this leave us?"

"I don't know," I say. "I suppose I will wake up before too long. I don't know when I will get back here. I'm not sure if I can. Maybe it will take some time. Or I hope so. I've never worried about time before."

"We'll leave it there, then," the cute guy says. "Good night, sweet Penny, and may flights of angels see you to your rest."

He walks off towards his office building on the other side of the street. As he leaves, all of the color drains away from the cityscape, and I am left alone in a gray emptiness. I close my eyes, once, twice, three times and sink back into unconsciousness.

# Useless Desires

## Ashlyn | March 29 | West Orange, New Jersey

I have wasted the entire morning arguing with Lindbergh about whether he will let me get back on the treadmill without the harness, and losing. I have logic and desire on my side, and Lindbergh has a medical degree, so I lose. The compromise is that I get to ride on the exercise bike. I have never been a big fan of the exercise bike to begin with, but it at least is going to help me bring up my cardio levels. I would say that it's helping me bleed off my frustration, but Nneka is watching me, and she won't shut up. For the first half hour, it's all about her current romantic fixation—a pharmacy tech she's been actively flirting with all week.

"He's from Botswana, though," she says. "They raise cattle in Botswana. I am a city girl. My father is a geologist, working for the oil companies. I've never been anywhere near cattle. If we get married, what happens if he asks for a dowry?"

I concentrate on maintaining my current speed. The bike is connected to a video feed that's showing the English countryside, which looks nice and flat and suitable for bicycle tourism.

"Of course, he may not be looking for another African girl, not here in America. You never can tell with African men here. A lot of them are here on visas, so they want to get married to an American citizen. I am not saying they are all looking for white girls, although some of them are."

The English countryside is looking better and better all the time. I take a swig of sports drink, the red kind this time.

"I am not saying that I would turn down a nice rich white American doctor, myself, though," Nneka continues. "It would help with the immigration paperwork if nothing else. Getting a doctor to even notice you, well, it's harder than you might think. This is where you have an advantage with Ben; he at least notices you."

I am concentrating on my cardio and don't have the breath to answer her. I do glance over towards the other side of the gym, where Ben is strolling easily on a treadmill. It won't be long before he's jogging, and then running.

"You are tired of hearing me say this, I know, so I will not bother repeating myself. You know what to do."

Nneka is not wrong about this, necessarily. If Ben walks out of here without me saying anything to him, I'm going to lose him. Maybe it's too soon for me to seriously pursue him. I want the relationship with Ben, but I'm not ready for anything serious, much less anything physical. It's not as though I don't have enough else to worry about, not with Penny still unconscious in the hospital and Lindbergh being stubborn about the treadmill.

The display on the exercise bike beeps, and the English countryside flickers out. I slow the pedals to a stop, and Nneka helps me to my feet. I manage a couple of tentative steps towards my wheelchair, and sink down onto it with a sigh. I shouldn't be this tired after what is moderate exercise, but I am.

Ben steps off the treadmill and heads over towards me. His new foot is apparently not causing him the same problems as the last one; he's not walking all that comfortably, but he looks not to be in any pain.

He walks over to me. "Ready for some lunch?" he asks.

"You know it," I say.

I get a turkey cutlet with a side of macaroni and cheese, and chocolate milk; Ben gets an arugula salad and the beef barley stew. "How's your sister?" he asks.

"Unconscious," I say, slipping all over the sibilant in the middle of the word. "Watching for rejection symptoms. Still on... breathing machine." There's a name for that, but I can't think what it is. *Ventilator*, that's it.

"Let me know if there's anything I can do," he says. "Well, maybe not me, but my parents aren't far from yours, if they need someone to look after the house or anything."

"Thanks," I say. "I'll let them know. How is your foot?"

He smiles, flashing those white teeth. "It feels great," he says. "My dad is picking me up on Saturday, and we're going to try to hit the Cherry Valley golf course if the weather is nice. I don't think I'll be able to play too many holes, but I'll be able to drive the cart, at least get outside for a little bit."

Golf. Boring. Not to mention cold; it's still March. Not the least bit interested. I take a big bite of macaroni and cheese, and a few noodles fall on my Carolina-blue sweatshirt. I reach over for a napkin and try to wipe off some of the cheese. I look up in time to see the girl.

She is tall, two or three inches taller than I am, with a long blonde ponytail. She has a dark-blue Duke windbreaker that looks almost tailored. She tiptoes behind Ben and puts her newly manicured hands over his eyes. "Guess who," she says, her voice all sunshine and honey.

"Is that Carissa?" he asks. She sits beside him, and beams at him, and gives him an ostentatious kiss on the cheek. "It is you," he says. "I'm so glad you came."

"Of course, I came," Carissa says. "As soon as I could get away, of course. May I join you for lunch?"

"Yes. Sure. Of course. It's hospital food, you understand, but it's not bad. It is so great to see you."

I am, frankly, staring at Carissa, mostly because of how out-of-place she is. It's as though part of the real world, the world outside the hospital, has shown up unexpectedly. She hasn't noticed me yet, because Ben is staring at her, too, as though he's seeing a vision. We might have sat there forever, enchanted by her presence, until Nneka breaks the spell. "Won't you introduce us to your friend, Mr. Shepherd?"

Ben blinks in surprise. "Yeah. Sure. Of course. Where are my manners? This is Nneka, she's a nurse here, and this is Cissy's friend I was telling you about, Ashlyn Revere. This is Carissa Buckley, she's my fiancée."

Fiancée.

In that moment, every thought I've had about Ben, every glance, every shared laugh, every stray desire, crystallizes into something as hard and white as the diamond ring on Carissa Buckley's finger.

"Of course," Carissa says. "How pleasant to meet you." Her voice is still honeyed, but with a drop of vinegar in it.

I open my mouth, and it's like swallowing broken glass. "Hello," I manage to say, and it takes an effort. Part of it is envy, part of it is betrayal, and part of it is the sudden understanding that Ben, handsome Ben, nice Ben, is the world's biggest rat.

"Ashlyn has speech issues," Ben says, not helpfully. "Since her car accident. She understands everything, but she sometimes has a hard time saying things." Yeah, like *oh, by the way, sorry I never told you, but I'm engaged to a pretty, smart, athletic blonde girl.* Those kinds of things are so hard to say.

"Ben has mentioned you several times," Carissa says. "Your story is... so inspirational."

Is she being sincere or condescending? I ask myself. Probably condescending. Well, then. Let's get the focus off me.

"Did you meet at Duke?" I ask. It's a dumb question, I know that, but it's the most inoffensive thing that I can come up with.

"Of course," Carissa says. "Freshman geology course. Rocks for jocks, as they say."

"Carissa is the captain of the basketball team. They missed out on the Final Four; that's why she hasn't been by to see me before now."

I'd heard the name but hadn't made the connection. Ben's fiancée isn't just cute; she's famous. Sure-fire first-round WNBA draft pick, daughter of a rich-as-hell United States Senator. Ben is engaged to her?

"The tournament committee," Carissa says dryly, "sent us to Norman, Oklahoma, and then to Sioux Falls. Lost to Arizona in the Elite Eight at the buzzer. Just as well. I would almost rather not be in the Final Four if that means I have to say nice things about Jennifer Lamb the whole time. I mean, of course it's sad that she died and everything, but the way the press is talking about her, you'd think she was some kind of saint or something. Believe you me, she wasn't."

I decide that I don't like Carissa Buckley very much.

"So, what did you get, Ashlyn? Macaroni and cheese? Looks yummy."

This is either condescension or sarcasm; I get that, but I have no idea why she's indulging in it. I can't even tell who or what it's directed towards. Nneka's expression gets very hard; if Little Miss Ponytail is expecting Nneka to get up and fetch her a plate of macaroni and cheese, then Little Miss Ponytail is in for a long wait.

"I don't recommend it," Ben says. "Let me go and get you something."

"I wasn't expecting that *you* would get anything for me," Carissa says. "Finish your lunch."

Nneka's expression goes from hard to hostile; she's not about to say anything mean-spirited, not to a patient's fiancée, but she is not moving one inch to fetch Carissa so much as a glass of water.

"You sure?" Ben asks. "No trouble at all. It's good exercise."

"If you wouldn't mind then. Maybe a club sandwich, extra mayonnaise."

"Okay. Be right back, sweetie. I'll miss you."

"Not as much as I'll miss you."

I have lost my appetite.

Carissa turns towards Nneka. "I was wondering if I could get a private moment to speak to Ashlyn," she says.

"I have a job, Miss Buckley, and that job is to watch out for Ashlyn. In case she chokes or something. I can't do that if I'm somewhere else." I appreciate that Nneka is being protective, but I expect she doesn't want to miss out on the gossip, either.

"It's okay," I tell Nneka. "S-she can talk for a minute."

"I'll be right over there, then. Let me know if you need me." Nneka shoots Carissa a glare, which she ignores.

Carissa stares at me, the way that a bad-tempered hawk might stare at a mouse. "I don't have a lot of time, and I want to make sure you understand what I have to say. Are you listening?"

"Yeah."

"Good. You will stay away from Ben from now on. Got it? No eating lunch together, no long talks, no late-night basketball-watching parties. He is off limits. He is my fiancée, and you are going to stay as far away from him as you can get. Do I make myself clear?"

"Crystal." I don't want your rat-fink boyfriend anyway, I think, not if he wants to spend the rest of his life with the likes of you.

"One more thing. Ben wants to invite you to the wedding. You are not going. Understand? This is my wedding, my perfect day, and I do not want some scraggly-haired, scar-faced accident victim in the background of my wedding photos. Don't show up, don't send a gift, don't even send a card. I don't want you or that wheelchair anywhere near my wedding. It's bad enough the groom is a cripple without having another one at the reception."

I have one thing to say, just one word, and there is no way I am letting aphasia or apraxia stop me from saying it, loud and clear: "Bitch."

Carissa looks at me and beams. "Of course, you would say that. Small-minded women have been calling tough-minded women that horrible name since the Stone Age. It's your crude way of expressing your inferiority and weakness. Now, if you'll excuse me, Ben is coming back with my lunch. I think it's best if you find somewhere else to go while we enjoy each other's company."

The grief I feel about the end of my relationship with Ben winds around the rage I feel towards Carissa. I tell myself that I can control my emotions. The last seven months have been a master class in controlling my emotions. Even so, it takes every bit of restraint I possess to keep from throwing my macaroni and cheese in Carissa Buckley's horrible face.

Ben, poor Ben, the rat, chooses that moment to walk up with a sandwich for Carissa. "The sandwich didn't come with mayonnaise, so I got you a couple of packets. What have you two been talking about?"

I can't look at him, can't talk to him, won't lower myself to give Carissa the tongue-lashing she deserves, not that I can do that anyway. All I can do is to put the wheelchair in reverse and motor away before the tears start.

Nneka steers me to a little patch of concrete out on the grounds that's littered with cigarette butts; presumably, this is where the nurses go to indulge their smoking habit. It's raw and windy outside, and the cold, lashing breeze stings my wet cheeks. Twenty minutes of ugly crying have not made me feel any better.

"I want to tell you," Nneka says, "that I am very sorry about this."

"Not your fault," I tell her.

"Isn't it, though? I should have spotted him for the dog that he is. I should have warned you away. He seemed nice enough at the time, didn't he? And I encouraged you. It was wrong of me to do that."

I blow my nose on my last clean tissue.

"Her fault. No need to be that cruel."

"He knows how cruel she is; if he doesn't know, he'll learn once they get married. Who knows, that may have been what attracted him to you in the first place. That you aren't a hard, cruel person like she is."

"It's not fair."

Nneka crosses her arms. "If this was a movie," she says, "this would be the scene where your nice, kind, Nigerian friend gives you some words of wisdom to help you cope. But I don't have those words. There aren't any words. Sometimes people are mean and filled with hate, and you can't do anything about it."

I blink back the last of my tears. "Thank you," I say. "You're a good friend."

"Because I am such a good friend, I will give you one word of wisdom after all. You have a great deal to carry. Physical injuries. Mental injuries. Your sister's condition. This is enough of a burden for anyone. Those cruel insults from that horrible woman? You do not need to carry those as well. You have enough to carry. Let them go. Set them aside."

This is good advice. I am not ever going to be able to take it, but it is good advice, nonetheless. I remember that Nneka has been sharing information about me with my dad and with Penny—and this is too good a piece of gossip to waste. Maybe I don't need to tell anyone about what happened, which is fine because I don't want to talk about it anyway.

It occurs to me, for the first time, that the exchange of information can go both ways. Nneka did say something, a minute ago, about Penny.

"What about Penny?" I ask.

"What about her?" Nneka replies.

"You said that I had to carry Penny. Why?"

"Oh. That. Because she is ill, that is all."

"What do you know?"

Nneka sighs. "Perhaps this is not the best time."

"She is part of my burden. I sh-should know."

"All we know is that she's got a fever," my father says.

"Rejection," I reply.

"We expected some issues; there's rejection in about ninety percent of cases. Morton is here; he says that everything is normal so far."

"I see." Dr. Morton is, well, not my favorite person; he had been a very vocal advocate for transplanting my lungs into Penny after the accident, even though I was still using them at the time.

"What Morton is worried about is the fever; he thinks it might be due to an infection. The lead surgeon doesn't seem too worried; they do a lot of lung transplants, they see it all the time, and they say there's nothing to worry about, that they have it under control. I am worried, though, and I know you are, and your mother is more worried than the two of us combined. We can't do anything other than worry, and pray, at this point."

"S-still unconscious?"

"Still unconscious, still on a ventilator for a few more days. It's nerve-wracking. I don't mean to dump it all on you, but I know that you want me to keep you posted."

"It's will be okay," I say, only halfway believing it.

"I know. You get some sleep, okay, Ashlyn? I'll call you tomorrow. Good night."

"Good night."

An hour later, and I am in bed, staring at the ceiling. The room is as dark as I can make it, but the corridor outside is bright and noisy. I try using breathing exercises to calm down, in through the nose, out through the mouth.

Since the accident, I have learned to live with apraxia and aphasia. Apraxia is annoying; you know what you want to say but it comes out wrong, you can't get the mouth movements of speech lined up the right way. Aphasia isn't mechanical like apraxia; it's mental. You can't find the words you want when you need them.

As long as I keep what I say simple and concrete, I can manage pretty well in most situations. It's a struggle to process anything more abstract or complex—and I am finding it hard to sort out my feelings, much less articulate them.

I know that I've lost Ben—or that I never had him in the first place. Ben, for me, was a constellation of possibilities that suddenly collapsed into a neutron star of anger and regret. It didn't have to be that way—he could have mentioned something, casual-like, about his fiancée. I would have been disappointed, maybe even hurt, but I would get over it, no problem. We could have stayed friends—I've been in the friend zone enough times to not have it bother me. Instead, he let me think... what? Why? I would have told *him* if I had a boyfriend. Not that I do.

That is what bothers me—not the fact that I don't have a boyfriend, but the idea that I might never find one. Carissa Buckley is a bitch, but she is at least honest. I am a scar-faced, scraggly-haired, wheelchair-driving hot mess. It was stupid of me to think that Ben was ever serious about me; whoever would be? Who could be? What can I ever hope for?

I feel a hot, shameful tear running down my face. God damn it. I shouldn't let her get to me, I'm better than she is, I'm better than the way I look and the way I feel right now. I know who I am and what I want, and it's useless to feel this way, useless to cry, useless to want things I'm never going to have.

I reach over to my nightstand for a tissue, and I wish suddenly that I hadn't. Lifting my head even a fraction off the pillow makes me feel unaccountably sick and dizzy. I take a shallow breath, and then another. I close my eyes, and the world cracks into jagged black shards.

I blink, slowly, and see the ceiling above me. My tongue is thick in my mouth. My body feels as though I was tossed from a car at high speed and hit the asphalt hard.

"How do you feel?" a voice asks.

I feel like I was beaten with a sack of oranges, but I can't even articulate that. I let out a long, lingering Wookiee moan.

"Well, you're entitled to feel like that. You've had a seizure."

I let out another groan. I would much rather be beaten with a sack of oranges.

"The good news is that it's been five minutes since the seizure ended," the voice says. "And you haven't had another seizure, and that's excellent. Not that seizures are any fun, but multiple back-to-back seizures can ruin your whole entire day."

"Great," I say.

"When was your last seizure? Do you remember?"

"August," I say. I had a seizure not too long after the accident, or so I'm told. I was busy being comatose at the time. Dr. Kingman told me, afterwards, that one seizure was to be expected. Any other seizures after that, though, and I'd get an epilepsy diagnosis, which would prevent me from driving a car. I feel the tears again, hot and unbidden.

"It's okay, sweetheart," the voice says. "I understand. Would you like a tissue?"

I nod, and she dabs at my face.

"Can you tell me how you're feeling?" she asks. I look up, and her face comes into focus; it's Roxanne Jenkins, a nurse on the night shift.

"Tired," I say. "Hurts."

"I'm asking, because it looks like your left hand is swollen. I think maybe you banged it on the side of the bed."

As soon as she says it, I start to feel it—not the usual soreness, but a lash of bright pain up the side of my wrist.

"Hold still," she says. "You'll need an X-ray. I don't think there's anyone in radiology, though, so you may have to wait until the morning. Let me get you some ice to bring down the swelling."

I blink back the tears and look up at the ceiling. I try breathing again, in through the nose, out through the mouth. It doesn't help. Nothing helps.

# Singular Deliverances

**Penny | New York City | Ten Years In The Future**

"Pikachu!"

The large yellow balloon floats high above us in the pale blue New York sky. The little girl is sitting in my father's lap, and I wonder how she knows about Pokémon.

My mother is sitting next to my father, and they are beaming with pride. Ashlyn is next to them, and she has a very slight scowl on her face that I attribute to being out in the November wind for too long. My brothers are on the other side of me, and they have grown tall and gangly, with oversized hands and feet; they're both wearing Montgomery High varsity jackets.

"When is Santa coming?" the girl asks.

"Soon," I say. "He's always the last float in the parade."

The girl is wearing a bright-pink parka, the color of Pepto-Bismol, with white woolen mittens and a matching ski cap. She has an adorable yellow scarf with blue stripes around her neck, and I can see her breath in the crisp November air.

"How are you holding up?" I ask. "Are you getting cold?"

"Not very cold," she says. "How long until Daddy gets here?"

"Two or three more balloons to go," I say. "Look, it's Thomas next."

"I don't like Thomas," she says. "I like James. Thomas is boring."

We are at the end of the parade route, in the bleachers, which are impossible to get under normal circumstances. My husband took care of it, of course, when he volunteered for the balloon crew at MetLife, they helped set it up for us. It's my first time at the parade; I never got to go when I was young because it wasn't good for my lungs to be out in the cold air that long. I've had my new lungs for ten years now. I've been able to do lots of things I've never done before. The transplant surgery was a singular deliverance for me, one that has opened all the doors that have led me to this point.

"Are you having a good time, sweetie?" my mom asks. There's a light in her eyes that I haven't seen for a long time, and there are smile lines crinkling around them.

"Can we come next year?" the girl asks.

"We'll see," I say, not wanting to make the promise, but we will, of course we will. My heart is soaring. I am surrounded by joy. My family is with me, safe and whole, and my little girl is happy, and what more can you ask for than that?

Then I see the Snoopy balloon, bobbing along, and I point it out to the little girl. "There's Daddy," I say, although I can't see him, yet.

"Where is he?" the little girl asks.

I wait for a long moment for the balloon crew to get closer, and then I spot him. He is tall, impossibly tall, with jet-black hair and a round face set on broad shoulders. He can't wave, as he needs both hands for the ropes holding the balloon down, but he catches my eye and smiles at me, and at the little girl, and he is having the time of his life.

"Daddy!" the little girl screams. "I see Daddy!"

"Not so loud in my ear, sweetheart," Dad says. "Like I used to tell your mother."

The Snoopy balloon sails on, and a marching band from Ohio follows in its wake, playing "Twist and Shout," right out of the Ferris Bueller movie. I sweep the little girl out of her grandfather's lap and we dance together, holding her close, feeling the warmth of her against me.

This is a dream, I tell myself, but it's a sweeter dream than I ever could have imagined.

# NOT BROKEN

### ASHLYN | MARCH 30 | RWJ HOSPITAL, NEW BRUNSWICK, NEW JERSEY

Torrez picks up the penlight and shines it in my face. "Follow the light with your eyes," he says, and I do. I have done enough of these neurological tests that I know the drill. My eyes do whatever they are supposed to do, apparently.

"Let's take a look at the burr hole," he says, leaning in closer to inspect his handiwork. Dr. Torrez did the surgery that saved my life last August, which is why he is doing the neurology consult before the surgery. He moves his finger around the edge of the surgical scar, which feels odd and cold.

"All right," he says. "I think you're recovering nicely, if that's any help at all. Your speech has improved markedly. Your motor skills are starting to return. I understand from Dr. Lindbergh that you've started walking. Your EEG is very good."

"The seiz-zhure?" I ask.

"Little trouble with the sibilants there, but that will get better in time. Okay. You had a seizure. That's two seizures in six months. You might go the rest of your life without having another one, or you might have one as you're lying here. The more seizures you have, the more data we have available to understand why you have them, what triggers them, and how we can prevent them. The problem is that we're looking at a small sample size. Ideally, I'd like to keep that a small sample size, but that's not something you or I can control."

I have been laboring—quite literally—under the assumption that at least a good part of my recovery was under my control. I thought I could, by sheer force of will, put in the work I needed to do to make myself walk and talk the way I had before, or at least as close as I could get. The seizure—again quite literally—shook me out of that delusion. I can control what I can control. That is not what you would call a comfort.

"All right then. Two things. First, I'm recommending general anesthesia for your surgery."

"Why?" I had been assuming that this would be a local anesthetic, although I hadn't thought it all the way through.

"While I think it's incredibly unlikely that you would have a seizure during the surgery, it's not impossible. Having a seizure on the operating table is something that I always try to avoid with my patients. It also means that we'll get to monitor your brain activity while you're out. That may give me more data to understand why you had that seizure, and to see if there's anything we can do to prescribe treatment."

"Okay." This at least is sensible, or more sensible than what I get from Lindbergh.

"The second thing. Were you wondering why I wanted to do this consult?"

"No."

"It is not, as you may have guessed, because I am vain enough to want to inspect my handiwork, although that's part of it. Surgery is difficult—that's why we say of any trivial task that it's 'not brain surgery.' It is a hard thing to do, an unnatural thing to do, to cut into someone's body, to drill into someone's skull. When it goes poorly, as it so often does, it's depressing. I had heard from Dr. Kingman that you were doing well, and I wanted to see you for myself. Not out of vanity, but for inspiration. You understand? It is incredibly heartening to see you alive, and prospering. It tells me that I am doing good in this world, by playing a small part in your recovery."

I shift uncomfortably in my hospital gown. "Thank you." I manage to get out the words a little more smoothly this time, and that, in its way, is a victory. And a reminder that I am not doing this to inspire Torrez. I am doing this for me. If another surgery is a part of that, then that is what I will have to undergo. One more setback. One more trial.

"You are most welcome. I have another patient waiting, so you must excuse me. Don't give up. You understand? This is a setback, but it's temporary. Giving up is permanent. Don't give up."

"Okay."

Torrez changes his facial expression ever so slightly, as to suggest the vague impression of a smile. "Good luck," he says, and he hustles out of the room.

For the second time in my life, I am flat on my back, seeing the universe as a series of ceiling tiles and fluorescent lights, on my way to surgery. The first time, I was dazed, in shock, in pain. I am more composed now, not feeling any pain. The only similarity is that I am again worried sick about Penny, and not able to do very much about it. The last report I had was that there was no change, she was still hanging in there, still trying to fight off rejection, infection, and fever. They wouldn't have told me any bad news, though, knowing I was going into surgery.

We are in a smaller operating room this time, or I think so. I have the haziest memory of my first surgery—and don't remember the surgery that Torrez performed at all. Dr. Kingman says that I told a nurse that Penny had cystic fibrosis, which helped him treat her. If Kingman says so, I believe him, but I don't remember either way.

"Welcome to your operating room. I am Dr. Kwon, and will be doing your surgery today." Dr. Kwon has dark, animated eyes over her pink surgical mask. She sounds alert and chipper, which I suppose is a good attitude for your surgeon to have. It would be much worse if she were morose and depressed.

"We're working on your left hand today, correct?"

"Correct." I have written NOT BROKEN on my right hand, to make sure they don't start fiddling around with that one.

"Very good. What we're doing today is removing the broken part of the hamate bone, setting a pin in the metacarpal, and removing the bone chips and any bone spurs in the left wrist. We'll get started after Dr. Lewis administers the anesthetic."

Dr. Lewis appears at the top of my field of vision. "I'm putting the mask over your face," he says. "All you have to do is breathe. Can you manage that?"

"So far, so good," I say.

"Let's keep it that way," he says. He puts the mask over my face, and I breathe in, and a gray curtain falls.

# GRAVITY

**ASHLYN | MARCH 30 | THE LAND OF SUMMERVALE**

I wake up under the World Ash Tree, on a sunny afternoon in the heart of Summervale. A warm wind blows in the tall grass and gently shakes the canopy of leaves overhead. Nicholas is snoozing in my lap, and I pet his black, glossy fur absently. There is a faint hint of lavender in the air, and a lazy drone from a far-off beehive in the background. I blink my eyes, thinking that I am about to doze off, until I remember that I'm already asleep.

Nicholas stirs, and hops out of my lap. His bright eyes twinkle in the dappled sunlight. "I hope that you are resting comfortably, Lady Ashlyn."

"It's a very relaxing place," I say. "I mean, there's no swimming pool. No frozen piña coladas. Other than that, it is very nice."

"Perhaps next time," Nicholas says.

"Don't get me wrong, it's very nice. Most of my experiences here have been, well, you know. Frantic, you might say."

"This is how Summervale is, most of the time," Nicholas says. "When you were young, Summervale was a quiet, peaceful place. As you grew older, and experienced more of the world, Summervale grew with you—and the troubles of your world became reflected in ours. There are still some corners of Summervale that are safe havens to heal and thrive, but much of it is dangerous now."

"I wish I could remember what it was like," I say.

"You will find the joys of your youth become harder to recapture as you grow older, Lady Ashlyn. That doesn't mean that they're not there. You have to seek them out with your heart, and hold on to them when you find them."

I stare out in the distance. I came here after the car crash, and I came back here when I was wounded and dying. It is a lovely place, still and peaceful, but I know that I can't stay here.

"I don't remember the last time I felt joy," I say. "I don't know where to find it anymore. Or else it's been running away from me."

"It will return," Nicholas says. "It may surprise you, or it may come in a disguise, but it is never that far away. You will learn to recognize it when it appears, and accept it when it comes."

A dark, sinuous shape appears over the horizon.

"Maybe it's that other emotions come to the surface."

"Destructive emotions are always easier. That is part of their power. You can let them have their way with you, or you can resist them, and through resisting them, grow stronger."

"I have been trying to grow stronger. Become mentally tough. The more I try, the closer I get to my breaking point."

Nicholas hops into my lap and presses close to me. "There is value in knowing where that breaking point is. You have come close to it, and remained whole."

"If it's all the same to you, I think I'll pass on any more learning experiences like that for a good long while."

"If all you ever learned in life was not to let cruelty and unkindness master you, then you would have learned much."

The dark shape on the far horizon comes closer, and sails higher in the sky. It is the familiar shape of a dragon, its wings outstretched, flailing this way and that, diving and swooping.

"I know that I can't repay evil with evil, pain with pain. I feel sad, and tired, and overwhelmed."

"None of these are bad feelings," Nicholas says. "It is all right to feel them, to experience them, but they will pass, as joys and sadness pass. The question is always the same: how do you respond to them? What actions will you take? How can you take the pain that you feel and transmute it into something positive?"

The dragon, a darker blue against the pale sky, bucks and twirls high above us. There is a rider athwart his broad neck. "It's getting closer," I say. "What can we do?"

"This is a place of deep power," Nicholas says. "The dragon knows that, and fears that, and yet the rider keeps pressing it onward. Dangerous, and unwise."

The dragon accelerates, snaps off a barrel roll in midair, and throws the rider off his back. I pull my wand from its holster and point it at the falling figure. "*Adagio!*" I cry, and the would-be dragon rider drifts to the ground, less like a leaf than a sack of leaves. She hits the ground rolling, dusts herself off, and makes her way towards the World Ash Tree.

"Much obliged there, Lady Ashlyn." It is C.J. Valentine. Her black hair is matted with sweat, and she has a large bandage wrapped around her left arm. "Thought I was a goner there for a minute. Greetings to you as well, Lord Atropos."

"You can call me Nicholas, Warden Valentine. Greetings."

"What was it like?" I ask. I've wanted to ride a dragon ever since I ran through the Pern books in fifth grade.

"I ain't going to lie to you, Lady Ashlyn. It was intense. Didn't have an alternative. Since you had that run-in with that blonde tart, the Eastern Marches have been hip-deep in monsters. I had to fight two octokongs and a griffin to get here. You ever fought a griffin? Hell of a workout. I think I pulled a hamstring, and I got my left arm torn to ribbons in the process. After that, riding a dragon didn't seem all that frightening."

I am maybe a touch embarrassed by this, but not enough to matter. "Okay, look, I am in surgery right this minute. I had a seizure. This has not been a fun couple of days for me, either."

"Be that as it may," C.J. says. "I ain't here for the conversation." She opens up a travel-stained leather bag hanging off her shoulder, and takes out a black envelope. "Special delivery, from the Dark Lord himself. For your eyes only."

I take the envelope. "The seal's been breached."

"Well. I admit I was a mite curious about the contents, you understand. It ain't every day the Dark Lord sends me on a mail run."

I open the envelope, and extract two small pieces of glossy cardstock. "This is a joke, right?"

"Not at all, Lady Ashlyn. That there is serious business."

"These are two courtside tickets for Madison Square Garden. The Dark Lord is inviting me to a Knicks game? I didn't think we were on speaking terms."

"He's not, and you're not. There's a job for you to do."

"Hard pass," I say. "I've got my own problems to deal with at the moment."

C.J.'s voice goes quiet. "I would think your sister might want you to. Or need you to."

"Penny is in New York?" I ask.

"As though you didn't know."

"I knew she was in New York—the New York in the real world. She's here in Summervale?"

"That's the tale that I heard told. It's not like you to hang back while she's in danger."

"Where is she in New York?" I ask.

"First things first," C.J. says. "Are you coming or not? We'd best hurry."

"Do you know a shortcut?" I ask.

"Do I know a shortcut? You're asking me? Please. I got my arm halfway turned into stroganoff getting here; you think that would have happened if I used a shortcut?"

"So how do we get there? Do we flap our arms and fly?"

C.J. rolls her eyes hard enough to see her frontal lobe. "I cannot believe this. Little Miss Sorceress over there, with a wand made from unicorn hair and a splinter off the World Ash Tree, is going to flap her arms and fly to New York City. Seriously? You have the next best thing to unlimited power there on your sword belt, and you're over there doing a pigeon imitation. I'm sorry I ever came all this way."

"Okay," I say. "I get it. Let me think for a minute."

"Think about what?"

"There's different methods. You can open a portal. Or a passage into another dimension, something like that. Or maybe something like a *Star Trek* transporter beam. Give me a second to figure something out."

"Oh, well, by all means, take your time," C.J. snarks. "Don't let me interrupt you."

Nicholas hops out of my lap. "Lady Ashlyn, do be careful," he says. "Whatever it is that you are planning, please think it through."

"I know, I know. I remember what happened last time I tried this, don't think that I don't." I had an army that time, and good leaders, and a plan, none of which I have now.

"I don't have all day, Lady Ashlyn," C.J. says.

"Okay. We're going to try to Apparate." I scoop up Nicholas and tuck him under my arm. "Take my other arm," I tell C.J., "and hold on."

"Have you ever done this before?" C.J. asks.

"Never."

"Lady Ashlyn," Nicholas interrupts, "I really must protest."

"Quit being a baby." I take C.J's arm, hold Nicholas tight, and think hard about Madison Square Garden. I give my wand an awkward flick and close my eyes.

We hit the ground hard, and when I look up, I recognize that we're somewhere in the vicinity of Hoboken, on the wrong side of the Hudson. Not that we're in Hoboken; we are where Hoboken would be if there were such a thing as Hoboken in Summervale. Everywhere around us is green and swampy, with no sign of human habitation. The familiar spires of New

York—together with some unfamiliar ones—loom across the river.

"Not too shabby," C.J. says. "You done good, Lady Ashlyn. Now all we need is a way to get across. You used a bridge last time, right?"

"Didn't work out so well." I had been on the receiving end of the Dark Lord's Laconian hospitality committee last time I was here. Even with an engraved invitation, I would rather not tangle with them again—especially without an army of my own.

Nicholas wiggles out of my arm and sits up on his haunches. "The Dark Lord likes to test people. He wants you here, but he is also not above keeping you out to prove a point. Perhaps Ms. Valentine can reveal his intentions."

C.J. snorts. "Beats my pair of jacks. Maybe we build a catapult and try to launch ourselves across."

"Good idea. You go first."

"Like hell, we will. I ain't your crash test dummy, Lady Ashlyn."

"You got a better idea?" I ask.

"Not me. How do they do it in your world?"

"Staten Island Ferry, but I kind of wrecked the ferry last time, so maybe not such a good idea. New Jersey Transit to Penn Station, or PATH train from Jersey City. Or else..."

"Or else what."

"Or else I'm an idiot. Hold on a second. Let me try something."

I turn my back to the skyline and focus my thoughts on my castle. "*Accio Dwarves!*" I shout.

Nicholas twitches his whiskers. "Dear, dear."

"Wait, is it going to start raining dwarves now?" C.J. asks.

"Might be. You need an umbrella?"

"What are dwarves going to do?"

"You want to get across the river? Best way to do that is a bridge or a tunnel. I'm voting tunnel. If you want to get started before the dwarves get here, feel free. I can even conjure you up a shovel. Or you can wait."

C.J. crosses her arms over her chest and glowers at me, as if all of this is somewhat my fault, and I suspect she's right. I hadn't planned on going to New York, not this soon, not this fast, not this way. If Penny is there, I don't have a choice. I will survive my surgery, but there's a fair chance that she won't. I don't know if there's anything I can do in this dream to reach her, but she showed up in my dream to reach me. Maybe it works both ways.

I look up into the western sky, and sure enough, I see a red dot and a black dot, both hurtling my way. I point my wand at the airborne dwarves and wave them in for a soft landing. They tumble as they land, and I stop them before they roll into the Hudson.

"What did you do?" Lincoln asks.

"Don't look at me!" Holland splutters. They are both covered with dirt and granite dust; I can barely tell them apart. "I didn't do anything!"

"Then what happened?"

"I happened," I explain. "Sorry, fellows. I needed help, and there wasn't an easier way to get you here."

Holland throws down his helmet and kicks it. "You chose a bloody inconvenient way to do that, Your Worship."

This causes C.J. to let loose a snort, which turns into a wave of giggles. "Your Worship," she splutters.

"For crying out loud," I say. "Get hold of yourself, if it's not too difficult. Holland and Lincoln, pay attention. We're over here, and I want to get there."

"Maybe you could build a catapult and launch yourselves across," Lincoln suggests, which leads to another wave of cackling from C.J.

"Not an option," I say. "I am thinking tunnel. Can you do it?"

"Under the river?" Holland asks. "Could be done. Lot of hard work. Easier to build a catapult."

"I would rather not travel by catapult," Nicholas says.

"Okay, you heard Nicholas. No catapult."

"A tunnel, Your Worship?" Lincoln says. "There's no way."

"Your names are Holland and Lincoln," I say. "This is your destiny. Let me know what kind of tools you need, and I'll get them for you. How long would it take?"

"The real Holland Tunnel took seven years," Holland explains. "The Lincoln Tunnel took over twenty years. We're only two dwarves."

"Maybe you can flap your arms and fly," Lincoln suggests. "It would be faster."

"Even with modern earth-moving equipment, which I don't think you can manage to conjure, it would take a week. You don't have that kind of time," Holland explains. "You need something quicker."

"Any bright ideas?" I ask.

"You're not going to like it."

"Try me."

The dwarves work faster than thought, cutting down the local trees and shaping them into a platform, rising six stories from a point about a quarter mile from the river. From the top of the platform, they have constructed a broad metal half-pipe, sloping down at a terrifying angle. They are at the top of the platform, ready to hoist us to the top.

"This is the stupidest thing I've ever heard of in my life," C.J. says.

"It's going to work," I say.

I look across the river; there's an exquisite panoramic view of New York, with the late evening sunlight glinting off the skyscrapers. The dwarves have managed to fashion a two-seater bobsled, dark green with garish orange stripes. "We couldn't decide on a color scheme, Your Worship," Holland explains.

"I am exceptionally apprehensive about this," Nicholas says.

"It's going to work," I say. I take my wand out and point it at the surface of the half-pipe. *"Lillehammer,"* I say, and the surface of the pipe is coated with thick white ice. In order to get into the spirit of the thing, I transform my clothes into a green-and-orange bobsled leotard, with matching helmet and goggles, and climb on board in the front seat, Nicholas squirming in my lap.

"Begging your pardon, Your Worship," C.J. asks, "have you ever done this before?"

"I did the bunny slope at Stowe once," I say.

"This does not fill me with confidence."

"It's either this, or wait a week, and walk through a wet smelly tunnel with billions of gallons of Hudson River over our heads, ready to drown us. Come on and get in, or I'll tell the Dark Lord you were too chicken."

C.J. glares at me, and then zaps herself into a matching bobsled outfit and climbs in behind me. "Any seat belts in this thing?" she asks.

"We thought about it, Warden Valentine," Lincoln explains. "We figured that if we miscalculated, and you fall into the river, you might want to exit the vehicle quickly."

"This sounds better all the time," she says.

"Okay," Holland says. "We'll help push you down the pipe, to help you get some acceleration. After that, gravity takes over. Any questions?"

"Are you sure you've thought this quite through?" Nicholas asks.

"Don't you have any confidence in me?" I reply.

"I would prefer not to answer that."

"Okay, then. On three. Let's do this."

Holland and Lincoln line up on either side of the bobsled and push us forward, and in a throat-clenching and stomach-heaving moment, we are over the precipice and rocketing down the half-pipe over the river. The bobsled shakes and rattles with the acceleration. C.J. screams out a banshee wail of fear behind me. I hang on, one hand on the bar in front of me, one hand on my wand, Nicholas scrabbling against my chest. The wind whistles past as the bobsled bumps off the half-pipe and into the void.

We are over the Hudson now, the white towers of the city coming into focus. "*Frigidaire*," I shout, and the river below becomes a flat sheet of thick ice. I grab onto the bar and brace for impact; this is the point where it could all go wrong. But the bobsled hits the ice at the right angle, and glides across it, its runners scraping against the frosty surface. I pump my fists in triumph as the bobsled slows to a stop, a few feet short of the piers. C.J. gets out of the bobsled first, and helps me up, and we hoist ourselves up over the rail and onto the pier. By the time my feet hit the wooden boards I'm wearing black jeans and a black leather jacket, looking like any other anonymous New Yorker, if you discount that I'm carrying a rabbit. I look across the river, but the bobsled run has vanished.

"I suppose congratulations are in order, Lady Ashlyn," Nicholas says. "You handled that splendidly."

"Next time," C.J. says, "I'm taking the bus. You got us here; that's what counts. You know where we're going, right?"

"This is Chelsea, right? Not too far now. Walk east from here, catch the 1 train to Times Square, and then transfer to the Q for New York Presbyterian. Or that's what you'd do in the real world."

"You want to take the subway?" C.J. says. "No thank you. I'd rather not deal with Rodents Of Unusual Size, for one thing. Besides, that's not where we're going."

"That's where Penny is," I explain. "I need to see her before we do anything else."

"No way, Your Worship. Madison Square Garden, then I take you home."

"First things first. First, I see my sister, then I do whatever errand the Dark Lord is asking me to do. That's non-negotiable."

"You want to watch how you talk to me," C.J. says. "That kind of humorous banter works out in the marchlands. This here is the big city. Get us to the Garden before I make you."

"You and what army?" I ask.

"You oughta know the answer to that," C.J. says. "Buncha tall Greek guys with spears."

"You are here at the Dark Lord's sufferance," Nicholas says. "If Miss Valentine thinks that you can help your sister by going to this Madison Square Garden place, then you should follow her instructions."

"You know this is a trap, right?" I say to Nicholas. "I don't trust her, or the Dark Lord."

"As you should not," he says. "Keep your wits about you."

# When I Get Where I'm Going

**ASHLYN | MARCH 30 | NEW YORK CITY, EIGHTH AVENUE**

C.J. isn't quite skipping down the near-deserted 8ᵗʰ Avenue, but if she isn't, it's the next best thing. She has ditched her bobsled outfit and is wearing a black-and-red New Jersey Devils hockey jersey. "You know what this errand is all about, right?"

"Not the first clue," I say. "The Dark Lord didn't tell you about it?"

"He told me to watch your back, and that you oughta be able to know what to do when you figured out the problem."

"I appreciate the confidence he is showing in me here."

"Sarcasm ain't going to help you do anything," C.J. says. "Whatever that might be."

"My guess is it's something unbelievably stupid, or else something incredibly dangerous. No middle ground."

"You might be right about that. Your Worship."

"You need to stop calling me that," I say.

"I am just sayin', you gotta be ready for anything. You've noticed, have you, that this street is well-nigh empty, right?"

"Yup."

"There's a reason for that. Nice day like this, the streets would be teeming with traffic. Depends on what you're feeling, what you're reading. Bunch of pirates wearing turbans not that long ago. Understand?"

"Whatever I'm feeling, in terms of anger, fear and anxiety, they could all be holed up inside Madison Square Garden, and I'll have to do something about that," I say. "Got it."

"All I'm saying is, be prepared, y'know?"

"I am worried enough about what might be in there without you standing at my elbow foreshadowing it, thank you very much."

"Happy to oblige, Your Worship."

Madison Square Garden is a big place, and I am somewhat cheered to see a door with a banner above it reading "Madison Square Garden VIP Access: Guests of the Dark Lord Only." I open the door and there's a bored-looking orangutan with a blue cap sitting on a stool. I hand him my tickets and he lazily waves the three of us inside.

We walk down a dull corridor decorated with photos. James Dolan. Reggie Miller. Renaldo Balkman. Patrick Ewing in a Seattle uniform. There's a framed copy of Allan Houston's contract. A photo of Stephon Marbury missing a free throw, and another of Eddy Curry eating a hoagie.

"All that's missing," I say, "is a picture of Isiah Thomas sexually harassing someone."

"Over to your right," C.J. says. "The Dark Lord has gotten a hell of a lot of mileage out of the Knicks over the years."

"I was right," I say. "Whatever is in here is stupid and horrible."

"Keep an even strain, Lady Ashlyn. We're almost there."

We keep going down the corridor, with photos of LeBron James in a Miami uniform and Kevin Durant in a Nets uniform, until we reach a glass door with gold letters. COURTSIDE PASS HOLDERS ONLY. I stop for a second and make subtle changes to my wardrobe, manifesting a thin chain mail coat under my jacket, sturdy boots, and a sword belt. C.J. is beside me, chewing gum, still wearing her Devils jersey.

"That's what you're wearing in here?" I ask.

"Dark Side. Gotta represent."

"Okay, then. Here we go."

I push open the door, bracing myself for an assault of sound that doesn't come. Inside the Garden is an unnatural wave of silence. I sweep my head back and forth, looking for danger, but I don't see anything but empty seats and dim light. Somehow, this is more unnerving than the thought of the arena being infested with griffins and wyverns.

"Something ain't right," C.J. says. "You see anything?"

"Over there," Nicholas says. There is a lone spotlight shining on the foul line of the basketball court, highlighting a shadowy figure.

"That could be it. You think?"

"I guess. How do you want to play it?"

C.J. frowns. "I figure you stun it with your wand, and I'll come in behind you and take it out with my sword."

"That would be most unwise," Nicholas says.

"It's one person. Maybe we try talking first. I'll go in, and you stay close."

I step onto the court, and the figure comes into focus. She is standing at the free-throw line, facing the basket, and she is wearing a familiar light-blue jersey, number six. The name on the back reads LAMB.

"Stand down," I tell C.J. "I got this."

I reset my clothes to my favorite North Carolina hoodie and faded jeans, and walk towards the ghost of Jennifer Lamb. I come cautiously up on her left side, the way you would approach a stray panther. If she notices me, she doesn't show it. She has a basketball cradled in her left hand, her right arm hanging loose and useless at her side. She launches the ball towards the basket, but it clangs remorsefully off the bottom of the backboard, nowhere near the rim. The ball hits the floor, bounces once, and then vanishes and reappears back in her left hand.

"Hi there," I say.

"Who are you?" she asks. There's a tense, distorted look on her face, as though she would run away if she could.

"My name is Ashlyn Revere. I played field hockey at UNC. I was two years ahead of you. I think we met once, at an athletics banquet in Chapel Hill. You're Jennifer Lamb, right?"

"That's right," she says, and the anxiety on her face lessens a bit. "Don't remember you, though. Unless— there was somebody on the field hockey team who was in some kind of car accident."

"That was me."

"I could tell, because of the scars. What are you doing here?"

"I was about to ask you that," I say.

"I have to make my second shot. We were in the bonus. I missed the first one."

"I remember," I say. "You were playing Michigan, in the second half."

"We were getting beat." She tries another one-handed shot, which misses the backboard by a foot before it reappears back in her hand. "Were you at the game?"

"No. I was watching, on ESPN. That was days ago. Why are you still here?"

"Because you ain't supposed to be here, is the point she's trying to make," C.J. says. "If you can kindly vacate, that would be enormously helpful from everyone's point of view."

"Maybe a little sensitivity," Nicholas says.

"What I'm trying to say, Jennifer, is that you didn't get to make that second shot. They had to take you to the hospital. You had a stroke."

"If I had a stroke, why am I still here?" Jennifer Lamb tries another shot, this one glancing against the bottom of the net before it clatters ineffectively on the hardwood. "This is embarrassing," she says. "I had a seventy-percent average until the postseason. Haven't made a single free throw in the tournament."

"It's not important now," I say. "Nobody's expecting you to make one free throw in a game that's been over for a while."

"That doesn't matter," she says. Her voice takes on a steely edge which masks a slight slur in her speech. "You ought to know that. It doesn't matter what the score is, what the situation is. You play. You perform. You fight. That's what matters. This is the last game of my career. I don't want to walk away on a missed shot."

"You want to tell her," C.J. says, "or do you want me to?"

"I think she knows," I say. "Let's try not to stress her."

"Maybe we don't have to." C.J. walks up behind Jennifer, unsheathes her sword before I can stop her, and tries to take Jennifer's head off her shoulders. The blade passes right through her; Jennifer doesn't even notice.

"Can we please not do anything else stupid?" I ask C.J.

"You got any better ideas?" she replies.

"Maybe one." I bite my lip; I want to say this the right way. "You realize you had a stroke, right? That's why your right arm doesn't work."

"I know what you're trying to tell me," Jennifer says. "Listen. It doesn't matter. Maybe I had a stroke. Maybe I died. It doesn't matter. I need to do this."

"Why is it so important to you?" I ask.

"Why is it so important to you?" Jennifer replies. "Why do you care?"

I stop for a second. *Because I'm supposed to*, I say, but that's not enough. *Because the Dark Lord asked me to*, and that doesn't make any sense.

*Because it helps my sister*. That's a reason, and it's a good reason, but Jennifer and I barely know each other; she doesn't have any connection to Penny that I can think of.

Unless.

"Because my sister is in the hospital. She had a lung transplant, with your lungs."

Jennifer's head snaps around to look at me, as though she's just noticed I was there. "No way. You're lying."

"My sister's name is Penny. She has cystic fibrosis and has been on the lung transplant list for months. She lives in New Jersey, which is close enough to New

York. She got called to New York Presbyterian the same night that you had your stroke. It makes sense."

"Stop it," Jennifer's ghost says. "Stop talking. I don't want to hear this. I want to make my last shot, and hit the showers, and go back to Chapel Hill so I can graduate and get a good job. You're keeping me from doing that."

"You signed the donor card, right? That means you did a good thing, a brave thing. Your life is over, but you live on in my sister, and who knows how many other people."

"I don't want to hear it." Jennifer rockets the ball towards the backboard, where it bounces off harmlessly.

"Maybe a little more sensitivity, there," C.J. interjects.

"My sister is lying in the ICU at New York Presbyterian right this minute. She got a new set of lungs. Your lungs. Her body is rejecting them, and if it keeps doing that, she'll die."

"That's too bad for her."

"My sister is going to live because of you, but you have to let go. Understand me? She can't live unless you walk off this court." I am extrapolating a little here, and I know that, but that's the conclusion that seems to make the most logical sense.

Jennifer tries another shot, this one underhanded, which goes off course almost immediately and reappears into her hand. "I don't know who you are, or your sister, and I don't believe you. Why should I? There's not anything you can say that will convince me."

I stand in front of her, blocking her view of the basket. "Yes, there is."

"What's that?"

"Carissa Buckley is a bitch."

The unquiet ghost of Jennifer Lamb stares at me, her mouth half open, and then she laughs. A deep, convulsive laugh that forces her almost to her knees. "Who told you that?"

"I told her that. She stole my boyfriend."

"You're kidding."

"Absolutely not. I saw that last game you played against Duke; you guys didn't seem like you liked each other."

"Hell, no," she says. "Couldn't stand her. Feeling was mutual, I guess."

"I'm telling you the truth, Jennifer. You had a stroke. You died. It's time to accept that."

Jennifer straightens up, the ball still in her left hand. "This isn't fair, you know," she says. "This is my last game. I was graduating from college. I was going back to Asheville and work in the hospital. I wasn't trying to make the WNBA, nothing like that. I wanted one chance to play in Madison Square Garden, and look what happened. It's not fair."

"Life ain't always fair," C.J. says.

"To hell with that," Jennifer says. "Absolutely to hell with that. Life isn't fair because people like you run around and say that life isn't fair instead of doing something about it. We accept things we can't change instead of trying hard to change them. I want to live. I want a family. I want everything you want, but I don't get to have it, and that's awful."

"I know," I say. "You're right. It's not fair, but it's not fair that my sister is dying because you're trying to hold on to a dream that's... already died."

Tears well up in Jennifer Lamb's eyes, and she drops the ball and wipes them away. "I want to hold on. I want to keep playing, maybe even up the score, but I'm not going to win. I get that. I don't want it to be over. It's a painful thing to do, to admit defeat. Even more painful when you realize all you could have had if you had won."

"Maybe I can help," Nicholas says softly.

"There you go," C.J. says. "Lord Atropos in the house."

"Nicholas," I say. "What can you do to help?"

"I can go with her."

"Okay, okay, okay. Unpack that for me, if you don't mind."

"This is my role. I am a comfort. I can go with her, guide her to the next place."

"And then you'll be right back?"

"No. I am sorry, Lady Ashlyn, but if I go with Jennifer, I will go with her all the way. That is how it works."

"Wait. Wait." I kneel on the court, to get on his level. "If you go with her, does that mean I would never see you again?"

"I would not say *never*. I would not leave you alone, not at the very end. It will be some time. Hopefully, for you, an exceedingly long time, until it is your time to go where Jennifer Lamb is going."

"Nicholas," I say. "You're not serious. You're my guide. My best friend in this whole world. You can't leave me like this."

"I can, and I must. If she stays, Penny dies. You would never forgive yourself."

"What am I going to do, here, without you to snark at me?"

"Miss Valentine seems to be doing an adequate job."

"Nicholas! You know what I mean. I'll miss you."

Nicholas climbs into my lap and nuzzles my cheek, and I give him a hug. "Don't leave me," I choke out, the words rough around the lump in my throat. "I couldn't bear it."

"I am always with you," he says. "Even if you don't see me, even if you don't hear me. I am part of you. I always will be."

I hold him close, feeling the warmth of his fur. "Take care of Jennifer."

"I will, and I will see you again, though it may be years. When you get where you are going, I will go with you. That is my promise."

Nicholas hops away, and his small body shudders. He resolves into the form of a tall woman with dark hair, wearing a conservative pale-blue pantsuit, who then walks to Jennifer and takes her elbow.

"Six," she says. "It's time to go."

Jennifer looks stricken. "Coach."

"I'm here. It's okay. It's time for you to hit the showers."

"I have to make that last shot, Coach. I can't leave until I do."

"Let me help," the coach says. She picks up the ball, puts it in Jennifer's left hand, and helps her line up for a set shot. Nicholas-the-Coach gives me a quick nod, and I pull my wand out of my jeans pocket, where Jennifer can't see me. I whisper an incantation, "*Jordan*," and the ball sails out of her hand and passes through the hoop, nothing but net.

"Okay, now," the coach says. "Time to go."

"Go where, Coach?"

"You've done your best, Six. You've been my rock, but it's time now. You know that."

"I'm afraid, Coach. I've never been afraid before."

"It will be fine, and I will be with you, every step of the way."

Nicholas leads Jennifer off the court, gently and deliberately, stopping short of the out-of-bounds line.

"Thank you," I say. "Thank you for saving my sister's life."

The ghost of Jennifer Lamb takes a deep breath, the kind you take before you do something that frightens you. She and Nicholas step across the line together and vanish into nothingness.

# Long Black Limousine

**Ashlyn | March 30 | Madison Square Garden**

"Ya did good, there, Lady Ashlyn," C.J. says. "Time to go home."

"Not yet," I say, tears wet on my cheek. "One more thing to do. I need to make it to where Penny is, let her know that it's okay."

"No can do," C.J. says. "You heard the Dark Lord. He gave you a job to do and you did it. Now I have a job to do, and that's to send you back home. No time to run any other errands before you leave."

"You were the one saying Penny was in danger. You were the one who persuaded me to come here."

C.J. smirks. "Worked, too."

I give her my best glare. "Call the Dark Lord," I say. "Ask him for me. He understands about Penny; he won't stop me from talking to her."

"I have my orders, Your Worship, and they involve escorting you straight off this island."

"You can't stop me, C.J. I'm going to find my sister."

C.J. leans on her sword. "Exactly how do you plan on doing that? Because I can tell you one thing, you're not getting past me."

"Is that a fact?" I ask.

"That's a fact."

"You're forgetting something," I say.

"What might that be?"

I pull the wand from its pocket. "You have to catch me first."

"I ain't too worried about that," she says. She cracks a cruel smile, then snaps her fingers. All the house lights in the Garden come up. The arena is filled with dark furry shapes, all of them wearing hockey sweaters.

"Maybe you can get past me, but all of them? Not seeing it, Your Worship. Best to come along quietly. I can be reasoned with, but werewolves, you know, they don't excel in the art of negotiation."

"I was right. This was a trap all along."

C.J. smirks. "That's as may be. Question is, what are you going to do about it?"

All right, Ashlyn, I think to myself. You against the Warden of the Eastern Marches, backed by twenty thousand werewolves. How do you get out of this one?

Assets: my brain, my sword, the most powerful wand in the world.

"What I wouldn't give for a holocaust cloak," I say.

"Old movie quotes ain't gonna help you any, love," Valentine says.

Fight or flight. Fight or flight. Fight or…

"*Accio Broom!*" I shout, and a push broom flies from somewhere into my outstretched hand. I climb aboard, and kick off the ground in one fluid motion. I rise into the air, wafted by a ragged chorus of howls.

Madison Square Garden turns out to be a pretty good place to learn to fly. No crosswinds, for one thing. I fly over the court in a lazy loop, about twelve feet up. The werewolves rush the court, but all they can do is mill around, waiting for me to fall. C.J.'s face is an unbecoming shade of scarlet, as she yells something at me that I can't hear.

I take a second loop around the court, rising until I'm level with the new bridges, which are lined with werewolves wearing Philadelphia Flyers jerseys and shaking their paws at me from behind the thick glass. I shake my fist back at them and feel the broom dip under me; apparently this flying thing takes a good bit of concentration. Either that, or the enchantment on the broom is dying out. Whichever it is, I need an exit strategy. I climb up to the level of an upper-level lounge and pull out my wand. *"Reducto!"* I shout, and the glass in front of the lounge explodes, sending shards onto the cursing werewolves below. As the werewolves duck for cover. I sweep into the lounge. The magic in the broom chooses that moment to sputter out, and I hurtle into the concourse.

Eight werewolves are standing there; they're waiting in line for beer. I spring to my feet, snap a curse in their general direction, and take off the other way. I'm too high up now. If I can get downstairs, maybe I can find an outside door that will let me out into the city. I have a vague idea where New York Presbyterian is from here; it's somewhere on the East Side over by the United Nations building. Another platoon of werewolves spots me from the other side of the concourse, and I blast a curse at them, but all it does is slow them down. I spot a stairwell, and race towards it. There's a horde of werewolves racing up it, and they spot me, and start howling.

*The enemy's gate is down,* I think. There's barely enough room in the center of the stairwell to fit through. I hold my left hand over my head, and give my wand a flick.

"Supercalifragilisticexpialadocious!"

I grip the umbrella with my left hand and vault over the rail, floating down the middle of the stairwell. The werewolves howl in frustration, and some of them try to swipe at me, but I manage to hold them off. I drift down all six stories, and land lightly on the concrete floor. There's a door that says, "Emergency Exit," and being chased by twenty thousand werewolves would seem to be a pretty big emergency. I fall against it, and it opens, and I am outside, in the still night air on 31st Street. I cross the street, dodging two tour buses (both thankfully werewolf-free, from the looks of them, or at least nobody was howling at me). I wind up in front of an Irish pub, next to a Vietnamese pho restaurant. I stop for a minute to catch my breath, and head east, racing past a parking garage and some kind of construction site. Seventh Avenue is up ahead. New York Presbyterian is northeast of here, up on First Avenue somewhere, if it's in the same place. Easiest thing to do is head east and hope for the best, then turn north once I get close to the East River. It's a plan, anyway.

Traffic has picked up a good bit, with the usual chaotic mix of police cars and taxicabs. I don't see any good way through. I look to my left, towards the Garden, and there's a crowd of werewolves, spilling out of the arena. They haven't spotted me yet, and I don't have a prayer of outrunning them if they do. I turn right, heading south, with the idea that I will cross over Seventh in a couple of blocks.

I don't get five steps before C.J. Valentine appears out of nowhere, chewing gum and wearing a ridiculous chauffeur uniform. She's holding a sign that says LADY ASHLYN REVERE, and is standing next to a sleek black limousine parked against the curb. "Get in the car," she says. "Unless you want to get up close and personal with my furry friends."

I have read too many Jack Reacher novels; I am not ever going to get into that limo. "Get out of my way," I say, brandishing my wand.

The door of the limo opens, and the Dark Lord unfolds himself from the interior. My stomach lurches at the sight of him; this is a battle I'm not prepared to fight right now. He is tall, and bald, with his undertaker suit hanging off him. "Miss Valentine is doing her job," he says. "Please don't abuse her any more than is strictly necessary."

"I am not here to abuse her, or to settle scores with you," I say. "That can wait. I'm here to see my sister."

"That is easily accomplished," the Dark Lord says, gesturing to the interior of the limo. I look inside, and there is Penny, sound asleep and curled up in a ball in the back of the limo, shivering in a green hospital gown.

My wand is out, but I can't think of any curse or hex that would be enough to blast him into oblivion for this. "She should be in the hospital," I say.

The Dark Lord blinks. "She *is* in the hospital, of course. In your world. In this world, the place you call New York Presbyterian is a warehouse; publishing companies and literary agents use it to store surplus rejection letters. Anyway, that's not important. What is important is that your sister is asleep—really asleep, by which I mean not REM sleep. She will wake up in an hour or so, is my guess, and much improved. Thanks to your banishment of that inconvenient ghost. You have nothing further to do here, and would be well advised to leave. Even better advised not to return, although I admit that I admire the creativity of the bobsled run."

"I'm not leaving without Penny," I say. "You can't hold her hostage like this."

The Dark Lord grins, the sharp tips of his yellow teeth showing. "Like every child, she is a hostage to fortune. You can't blame me for that."

I can feel the anger rising against the backdrop of the screeching werewolves behind me. I point my wand in their direction, and shout a curse. *"Igneous!"* A pool of lava erupts in the middle of Seventh Avenue, and the howls of the pack turn into yelps of pain.

"That was unnecessary," the Dark Lord says. "They would not have hurt you without my leave."

"There's no need for anyone to be hurt today, least of all my sister. If you can't let me have her, you can at least let her go."

The Dark Lord shakes his head. "That would show exceptionally poor judgment on my part. You are leaving without her, no matter what happens."

"Don't be so sure," I say.

"I am sure," the Dark Lord says. He pulls back the sleeve on his suit jacket and checks a gold watch. "It's seven-fifteen. The orderly brought in dinner for the room across the hall. He'll be waking you up any second now."

"This isn't over," I say.

"It is for now." The Dark Lord snaps his fingers, and the towers of Seventh Avenue dissolve into smoke and ash behind the Dark Lord. I get a last glimpse of Penny, silent and helpless in the back of the limousine, before reality comes crashing in and erases the New York of my nightmare.

## Ashlyn | March 30 | RWJ Hospital, New Brunswick, New Jersey

I wake up with a start, heart racing, with my right hand gripping the handrail of the bed.

"Didn't mean to wake you up like that," the orderly says. "You should eat something, though. I've got macaroni and cheese, if you think you can handle it."

I gulp in a lungful of air. My hospital gown is soaked in sweat. I try to brush away the droplets on my forehead with my left arm, forgetting for the moment that it's in a cast. I stop before I bash myself in the head with it.

"Water," I ask. "Please. And my bag."

The orderly looks like he's going to shoot off a smart remark, but he swallows it and nods. He pours me a drink from the pitcher on my left, and hands me my bag. I open the side pocket, retrieve my phone, and manage to enter my access code one-handed. I call my dad, who picks up on the first ring.

"You're awake," he says. "Good. I was wondering."

"How is Penny?" I ask.

"She took a real turn for the better about an hour ago. Morton thinks that the anti-rejection drugs started working. She's not out of the woods yet; she still has a fever and they're not sure whether the virus she has is antibiotic-resistant yet or not. She's still alive, though, that's all that matters."

I collapse back onto my pillow, exhausted. "Is she awake?" I ask.

"Not yet, but Morton says soon. We're on our way over to ICU. I'm not planning on telling Penny you're in the hospital, too, no need to stress her over that. Understand?"

"Of course."

"How are you doing, though? Dr. Torrez texted me and thought you had come through okay, but he didn't do the surgery, so I wasn't sure."

"Fine," I say. "Fingers all there." The pinky finger and ring finger are encased in the cast, which goes halfway to my elbow, immobilizing the wrist. My other two fingers and my thumb are free, which is at least something.

"That's a plus, in case you need to ever use the Yellow Pages. Look, we're almost there. You need to try and eat something, get your rest. I'll get you an update in the morning."

I put the phone down on the bedside table and try to sit back up.

"Are we good with the macaroni and cheese?" the orderly asks.

I take a long, cool sip of water, to try to chase the foul taste of the city out of my mouth. "Yeah. Sounds good."

# Every Breath You Take

**Penny | March 30 | New York Presbyterian Hospital ICU**

I open my eyes a crack, and immediately regret it. For one thing, they're covered in goop, and I can't move my hands to wipe it all away. For another thing, all I can see is ceiling tiles and one square of fluorescent light. Might be better off asleep.

"Good morning, favorite patient," Morton says.

I try to release a groan, but nothing comes out except a dry rattle. I taste the hard plastic of the ventilator tube, forcing air into my new lungs.

"Relax," he says. "Don't try to move. You've been unconscious for two days."

This is an easy instruction to follow. I have zero motive power remaining in my body. I couldn't fight off a second grader armed with a throw pillow.

"You've weathered the experience very well so far," Morton says. "It was touch and go, I admit. The anti-rejection drugs didn't work very well at first. You hung in there, and you're looking good at the moment. Enough to have you wake up for a few minutes, anyway."

I take another machine-assisted breath. It doesn't feel any different with the new lungs, not yet. I suppose I will get used to them eventually—every breath I take will be with them from now on. They don't feel different, or alien, or anything except sore, like the rest of me. I wanted this moment, wanted to feel my new lungs inside me, wanted the freedom I hoped they would give me, but here I am, and all I am feeling is pain and bone-deep fatigue.

"Your parents are waiting outside, if you're up to seeing them."

I give a slight nod, which is about all I can do right now. Morton claps his hands. "Very well, then. I will see you in the morning, favorite patient."

I open my eyes wider, and see my parents framed against the ceiling tiles. Dad is tired and careworn, while Mom looks pale, almost chalky. "It's so good to see you, Penelope," she says. "You had us so worried."

All I can do is blink, and try to look pleased.

"You've had a rough couple of days there," Dad says. "We all have."

"We wanted to drop by and say hello," Mom says.

The ventilator continues its slow hissing. I can feel my lungs rising, feel my mom take my hand and squeeze it. I squeeze back a little, all I'm capable of at the moment. I close my eyes and fall back into darkness.

## PENNY | NEW YORK CITY | TEN YEARS IN THE FUTURE

I wind a towel around my hair and then step out of the shower. The little girl is there waiting for me.

"What are you doing here?" I ask.

"Daddy told me to tell you we were out of grapefruit juice," she says.

"Why couldn't Daddy tell me that himself?" I ask.

"He went down to the bodega to get it. What's a bodega, Mommy?"

I grab the other towel and start drying myself. "You've been there before. It's the little store where Marco works."

"But what does it mean? Bodega?"

"I don't know. It's Spanish."

"Like *uno, dos, tres,* that kind of Spanish?"

"Right. Now go back to the kitchen and wait for Daddy to get back. I'll be there in a few minutes."

"What's that on your chest?"

"I've told you a million times already, sweetie. It's the scar from my lung transplant. Can you please let me get ready in peace?"

She is not going anywhere, not while she has more questions to ask. I worry that she's going to grow up to be a lawyer. "Did it hurt?"

"It hurt a lot," I say, wrapping the towel around me. "It doesn't now."

"Am I going to have to get one someday?"

"No, sweetie. Thank goodness." We had her tested when she was three, and the genetic scan showed that she wasn't a carrier.

"Can they fix the scar?"

"No. I don't think I want them to." Most of my friends don't even know that I've had a lung transplant, or that I ever had cystic fibrosis. It's not part of my life anymore. The scar reminds me of that, reminds me of the sacrifice the donor made, and I don't want that erased.

"What are we doing today?"

"I have some research to do."

The little girl stares daggers at me. "Not the museum."

"What a great idea!" I say. "I never thought about the museum. I could do my research there. We could go together. Won't that be fun?"

"I don't want to go to the Frankenstein room."

"Not Frankenstein. Frank Lloyd Wright. Afterwards, if it's still sunny out, we could go to the park. Would you like that?"

"Can we climb on the rocks?"

"Of course."

"And get ice cream?"

"That depends on whether you can leave me alone long enough to get dressed."

"Okay, Mommy. I love you."

"I love you."

I drop the towel and trace the long scar. It's worth it, I think. All the pain, all the fear, all the work that lies ahead. It will all be worth it one day.

# A SORT OF HOMECOMING

## ASHLYN | MARCH 31 | MONTGOMERY, NEW JERSEY

I am eating the last bite of my hot dog while riding in the rehab hospital van. They picked me up right before lunch, after the RWJ doctors gave me a clean bill of health. Nneka came along with Marcus the driver, and she suggested that we hit the Sonic in Franklin for lunch. I'd been reading my new assignment for work—some sort of Regency steampunk thriller—and I notice that we don't seem to be headed back towards East Orange. We're on a country road, trees in every direction, headed where I do not know.

"Where are we?" I ask.

"I got a text from your mother," Nneka says.

"Great." This is what I need in my life; my mother signed up for the Radio Nneka news service.

"She asked me if we could stop by your house for a moment to pick up some spring clothes for you. You don't mind?"

"Home?" I squeak. I haven't been home since last August, since the day I pulled the Volvo out of the garage, with Penny hiding in the back seat. I was going to New York City for a job interview but I never made it. It's been all hospitals ever since. I was supposed to come home for Christmas; that's what I wanted, to walk in the front door with a loving family waiting for me.

Now I'm coming home in a wheelchair with a cast on my arm, home to an empty, quiet house. It's exactly what I wanted, just not the way that I wanted it.

"Are you all right, Ashlyn?"

"Home," I say. "S-sure. Let's go home."

It doesn't take long for Marcus to find the development. He pulls the hospital van into the driveway and he and Nneka help me exit. I punch in the code for the garage door; it's still my dad's birthday, 0518.

Inside the garage, there is a long metal ramp leading up to the laundry room. It hadn't been there before; it takes up so much space that you can't park a car here anymore. I hadn't even thought how I would get inside. I wheel myself up the ramp and open the door.

The kitchen is brilliant in the afternoon sunshine. This is where I had breakfast that morning; my mom had made me French toast in the waffle iron, of all things. I know the refrigerator is full of Coke Zero, and that my dad has his stash of Cherry Garcia ice cream hidden in the freezer.

"Your mother told me the clothes were upstairs in your room," Nneka says. "Something about a blue duffel bag. I will go fetch them for you."

"Okay," I say, looking around. Not much has changed. They have a new coffeemaker and a new air fryer, it looks like, probably Christmas gifts. There's a teetering stack of books on the corner of the coffee table in the family room, and I wheel myself over to look at them. Most of them are from some series called *Wings of Fire* that I'm not familiar with. A couple are my old Harry Potter books, which look to have sustained a bit more use.

My graduation pictures are on the bookshelf—high school and college, and in between them there's a homemade candle from a middle-school project. It was less than a year ago that I graduated college, I realize with a start. The girl in the picture looks so different, so alive.

It's like a shrine, I think. A shrine to a dead girl.

I hear Nneka making her way down the stairs. "Anything else you need, Ashlyn?"

I am crying, hot salty tears.

Nneka is carrying my old field hockey bag, and drops it when she sees me crying. "Oh, poor child," she says. "How can I help?"

"You can't," I say. "It's not... anything anyone can fix." Or that's what I try to say, it comes out jumbled.

Nneka finds a box of tissues and hands me two; they're not enough.

"I will not try and talk away your sadness," she says. "It will pass soon enough. I can wait here with you, or go back to the van with your bag."

"Go," I ask her. "I need a minute."

I could stay here, I think, as Nneka makes her way outside with the bag. There's enough food here. I could sleep on the couch. I could ask Aunt Stephanie to bring the boys back. It would be all right to do that. Not what I want, but it's something I could have for a while.

I wheel myself over to where Nneka left the box of tissues, and dry my face as best I can. I can't stay here. I have to go back. They're teaching me to talk. They can teach me to walk, once my hand heals. I can walk back in next time. I won't need the ramp.

You're supposed to wait, and not take the marshmallow right away, so you can have two marshmallows later. But that's hard, and it's really hard when the marshmallow is all you think about, all you want, all you can't have.

When I left here the last time, I wanted to leave, and I wanted to come back. I wanted my own life, independent of anyone, working in the city, working on beautiful, meaningful books, building a life for myself, but always coming back home again. Now I'm here and there's nothing for me to do but leave.

I wheel into the kitchen and open the junk drawer. There's a mini legal pad inside, and about a thousand pens. I find a big thick one and write on the legal pad, "Love you guys, Ashlyn," I write. My handwriting is big, almost cartoonish, but occupational therapy has made it almost readable. I leave the pad on the kitchen counter.

Nneka pokes her head back in the door. "Is there anything else I can get for you while we are here? Anything at all. Tell me where it is and I will get it for you."

I think about this. I have a thousand books, but I can't read any of them. Board games, but no one to play them with. Memories, but nothing I can hold on to.

"I wish there was something," I tell Nneka. "I can't think."

"Let us go, then. You can always come back. The rest of your life is out there, waiting for you. Give it time. You'll catch up with it."

# PULSE-OX

**PENNY | METROPOLITAN MUSEUM OF ART | TEN YEARS IN THE FUTURE**

"Mommy, I'm bored."

I am down on my hands and knees in the pale beige carpet, looking at the thirteen-foot library table in the Frank Lloyd Wright room in the Met. It's early morning on a Thursday, so the room is deserted. The girl can be counted on to look out longingly out of the leaded glass windows into Central Park, but she's restless this morning. I want to figure out how Wright put the table together so seamlessly a hundred years ago, but I also need to keep the girl from breaking anything valuable, such as the winged plaster angel on top of the table.

"Did you know this room used to be in Minnesota? It was someone's lake house, and they hired Frank Lloyd Wright to design it."

"Mommy, no."

"When the next generation of the family decided the house was too old and too big, they gave this room away to the museum. They went up to Minnesota, put everything in crates, and reconstructed it here. Well, most of it."

"I know, Mommy. You told me last time."

"Well, I'll say something new this time. This table is over a hundred years old, did you know that?"

"Can we go climbing rocks now?"

"Frank Lloyd Wright was an architect, but he was also a great designer. Look at the way this table was constructed. You can't tell how it was even put together."

"Mommy. Why do we always come here?"

"Here's the thing. This building is filled with art. Most of it is paintings, and paintings are one way to make a room beautiful. Even if you have an ugly room, a beautiful painting is still beautiful."

"So?"

"So, Frank Lloyd Wright came along, and he said that 'the mission of an architect is to help people understand how to make life more beautiful, the world a better one for living in, and to give reason, rhyme, and meaning to life.'"

The little girl frowns. "What does that mean?"

"He didn't just want beautiful paintings on an ugly wall. He wanted the room to be beautiful—the windows, the furniture, everything beautiful, everything in harmony with nature. That's inspiring, don't you think?"

"I think I want to climb on rocks and then get ice cream."

"I know, sweetie. We've been here long enough. Let's go play outside in the park."

"Yay!"

**PENNY | APRIL 1 | NEW YORK PRESBYTERIAN HOSPITAL, ICU**

I wake up from a beautiful room to an ugly one, to the sight of ceiling tiles and fluorescent light. On the plus side, this means that I'm still alive, which is overall a good thing. Every cell in my body is crying out for a Sprite, a jelly donut, and a deep-tissue massage. I am prepared to settle for whatever sludge they're feeding me through the nasogastric tube. (I read the ingredients once; it's basically corn syrup and soybean oil with a crushed multivitamin mixed in, you could make it at home yourself if you were a big fan of flavorless sludge.) The ventilator tube is still in, too, which means that I'm not making as much progress as I thought. *It will all be worth it one day*, I think to myself again, but today is not that day. Tomorrow is not looking good, either.

Katie the transplant coordinator materializes in my field of vision. "Good morning, Penny. How are you getting along?"

I am supposed to give her a thumbs-up at this point, but that would involve moving a muscle, which I have no desire to do at this point. I blink in what I hope is a communicative way. "I hear you," Katie says, which is vaguely reassuring. "Let me clean you up a little." She vanishes, and then reappears a minute later with a warm, wet hospital washcloth, which she uses to clean up the gunk around my eyes and the corners of my mouth. "Feel better?"

I nod my head a fraction.

"Okay then. Dr. Cotton is going to swing by and check on you here in a minute. If she's satisfied by what she sees, we'll try taking you off the ventilator. It's temporary, you understand, to see where you are in the recovery process. If you have any breathing issues, we'll put it back in, so there's no risk. If you can manage to talk, and have any questions, you can ask them, okay?"

This sounds good. This sounds great, actually. I've always grown up with the idea that the ventilator is the enemy, that my independence and freedom depend on staying off machines that breathe for me. I am one hundred percent down with getting the ventilator tube out of my throat, even if it is for a minute. I make the thumbs-up this time, even though it's an effort.

"Okay. Great. The doctor will be here in a bit."

Katie vanishes again, which prompts me to reflect. There is a reason why smart, forward-thinking, progressive hospitals like New York Presbyterian hire people like Katie, and that is because smart, forward-thinking progressive hospitals like New York Presbyterian understand the fundamental truth that doctors are arrogant jerks. I don't know a single thing about Dr. Cotton, much less whether she is an arrogant jerk, but that's the way to bet. (Morton is arrogant, and a jerk, but he is one or the other, not both at the same time, which makes him at least tolerable, for a quack.) I know too many doctors, and their arrogant jerkhood is part of the package.

Some of them are born arrogant jerks, but being an arrogant jerk from birth doesn't make you a doctor. I know plenty of arrogant jerks in my high school class that aren't smart enough to take a splinter out of your finger, much less take your entire awful, corroded lungs out of your body and replace them with nice fresh ones. It has to come from medical school, I think, or residency. What it is not so much as an attitude as a form of professional armor, a façade that you present to your patients so that they never discover that you're a fallible human person. And that's sad.

I close my eyes for a minute to shut out the pale brightness of the fluorescent light, and open them to see Morton's blank grim face. "Don't worry, favorite patient. Dr. Cotton will be here in a minute. I thought I would observe, you know, keep you from biting her when she takes out the tube."

*Quack*, I think, as loudly as I can. Morton shifts to the right, and Dr. Cotton appears. "This is Dr. Cotton.

Dr. Cotton, meet Penelope Revere, the Children's Hospital of Philadelphia homecoming queen."

"Call me Meredith," she says. "Hello, Penny. It's a pleasure to see you again. How are you feeling?" She has a no-nonsense English accent, something like Helen Mirren.

*I can answer that,* I think, *after you pull that tube out of my throat.* Of course, I can't say it, so I try something that I hope looks like a smile.

Cotton smiles back. She's older, with light blonde hair like Ashlyn's, except that it is turning to silver. "I know. You've been through the mill, you have. Katie told you we were going to see if you could breathe on your own, right?" I nod at this, and then spot a nurse over on my right-hand side. The nurse unhooks the ventilator tube with one swift motion, and I feel my lungs deflate. I take in a tiny sip of air, all I can manage, and the air flows in and flows back out. In and out.

"Very good," Cotton says. She looks at the pulse-ox monitor. "Try breathing a little deeper," she says.

I try. I am a little afraid of stretching whatever stitches are hidden under the hospital gown, but I don't seem to be doing that. Deeper this time, trying to keep my breath slow and even. I don't hear the usual rattle and wheezing sounds when I breathe, which is beautiful by itself. Cotton looks back at the monitor and frowns.

"Penny, can you try saying something for me?"

"Thirsty," I say. "Sprite."

"She's asking for junk food," Morton says. "That's a good sign. Next she'll be telling you how incompetent I am."

Cotton is frowning at the monitor. "I'm afraid we'll have to put you back on the ventilator for the time being, Penny. It shouldn't be for much longer. Rest comfortably, love, and I'll check on you in the morning. Understood?"

I am not best pleased about this, but if the doctor is seeing bad numbers on the pulse-ox machine, that's not good news and it means I need oxygen. Ventilators are awful but they get you oxygen when you need it and keep you from dying, so they have that going for them. I nod as best I can and let the nurse stick the tube back down my throat. Morton holds my hand for a minute and then leaves quietly.

Katie is the one who comes back. "You want to know what's going on, right?" she asks.

I give her my most emphatic nod.

"Okay. There can be several reasons why pulse-ox is low after a transplant. One of them is that you're very weak afterwards. That's why she was asking you to talk, to see if you could manage it. You're maybe a little weaker than you should be at this point. That's not abnormal, necessarily. You're in recovery, you'll get stronger, and the muscles that control your breathing will be able to do that better. The better you breathe, the better your pulse-ox gets. With me so far?"

I nod again.

"If that's all it is, then that's all it is; we have to wait for it to improve over time. But there's also a possible complication she's worried about. When they reattach your new lungs, they don't attach all of the blood vessels that were there before. They do the main ones, the ones that lead to your heart, but not all of them. The smaller vessels have to reconnect on their own. If that doesn't happen, your new lungs can't get enough oxygen into your system."

I do not like the sound of this, and have no way to communicate that, but Katie gets it.

"It's still too early in the process to worry. All you can do right now is rest and try to get stronger, that, and stay away from infection. It will be a tough week or so, but you'll be breathing on your own before too much longer. Keep working with me and you'll be fine. Okay? Can I get you anything? I'll have a cold Sprite in the ICU fridge waiting for you when you're ready to drink something."

Katie squeezes my hand and goes back to wherever it is she goes, and I am left staring at the ceiling tiles again. Ten thousand little bitty blood vessels have to decide whether to reattach themselves to my new lung, and I don't get a say in whether they do that or not. I listen to the ventilator sound for a long time, and then drift back to sleep, back to Central Park, where a little girl climbs rocks on a bright spring morning.

# YOU ARE NOT ALONE

**ASHLYN | APRIL 2 | WEST ORANGE, NEW JERSEY**

"I'm very impressed," Lindbergh says. "They did a fantastic job." He's looking at the X-rays of my hand and beaming. I am trying hard not to stab him with his pen and pencil set.

"Are you feeling any pain there, under the cast? Any numbness?"

"A little pain. Sore. Swollen."

"Anything like a bone rubbing against bone, though?"

"No," I say.

"Okay. We can re-look at it in six weeks, let it heal, and then work on strength and stability. In the meantime, we can get you back up on the treadmill, using the harness, and intersperse that with some cardio work on the exercise bike. Does that sound like a plan?"

I suppress a heavy sigh, and it comes out as a slight hiss. I will not drown myself in self-pity, will not let my feelings get in the way of what I want to do, but I do not want to sit here one minute longer and listen to Dr. Lindbergh talk about my wrist. I know he's not trying to make me feel bad or anything, it's that he's a symbol of everything that's frustrating me right now.

I think he understands this. "I wish you didn't need this surgery. I know it's a setback. All we can do is use the time wisely, then by the time you're healed, you'll have the strength and the stamina and the cardio all built up so we can get you back on the road again. Sound good?"

"Good."

"One other thing. Did Nurse Nneka come back with you from the hospital? I thought I saw her get into the van the other day."

"Yeah."

"You spend a lot of time with her, right?"

"Yeah," I say.

"You guys talk a lot?"

"Sure."

"I mean, there's nothing wrong with that. Nurses and patients need to have good relationships. I'm just wondering, you know."

I have no idea what he is wondering, and I desperately do not want to know.

"I mean, you guys talk, right? Gossip, maybe?"

"Nneka and I talk, sure." *She has a big fat mouth,* but that's not Lindbergh's concern.

"You know, she has kind of a reputation around here."

I definitely desperately do not want to be here for any of this conversation. "S-sorry," I say. "Speech therapy. Can't be late."

"I'm not trying to make you uncomfortable, and I'm sorry if I have. I was curious... I mean, has she ever said anything about me?"

"Excuse me?"

"She's very attractive, and I know that she's, you know, got an active social life." Lindbergh's pudgy face is beet-red now.

"This is..." I can't say the next word. It's either *uncomfortable* or *inappropriate*, but whichever it is, I can't spit it out.

"I'm sorry. I'm speaking out of turn, I know that, but, well, if you get the opportunity, put in a good word for me? Please?"

*Good Lord, I'm back in middle school.* "Sure," I say. "Therapy. Gotta go."

I am doing exceptionally well in speech therapy. That is what Emily the speech therapist keeps telling me, and I want to believe her.

"What you're doing is retraining your brain to speak the way you want to speak," she says. "That's an ongoing process. When I was little, my mother started reading me the *Narnia* books, and she would try to use the English accents for the characters. Since she's from Quebec, she was bad at it at first, but the more she read them, the better she got at the accents. We had to switch to something else because she was starting to use the accent when she wasn't reading."

"Cute," I say.

"You're starting to sound like yourself again. It takes practice and repetition. One thing you might try is to start reading books out loud—I know you do a lot of reading at night."

"I have a job," I say. "Unpaid internship, anyway." They currently have me reading a very obvious *Harry Potter* knockoff where the main character is a claims adjuster for a magical insurance company.

"The more talking you do, the better you'll get at it. Is there anything you want to talk to me about? I know you're not feeling very positive now."

"No," I say.

Emily frowns at me, which is about as surprising as if the *David* in Florence were to put his sling down for a minute and went to get a pair of marble boxer shorts. Her face isn't built for frowns. "I know how you feel," she says.

I give her my coldest look, one that would split a boulder in half at medium range.

"I was supposed to go to Boston in two weeks for the marathon," she says. "I was out training last weekend, and I started feeling pain in my left foot." She gestures over to the corner, and there's a pair of crutches there that I hadn't noticed before. "I'd managed to get a tear in one of my tendons. The doctor said that I had to rest for the next month, not put any pressure on it, and it might heal on its own. If I didn't, the tendon would rupture, and I'd need surgery."

This elicits maybe a half a point of sympathy.

"I know. It's not the same. You've been through worse; every one of my patients has. I know I shouldn't complain, but I always wanted to do Boston. The problem with Boston is that it's so early in the year; if you want to train for it, you train during the winter. New York is easier, you have nicer weather to train in for that. I've never done Boston before, not until this year, and now I can't."

I know I ought to say something here. *That's too bad. That sucks.* I can't manage it, can't manage that degree of empathy for someone who gets to walk out of here every day and go home.

"I'm not expecting you to feel sorry for me, Ashlyn. I get that. I shouldn't be offloading all this right now; it's not fair to you. But it helps to talk about it to somebody. You're allowed to do that. You're allowed to ask for help, and to get help if you need it. Part of speech therapy is finding your voice again, and one reason for doing that is so you don't suffer in silence."

"Don't know what to say."

"Don't talk about your medical condition. Or your sister. You can gripe about the hospital food; Lord knows everyone else does. Or how the Knicks are doing. Come on. Talk to me."

"Lindbergh asked me to help him ask Nneka out."

"You're not serious."

"Truth."

She coughs, trying to hide the laughter, but it doesn't work. "What on earth is he thinking?"

"He likes her. She's cute."

"Well, sure, I get that, but come on. You know what she's like. Poor Lindbergh isn't going to know what hit him. She's going to chew him up and spit him out."

"What s-should I do?"

"Let them find their own way, without getting run over in the process. Come on. Five minutes to lunch. Let's get to work on those sibilants while we still have time."

I call my dad while Nneka is in the cafeteria line; Penny is holding her own and should be breathing on her own sometime later this week but not yet. Lunch is chicken tenders, lettuce and tomato wrapped in a whole-wheat burrito, which I can eat with one hand. Nneka spends the time chattering about some boy she knew in high school who is studying at the London School of Economics. "I should never have let him get away," she says. "London is supposed to be nice, and any big city always needs nurses. I am not saying there is anything wrong with New Jersey. New Jersey is very nice. It is cool and green and quiet. A large city has its charms as well, but so expensive! You need to be married to a rich doctor to enjoy London, or even New York."

I think about this for a minute. Is Lindbergh rich? It doesn't seem like he could be. Maybe I would be doing Nneka a disservice to push her towards a poor doctor. Maybe he could do better if he had a wife to support. "I talked to Lindbergh today," I say. "He likes you."

"As well he might. I have been flirting with him for nine months now. I thought maybe he was blind or something. It must be that he is not brave enough to talk to me. Brave enough to talk to you, but not to come to me directly."

"That sounds right," I say.

"He does not need to be brave, though. It would help if he were rich. Young doctors have student loans to pay off."

"What should I tell him?"

"Tell him? You do not tell him a thing. This is my decision. I have to think about it, though. If he is not brave, I worry if he has the stamina."

"Oh."

"He has to be able to keep up, you know." Nneka's dark eyes twinkle at this. "I move fast. Come on, hurry up, finish your lunch. You have a date with the treadmill."

I am back on the treadmill, back in the harness, and after half an hour of solid work, I am feeling distinctly uncomfortable. There's sweat running down into my cast, and it itches like anything. The area under the harness is, if anything, worse. My legs feel like they're on fire, even though the treadmill isn't running all that quickly.

"Two more minutes," Gretel says. "Then you can rest."

I glance over her, and her face looks stern. I don't want to keep walking but I can't face her scorn. I pick up the tempo, enough to finish strong. A deep breath, and then another.

"Looking good," a voice says from across the room. I don't have to glance over to know that it's Ben, so I don't. I keep my eyes front, doing everything I can to ignore him. It's not too much longer before Gretel shuts down the treadmill. I grab the rail with my good right hand for support, while Gretel brings over my wheelchair and places it behind me. She takes my left elbow and I sink down into the chair. Gretel undoes the harness and moves the lift over to the far side of the room.

"You got a nice workout there." Ben's voice is closer, but I will not look in his direction. "And quite the cast, too. I was sorry to hear about that."

I am not giving him anything, not even the opportunity for small talk. He will not be here much longer, and I won't put up with him if I don't want to.

"Good work," Gretel says. "Don't let yourself slow down. You are doing very well; the muscle memory is still there. More training, harder training, that will help."

Ben is over to my left, so I push the joystick over to the right. He is quicker than I think he is, on his titanium foot, and steps in front of me. "Why are you in such a rush?" he asks. "I just wanted to say hi."

I look up at his big, stupid face as he drops to one knee to get to my level. I don't say anything; there isn't anything to say.

"I'm leaving in a couple of days," he says. "I didn't want to go without at least saying goodbye."

"Please excuse us," Gretel says. "She has to get to OT." I don't have to be at OT right away, but I appreciate the assist.

"Look," Ben says. "I guess you're mad at me. I get that. And I heard Carissa supposedly said something horrible to you, and assuming that's so, then I'm sorry about that."

Ben does not get to apologize for Carissa. There is no way I am taking that from him. I don't want to run over his new foot, so I back the chair up slowly.

"Wait," he says. "Wait wait wait. I get it. Look. You have to understand something about how Carissa's mind works."

I cannot think of anything I want to understand less in this world. I wish Nneka were here—she's on her break—to squash him thoroughly, but she isn't. Come to think of it, how did Ben know what, if anything, Carissa said to me? Nneka must have told him. *Drat her anyway.*

"Carissa is a team player, but she takes it to the nth degree, like she does a lot of things. You are either on her team or you aren't, and if you aren't, she sees you as a threat. Even if you can't possibly hurt her, even if it doesn't make a lot of sense. That's the way she is."

Then she can go be that way somewhere else. "Thank you," I say. "Goodbye."

"I want to explain; I wanted you to know how badly I felt about it. I wasn't trying... I should have told you about her. I know that. We watched a game or two she was playing, and I could have mentioned, you know, that's my fiancée, and I think that would have been better than me not saying anything at all. It's just that... she was focused on the tournament, and didn't have any time for me. Not since the amputation. I wasn't sure if she was going to call off the wedding, honestly."

I will not let myself feel sorry for Ben. Period.

"What I'm trying to tell you is—she's not really the way she comes across. She's focused and driven, but deep down, she's not a horrible person."

That tears it. I was not going to say anything, but there is no way I can let him get away with that.

"Ben, nobody starts off being a horrible person," I say. "They get that way because being horrible works for them. Do you know how they learn that it works for them? It works for them because people like you let them get away with it. So... so don't stand there and tell me that your horrible fiancée isn't really a horrible person, because every time you make excuses for her, she gets that much worse."

I turn my wheelchair around and head for the opposite door out of the fitness center. Gretel races after me and pulls up next to me in the hallway. "Good for you," she says.

I don't see Ben the rest of the day. I get through OT without any problems, and tear through a plate of the bland hospital-food baked ziti for dinner. I don't say anything the rest of the day. Have I had the sudden improvement from my aphasia that the speech therapist said might happen? Or did my anger at Ben and Carissa temporarily smooth out the barriers that keep me from speaking normally? I am not sure, and also not sure that I want to find out.

I get back to my room, and there is a tiny vase of flowers on my nightstand, which turns out to be a welcome-back-to-the-hospital present, with a card signed by Nneka and my other nurses. I look at the back of the card. Someone has written there, "You are not alone."

I change into my pajamas, get in bed, and turn on my iPad. As Emily suggested, I start reading out loud from the horrible fantasy book I'm reading for my job.

"I didn't get very far into the warehouse before I knew I made a mistake," I recite. "Whatever the Arcturan Order was storing inside, it was far more deadly than I could have imagined. A large steel cauldron in the center of the room was bubbling, with a thick, viscous black liquid dripping onto the floor, where drops of fluid had etched a deep gash in the concrete. The room s-smelled of petrol and imminent violence."

It isn't a completely smooth performance but if anyone had been listening, they would have, I think, understood every word. I try another paragraph, same result. Emily had explained about sudden remission from aphasia, but I hadn't quite believed her until now. I am talking. Soon I will be walking. I feel a surge in my heart that is something like hope.

# Borrowed Time

## Penny | April 4 | New York Presbyterian Hospital ICU

It has become a drill now, a thing that I do from time to time. I wake up, blink my eyes, stare at the ceiling tiles, and wait for the medical entourage to show up. I have a hard time keeping track on what time it is, but I think that Dr. Cotton is there most mornings, and there's a resident, Dr. Shaw, who is there at night. Morton is there most of the time, but not always. I figure he still has patients at CHOP and is checking in on them, something like that. Since I am basically asleep twenty-three hours a day, it's hard to keep the thread of the story. All I know is that since Dr. Cotton is here, and my body is screaming for caffeine and sugar, it is probably morning.

"Don't try to talk, dearie," Cotton says. "Just breathe."

I comply. I want to be a good breather, get good use out of my new lungs. I breathe as heavily as I can, which is not something I am used to doing. Cotton has me sitting up for this, which makes me feel light-headed.

"Calm down," Cotton says. "Don't hyperventilate. Breathe normally as best you can. Try not to overthink."

*Easy for you to say,* I think. *You're not the one being graded.* Because that's what this is, a test, and I have test anxiety coming off me in waves. Cotton is right, I am overthinking this, but I can't do anything but overthink.

"Maybe we can take your mind off the breathing for a minute. Is there anything we can get for you?"

"Coffee," I say.

"Maybe not coffee right away. We don't want hot liquid going down the wrong pipe right at the moment. Sprite?"

"Sure."

I work my way up to something like a sitting posture, and Katie puts the straw to my lips. I take a sip, but cough it out as soon as I drink it.

"Carefully," Cotton says. "Take it easy. No one is rushing you. Take a sip, and then tell me how you're feeling, if you can."

I try again, and manage to get a little liquid in my mouth and swallow. "Better?" I ask. I can't see my pulse-ox score from here, so I'm not sure. I don't feel any better, but I can't feel the arteries and veins and capillaries attaching themselves to my new lungs.

"Sounds promising." She breaks out the stethoscope, which she hasn't done before, and I seize on this as a hopeful sign. "Try to breathe deeply."

I do the best I can, attempt to develop a steady rhythm.

Cotton bites her lower lip and puts her hand on my forehead. "Pulse-ox is good, although it could be better—should be better at this point. We can leave the ventilator off for a bit, maybe see if you can tolerate a morsel or two of breakfast. That's the good news."

"Bad news." It isn't a question.

"Your blood pressure is down a bit. Heartrate is slow. Couple of things that could be causing it; I don't know at this point. We'll have to run some tests."

It's never good when they have to run tests. She's holding something back. Morton is a quack but he's honest; he would tell me if I was in trouble. I look over at Katie, who is standing there, quietly, ready to give me more Sprite if I want it.

I take a deeper breath. "Full. Disclosure. Please."

Cotton cocks her head and looks at me as if I'm a bug on her plate. "Young lady, don't know means *don't know*. There's no point in speculating about everything it could be. When I run the tests, I'll have a better idea."

"How serious?" I ask.

Cotton's features soften, except for the worry line in her forehead, which gets deeper if anything. "You're at a delicate point," she says. "Every transplant patient lives on borrowed time—borrowed from someone else whose time ran out. If I had to guess, I would guess it might be a cardiac infection—treatable, but it extends your hospitalization. I want to tell you everything is going well, but I shan't lie to you, either. We'll see what the tests say and go from there."

This is annoying, but I'm not getting anywhere with her; I'll have to wait until Morton shows up. Cotton's phone goes off in her pocket, and she ducks into the hallway. I look expectantly at Katie. "Breakfast?" I ask.

"We need to start simple," she says. "Something like saltines."

"Okay." I would rather have a bagel but that's not realistic at this point. "Where's Morton?"

Katie's face goes blank. "Didn't Dr. Shaw tell you? He had to leave last night."

"Back to Philly?"

"No. Boston. His oldest daughter is a resident at Mass General; she had a miscarriage last night."

"Oh, no," I say. Poor Morton. I ought to remember to feel sorry for him once I get to the point where I stop feeling sorry for myself.

An orderly comes in with a tray. "You're in luck," Katie says. "Ritz crackers. Ready to try a bite?"

"Sure," I say. Katie breaks one in half, and I bite down. I have an unhealthy relationship with Ritz crackers. I chew deliberately, not wanting to block my airway, and take a sip of Sprite. It tastes good but I have a corner of a cracker in the back of my throat and I cough a little bit to dislodge it. Then I cough again. Then a big hacking cough, and a fine mist of blood mixed with cracker crumbs comes out of my mouth and splatters Katie in the face.

"Oh, my God," Katie yelps. Her face turns white, and I think that she's going to be sick, but she finds her composure. "Dr. Cotton! Stat! She's aspirating blood."

Cotton races over. I cough again, and manage to get my hand over my mouth this time. My hand is dripping red.

"She's got an internal bleed somewhere. We need to get her into surgery." She barks into her phone. "This is Cotton. We need OR nine stat. Emergency surgery. I need it prepped right away. Find Armstrong or anyone else you can find for the anesthesia."

It takes me a minute to process this—I've had cystic fibrosis all my life; I'm used to coughing up blood. Maybe not *that* much, and not *on* people, you understand—I certainly didn't mean to do that to poor Katie. Yeah, okay, new lungs, maybe there's an internal bleed, and hey, that explains the low blood pressure and maybe that means it's not a cardiac infection and the world goes white around me and I fall back into nothingness.

## Katie | April 4 | Staff Locker Room, New York Presbyterian Hospital

Katie Wright is in the shower, washing the blood out of her hair. *Lather, rinse, repeat.* The last time she got blood in her hair was, goodness, four years ago, from a psych patient at Bellevue. What was her name? Wallace, she thinks. Heather Wallace, who had managed to get hold of a soda can and had used the pop-top to slash her wrists. Katie had tried to restrain her and gotten blood smeared in her hair for her troubles. It's a horrid feeling. Katie was inured to blood and pus and other bodily fluids since forever, but blood in her hair is not something she can deal with effectively.

*Four years ago*, she thinks. *That was... that was right around the time you went back to Memphis.*

She'd fallen in love with New York in grad school, after she'd unexpectedly gotten into the NYU nursing program. After one too many nerve-wracking nights at Bellevue, she'd sent an email to the two people she still knew at St. Jude's—both of whom had made their careers there, and were in good positions to recommend her. She'd gotten the interview right away, and had taken the first flight south. She'd always told herself that she wanted to do pediatric oncology, to give something back, and St. Jude's was a logical choice—at the same salary, which goes much farther in Memphis than in Manhattan.

She'd parked the rental car at the parking garage, walked into the lobby, and was initially startled that she didn't recognize anything, as the complex had changed so much. In the important ways, though, it hadn't. Sick kids and nervous parents, everywhere you look. She was hyperventilating before she made it to the elevator. She still doesn't know how she made it back to the hotel room, but she did, and spent twelve solid hours there, crying her eyes out. The HR staff at St. Jude's couldn't have been nicer about it, but they let her know that pediatric oncology was not the career for her. As soon as she was able to locate her rental car, she was on the next flight back to JFK.

She'd sought out help, which at least at Bellevue was close to hand. She told the counselor the truth; she had seen her face on the face of every child there, seen herself, alone and frightened and trying to keep her family together even though it wasn't her job.

That's what she'd seen this morning, her face on Penelope Revere, there in the moments that she was choking on her own blood, and a chill runs down her back even in the hot shower.

She'd left Bellevue for Presbyterian, made a career for herself, mastering the technical details of the transplant process, helping and guiding patients through the anxiety and the pain. The fear is still there, and Penny had seen it from the first time they'd met.

Twenty minutes later, her hair spotless, dressed in dark blue hospital scrubs, she makes her way to her office. There's a card in her purse, a number she hasn't needed to call in three years. There's no answer at first, but a couple of minutes later her phone rings. "Sorry," she says. "I was on the phone with my periodontist. What happened?"

"I had a patient this morning," Katie says. "A lung transplant patient; she aspirated blood all over me."

"Goodness," the voice says. "Is she okay?"

"They took her to surgery; she's still there as far as I know. I just realized that no one has told the parents yet."

"You should definitely tell them now. I know you feel awful about it, but we talked about this. You have to compartmentalize. The parents need to know."

"I saw my face again. On her. I haven't seen that since Memphis. It scares me."

"I know, but her parents are more scared than you are, trust me. Talk to them, and then call me when you can."

"What if—"

"Katie. Listen to me. You've been through more than I want to think about in your life. We can't change your past. All you have is the present, and in the present, there are two scared parents out there who deserve to know that their daughter is in danger. Even if they can't help her, even if you can't help her."

"Right. Right. I know."

"Go tell them, and call me back."

"I will. Promise."

"You're a good person, Katie Wright. A good nurse. You can do this." *Click.*

Katie dabs at her eyes with a tissue, and then gets out of her chair, heading towards the Presbyterian's guest quarters at a fast walk.

# Carolina Blue

**Ashlyn | April 4 | West Orange, New Jersey**

I had a few minutes to myself after breakfast; a rare luxury. The occupational therapist has jury duty today, so I am cleaning out the duffel bag that my mom packed for me. Underwear and socks in the top drawer, T-shirts and shorts underneath. There is an immaculately folded sundress at the bottom, which I will be sure to wear to the next hospital garden party. I lay it on the bed for the time being until Nneka comes to pick me up for physical therapy and I can get her to hang it in my closet.

I look in the front pocket of the duffel bag, and sure enough, there are two Carolina-blue wristbands in there, still smelling faintly of salt. I remember how bad my left hand itched on the treadmill yesterday. Maybe the wristband can help. I try to put it on over the cast, but it won't stretch that far. I am trying—and failing—to slip it over my thumb when my phone rings. It takes me a minute to spin my wheelchair around from the dresser to the bed, but I manage to grab it before it stops ringing.

"It's Penny," my dad says. "She's back in surgery, and it doesn't look good."

I respond with an unladylike, but appropriate, profanity. "What happened?"

"She's got internal bleeding somewhere in her lungs. They finally were trying to get her to eat something, and she coughed blood everywhere and collapsed. She's been in surgery for the last half hour; they finally got around to telling us."

"Is she going to make it?"

"I don't know, sweetheart, I just don't know. She has been very weak, and the loss of blood isn't helping her. I'm going down and donate a pint, in case she needs it."

*At least he can do something*, I think. "How are you guys doing?"

"Worried half to death. Your mother is... well, you can imagine. The longer it takes them to find the bleeding, the worse the odds get. There's the possibility of reinfection, if she survives the surgery. All we can do is wait and pray."

"At least it happened in the hospital."

"That's true. Her doctor was right there; if she'd started bleeding in her sleep, she wouldn't have been so lucky. If you can call it that. Ashlyn, is your speech starting to get better?"

"A little bit. It's not important now."

"Holy cow. You sound so great. Look, I need to keep the phone line open in case they call."

"Okay. Love you both."

"Love you. I will let you know when I know."

"That Doctor Lindbergh. You would not believe..." Nneka stops as soon as she sees that I am sobbing. "Oh, no. Not your poor sister."

"S-she's back in surgery," I say. "Internal bleeding." *I am responsible for her*, I think for the thousandth time, *but there's nothing I can do about it*. It's a thoroughly miserable feeling, on top of every other thought that's rattling through my brain.

"That is terrible news. I am so sorry for you, and your parents as well. What are they telling you?"

"Doesn't look good," I say. "The sooner they find the bleeding, the better."

"Of course. You are sounding much better today."

I appreciate hearing that, but it's not important, at least not while Penny's life is on the line. "Thanks."

"What is that on your hand?"

The wristband is still there, wrapped around the cast. "Can you help me take this off?" I ask. I have to find another way to deal with the itching, I suppose, but again it's not important. What's important is Penny being all right, and I have no way to make that happen.

"We will get you up on the treadmill. Exercise will take your mind off your troubles, for a while, anyway."

I take another tissue and wipe my tears from my face. "What about Doctor Lindbergh?"

"He invited me to a picnic! Would you believe? A rich doctor, and instead of taking me out to a nice restaurant, he wants to eat outside. On a blanket. With ants. What is romantic about that, I ask you?"

"Try one more paragraph," Emily says.

I scroll to the next page of the galley on my tablet. "Magic is a powerful force, but like all powerful forces, it has its limitations. Magic can change toads into teacups and back again, but can't change the forces that s-shape our world. Magic can take us to the corner store or the four corners of the world, but can't bring back those we've lost. Magic can fix a broken plate, but it can't f-fix a broken heart. Only love can do that, and it's the one form of magic I've never been able to master."

"That's amazing," she says.

"It needs work," I reply. "The author is trying too hard to be profound."

Emily smiles. "That's not what I meant. You sound so much better. It's remarkable. I mean, there's still a lot of work to do with the apraxia—sibilants are still a little loose, and you tripped over some of the plosives. Whatever rewiring needed to go through in your brain seems to have rerouted itself."

"I don't have to think about what the next word is, reading out loud."

"Even when you're not reading, you're not struggling the way you were. The thoughts are coming out in complete sentences. It's excellent. You should be proud. You've put in the work, and now it's starting to pay off."

"Yeah. It's just that..."

"I know. Your sister. Nneka told me."

"Nneka has a big mouth."

"I'm aware. Look. I know it hurts. I know you don't feel like celebrating now, but this is a big step forward for you. You love your sister, but you can't be there for her, and that hurts. You've gotten an important part of your life back. You can't take that for granted."

"I don't want to lose her. I've lost so much."

"I wish there was something I could do, Ashlyn. It's difficult."

My phone rings. I don't want to pick it up. I don't want Penny's story to end here, with me on the wrong end of a phone call. I don't want to break down in front of Emily, but I don't have a choice. I have to know.

"She came through surgery," my dad says.

"Thank God," I say.

"I don't have the details, other than there was a blood clot around the sutures in one of the arteries. If the doctor hadn't been right there, she could have bled to death. Came pretty close as it was. It's touch and go, but she passed the first hurdle."

"So then we wait," I say.

"Waiting and praying. It's all we can do. I know you feel powerless right now. I do too. but she's in one of the best hospitals in the world, with trained doctors who know what they're doing."

"I know."

"We have to have faith at this point. I need to call your Aunt Stephanie and let her tell the boys, and then call Dr. Morton—he's up in Boston dealing with a family crisis. Okay? I'll call you when I know more."

"Okay," I say. "Love you guys."

"Love you too."

"Good news?" Emily asks as I put down the phone.

"For now. Getting through s-surgery is the best we can hope for."

"Then let's keep hoping. We still have ten minutes more. Why don't you read a while longer?"

**ASHLYN | CHAPEL HILL, NORTH CAROLINA | TWO YEARS IN THE PAST**

In my dream, it's a bright spring day, and I'm walking onto the field at the new field hockey complex, the one located past the right-field wall of the baseball stadium. I'm wearing my Carolina-blue uniform and carrying my best field hockey stick. The Duke team is on the far side of the field, doing stretches, loosening up. I take a practice swing with my stick. The grass is wet and slick, and I will need to watch my footing. The assistant coach runs up to me, her ponytail streaming behind her.

"Ashlyn, you know you don't have to play today. We can get by without you."

"I came here to play," I say, "and I'm playing."

"We don't want to pressure you into coming back too soon," she says. "What happened to your sister was tragic. If you need time to grieve, you should take it."

"My sister is fine," I say. "She had emergency surgery, that was all. Critical but stable condition, that's the last thing I heard."

"It's okay to be in denial after a loss like that," she says.

I stand there, gaping at her, open-mouthed. The other members of the team wander over—Rose Barrington, the captain, Tess Duckworth, the goalie. Jennifer Lamb is there too, which doesn't make sense as she's on the basketball team.

"We know how much you loved Penny," Rose says. "I'm sorry that she's gone. We want you to know we care about her, and we're dedicating this game to her."

"Penny isn't dead," I say. "What are you talking about?"

"It's an awful thing," Tess says. "To lose someone that young."

"Stop. All of you. You don't know what you're talking about."

A whistle blows, and we all line up for the start of the game. A voice comes over the loudspeaker. "Please stand for a moment of silence to honor Penelope Revere, sister of forward Ashlyn Revere, who died yesterday of complications from lung transplant surgery."

"No," I say. "Wait. Stop. You've got it all wrong."

Carissa Buckley walks over to me, wearing her dark blue Duke uniform. "I'm sorry your sister died," she says. "But she was weak. Just like you."

I slap her, as hard as I can, hard enough that she screams. Then everyone screams.

## ASHLYN | APRIL 4 | WEST ORANGE, NEW JERSEY

"It was just a dream, Ashlyn. Just a dream. Try and calm down."

I am sitting up in my bed, hyperventilating. Roxanne the night nurse is holding my hand.

"Penny. In the dream. They said she died."

"That's the anxiety talking. Your sister is all right. They would have told you otherwise, you know that."

"It felt real." I am trying hard to breathe, to calm down, but everything in the dream was so real, and so painful.

"Take a minute. Nothing bad happened. It was just a dream. Maybe drink a sip of water."

I find that I'm gripping her hand like I'm holding on to the last threads that are keeping me together. I let go, gradually, and she moves over to my bedside table and pours a cup of water. I drink it, half of it sloshing down my front.

"That's it. Easy, girl. Take your time."

I take one deep breath, and thank a merciful God that I didn't have another seizure. I take a careful sip of water. Roxanne gets a tissue and wipes my face.

"It will take time for your heart rate to go back down. Nightmares like that push adrenalin through your system, and that puts your whole body on high alert.

Even though they aren't real, it takes a while for the body to adjust."

"Thank you," I say.

"Don't mention it. What I want you to do is lay back down. Don't try to sleep just yet. Try thinking a happy thought, something that doesn't have anything to do with your troubles and your cares. Hang on to that thought. Your body will respond, and you'll go back to sleep. May not even remember it in the morning. Okay?"

All my happy thoughts are about being home with my family, or else in Summervale. This is the first dream that I've had since the accident that wasn't in my fantasy kingdom, and I don't understand why I didn't go there when I fell asleep. Penny saved me in my dream; can I save her in hers?

I take another sip of water, and put the cup down. "I feel better now," I say. "I think I can go back to sleep."

"Let's hope so. Good night, Ashlyn."

"Good night."

# A Circle of Moonlight

**Penny | New York City | Ten Years In the Future**

"The gorilla did not want to go to sleep. He wanted to stay awake, and he wanted all his friends to join him. He took the key from the zookeeper, and followed him around the zoo. Every time the zookeeper locked one of his friends away for the night, the gorilla would use his key, and let them out again."

"Mommy, you're not telling the story right."

"Of course, I'm telling the story right. There's the gorilla, see?"

The girl squirms in my lap. "That's not how Daddy tells it."

"Daddy is in San Francisco. You just got off the phone with him."

"But he tells it different. He talks about the different animals."

"There aren't any words on the page, sweetie. I can tell the story any way I want."

"But Daddy does it better."

"I cannot believe you said that, young lady."

"But he does!"

"So that means I should stop reading then, doesn't it?"

"No, Mommy. You can read."

"Okay, then. So, the gorilla..."

All the lights in the bedroom go out at once.

"What happened, Mommy?"

"I think we had a blackout. Before you ask, a blackout is when the electricity goes out all over the city."

"What makes the electricity go out?"

"I don't know. This is what we're going to do, okay? Can you listen for a minute, and do what I tell you?"

"I don't like it when the electricity goes out."

"I know. I don't either." The darkness in the room is absolute. "I will help you climb into bed. I want you to stay there, and not move. I'm going to get my phone out of my pocket. I can use the light on the phone to go into the kitchen, and find the flashlight. Then I'll come back, and we'll finish the story, and you can go to sleep. Does that sound good?"

"No, Mommy. I'm scared."

"There's no need to be scared. The dark isn't going to hurt you. You're safe in your warm bed. I'll be in the kitchen, and I'll come right back. Promise."

"But why did the electricity go out?"

"It happens sometimes. Something goes wrong with the electrical wires. It's not scary, it's just a little different. Can you get into bed now, sweetie? Please?"

"Can I help find the flashlight?"

"No. You get in bed. Mr. Cheetah is up there waiting for you, you can give him a big hug and tell him it's going to be okay. Can you do that?"

"Okay, Mommy."

"I'll be right back."

"Promise?"

"Super-promise."

The girl climbs out of my lap and I boost her into bed and help her find her stuffed cheetah. I fish my phone out of my pocket and turn on the light. "I'll be right back."

"Hurry, Mommy."

The flashlight is on top of the refrigerator; I go up on my tiptoes to reach it. Thankfully, the batteries are in good shape. I hurry back to the bedroom, where the girl is huddled in the bed, shaking.

"I told you I'd come back. Are we ready to finish the story of the gorilla?"

"No, Mommy."

"If you want to go to sleep, that's all right."

"Mr. Cheetah wants to know if we can sleep with you, since Daddy is in California."

"Mr. Cheetah wants to know that?" I ask.

"Mommy. Please?"

"The last time we did this, I ended up black and blue all over, because you were kicking me all night."

"I'll be good this time. Promise."

"Super-promise?"

"Super-promise."

"Okay. This one time. If the lights come back on, you go back to your bed. Fair?"

"I guess so."

"Okay then. Take my hand, and bring Mr. Cheetah."

We make our way through the darkened apartment. The apartment is tiny, but it has a spectacular view of Central Park, and the stony landscape of the Upper West Side behind it. Tonight, all is dark, save for the full moon hanging far away over New Jersey. "Look," I say. "See what I told you? The whole city is blacked out."

"The moon is a circle, Mommy."

"Yes. It isn't always, but tonight it is. And that's good. It gives people some light to see by."

"Can Daddy see the moon?"

"Maybe. I think so. It's still early in California."

"I'm glad for the moon. It's too dark out there."

"If you look closely," I say, "in some of the windows, you'll see some lights. Candles and flashlights. Everyone is looking for a ray of light, even when it's dark outside."

We sit together on the couch, snuggling together under a warm Hudson Bay blanket, watching the flickering lights of the city for a long while.

"Are you scared, Mommy?" she asks.

I am not just scared. I am terrified. I know this is a dream, I know I am lying in a hospital bed after God-knows-what surgery I've endured. I don't know how close I am to death, but when you're in a dream where all the lights go out, that can't possibly be good, you know, from a symbolic point of view.

That's what happened when I was in Ashlyn's dream, when she was dying, I think. All the lights started going out.

My world has dwindled to one little girl and a circle of moonlight. I hold the girl as close as I can, feeling her warmth against me. I am going to keep holding on, as long as I can, even if there's nothing more I can hold on to.

# The Better Angels

**Ashlyn | April 4 | West Orange, New Jersey**

"Try this," Gretel says. She has taken a Velcro headband and wrapped it around my wrist twice, snug to the cast. "It should help."

"That's very smart," I say. "Thank you."

"How is your sister this morning?"

"As well as can be," I say. She is still unconscious, still on a ventilator, hanging on by her fingernails but still hanging on. "She's either going to pull out of this or she's not," my dad had told me this morning. "Nobody has any idea one way or another."

Gretel walks around me to fit the harness around me, fastening it around my chest. "Good to go?"

"Good to go."

I hold my feet wide apart, and push with my right arm against the arm of the wheelchair. I am standing on my own, the cord that attaches to the lift slack against my back. Gretel takes my elbow and helps me make the step up to the treadmill, and then tightens the cord, lifting me up a tiny amount. I tense up for a second, as Gretel turns on the machine.

Left foot, right foot. Left foot, right foot. Finding a rhythm, settling in. I am breathing purposefully now, breathing with intention.

Running was always the best part of my game. I couldn't stand the monotony of being on a track, where the scenery never changed. Running somewhere, running for a reason, running to chase something, that I loved. I grew up playing soccer, aggravated because my third-grade teammates would gather in an amorphous lump at midfield, kicking each other's shin-guards trying to get the ball. On those rare occasions where I could break the ball loose out of the pack, kick it down the field and chase after it, that was what I played for, what I wanted. I discovered field hockey in middle school, and played against mean, tough girls who would knock you over without thinking about it. I had to learn to run to get away from them, get past them, get the ball into the goal. When they had the ball, I could chase them down, get it back, keep the game going. I shed my pudgy curves and became lean and sleek, a lioness on green turf, armed with a stick.

Whether I will get that back, I do not know. I've accepted that my field hockey career, such as it was, is long over, but I can try to come as close to it as I can. Walking on my own is the first step towards building the life I want.

"Can we make it faster?" I ask.

Gretel nods, and pushes the button with the up-arrow.

I need to walk, need to build up my endurance, but I also need to tire myself out. I was able to get back to sleep for a little while after the nightmare, but it was a light doze and I was up and awake at sunup. I don't know if I can rescue Penny or not. I don't know if it will make any difference. I can try; that is all I can do. I grip the right-hand rail of the treadmill.

"Faster," I say.

"Don't overexert yourself."

"Okay." I want to find the right speed, the lane between a light workout and a punishing pace. Gretel puts it up to 1.8 MPH, which is how fast you'd go on a slow walk around the park, but is faster than I've gone on the treadmill so far. If I can sustain this for the next half hour, I should burn off a lot of the stress hormones that are keeping me awake at night.

"That's good," Gretel says. "Let's keep in there. You want to keep going, yes?"

"Yes."

Gretel walks over and loosens the cord to the lift; it's still taut against my back, but less so. "You are supporting more of your full body weight," she explains. "It will take more effort, but you will grow stronger. The harness will still catch you if you fall. Good?"

"Good," I say.

"Walk, then," she says. "Keep up the good work."

**ASHLYN | APRIL 5 | THE REALM OF SUMMERVALE**

I open my eyes and I am on a modern couch, clutching a green throw pillow, staring into a fireplace, the embers blazing bright, the orange light reflecting on the large round red kettle to the left. The Lord of Light is hunched over, sorting through the firewood, looking for just the right log to place on the flames.

"You made it," he says. "A pleasure to see you again."

"I am glad to be back in Summervale," I say, "but I am a long way from where I want to be."

"Nonsense. You're doing very well, you know." He places the log on the fire, giving it a little toss, and it lands perfectly in the midst of the blaze.

"That's not what I mean."

"I know what you mean, and you need to listen to me. One of the worst things that people can do is minimize their accomplishments. You've worked hard over the last few months. Your speech has improved. You're very close to being able to walk again. Your brain functioning is improving, although it's not obvious, and I don't think you're even aware of it. You have a job, and you are doing it to the best of your capacity. All of these are good things, and they've come about because you willed them. Other people would have given up, accepted the damage, and moved on. You wanted to be more than that, and here you are. It's remarkable, and you're doing yourself a real disservice if you discount that."

"All of that is true in my world," I explain. "I'm here in this world, and I'm here for a reason."

"To rescue your sister, who may not even need rescuing."

"You don't know that."

"Neither do you."

"She rescued me when I was dying. I have an obligation to return the favor. Even if that means going back to New York, and facing down the Dark Lord and his armies. Even if that means going in alone."

The Lord of Light dusts a speck of sawdust off his hands. "That's another thing. You're not alone, and if you think you are, then you're wrong. You know that. Even talking about your sister, she's being cared for by top-flight medical professionals."

"They can only do so much. And she's my responsibility."

"That is noble of you. We are in a time where nobility is not valued. Do you know why that is?"

"Because nobility is difficult."

"Partly, I suppose. Nobility is not valued because it is confused for privilege. In a democratic society, privilege is looked upon with suspicion. Privilege is just one face of the coin—the face that most people see. The other side of the coin is sacrifice. The rewards of nobility, such as they are, are paid for by the sacrifices that nobility requires. *Noblesse oblige* and all that."

"With great power comes great responsibility."

"The problem with that little statement is that people then conflate power—or superpowers, in the comic book sense—with nobility. You do not have to have power to be noble, and many who are powerful have no conception of nobility—no true willingness to take up their obligations and discharge them as they see fit. That always takes sacrifice, there is no other way."

"My sister's life is worth whatever sacrifice I must pay."

"Then listen well." The Lord of Light sits down on the rough boulder to the right of the fireplace. "Summervale is a kingdom in conflict, riven between your subterranean desires and the better angels of your nature."

"A house divided against itself cannot stand," I reply.

"Can't it?"

"Lincoln said no. It will become all one thing or all the other."

"I wonder. You may choose to go back to New York, battle the Dark Lord, win back your sword, and leave as a conqueror. This will not end all your negative thoughts or deeds, of course, but you will know you can rise above them. Or you can fight as hard as you can and still lose. The Dark Lord will rise like a wave across the kingdom, and everything you love here will pass away."

"What will happen to me?" I ask. "If the Dark Lord wins?"

"You will wake up," the Lord of Light says, wryly. "But you will not be able to return to the Summervale that you know. You will lose a safe place, a happy place. Even if you succeed, you will replace the happy fantasy land of your youth with something else, harder and colder and farther away."

"For my sister's life, that's a price I'm willing to pay."

"There is another way. A third option. A rescue mission."

"How do you mean? The Dark Lord has Penny in his power. How can I rescue her without defeating him?"

The firelight twinkles in the old man's eyes. "Never forget, the Dark Lord is an accomplished liar. You saw what he wanted you to see. Your sister is free of the Dark Lord's influence."

"She's safe?" I ask.

"I did not say that. If you try to rescue her, you would be placing yourself in danger. There is no guarantee of success. Quite the opposite. Even if you do all you can, all you're capable of, you may not be able to save her—and this realm will still fall. Or you may stay here, warm yourself before this remarkable fire, and rest, and return to the Vale of Summer as you wish—trusting in your sister's doctors to save her. It is your decision."

"Can you tell me where she is?"

The Lord of Light nods. "I will give you all the help I can, but the most important advice I can give you is this: people get caught in a cycle of recurring dreams because they always act the same way towards the same stimulus. Don't fall into that trap. Be unpredictable."

"What can I do to tip the odds in my favor?"

The Lord of Light stands up, a light sparkling in his eyes. "I thought you would never ask," he says. "Are you afraid of the dark?"

"Not anymore."

"Good."

# HOT LZ

**ASHLYN | APRIL 5 | NEW YORK CITY, THE REALM OF SUMMERVALE**

I am not afraid of the dark, but it turns out that I am very much afraid of falling in the dark. Or at least that is what I thought I was doing, what with the wind whistling round me, and not being able to see anything, and the intense feeling of impending doom in the pit of my stomach. There is a sound coming from somewhere that sounds very much like a scream.

It is coming from me.

I am holding on to something round, and wooden. Some kind of stick. Well, when you're falling to your certain death, a stick is not what you need.

Unless...

I pull up on the stick, and my stomach stops its downward plummet and relocates into the back of my mouth. *Okay, so that's a broomstick. Got it.*

I am momentarily glad that I'd had my first solo test flight on a broomstick in the relative peace and quiet of Madison Square Garden, so I am only somewhat terrified. Here, I can't see anything, and I'm not sure about my relative speed or my altitude or anything else. I look around for a landmark, and then realize that I am a few feet away from impacting into the Chrysler Building, rising pale in the light of the full moon. I swerve left to keep from going splat against the Art Deco stainless steel.

I raise my altitude enough to keep from becoming permanently embedded in the New York skyline. The Lord of Light has solved two of my problems: how to get to New York without the Dark Lord finding out, and how to move around the city without falling afoul of his minions. The city below is dark, completely blacked out, with nothing but the full moon shining over New Jersey to light the way. The next step is to figure out where Penny might be, and to land without killing myself, in total darkness, in a city dominated by tall buildings.

I will get the Lord of Light for this if it's the last thing I do.

I circle back around and find the Chrysler Building, which is, what, 42nd and Lexington. Okay. Rockefeller Center should be over to the left. I hover for a minute, long enough to pull my wand out of the pocket of my hoodie. "Where's Penny?" I ask the wand, and then feel totally ridiculous. It's an immensely powerful magic wand, but it didn't come with Alexa.

And yet, the stupidest incantation imaginable seems to be working. The wand emits a thin beam of copper light, pointing north towards Central Park. Okay then. I'm not crazy about the notion of trying to land on top of the Rockefeller Center ice rink anyway. If I can make it north, I ought to be able to find the park and land there. I look over to the moon to get my bearings, and a long, sinuous shape passes in front of it.

Oh, yeah. Here be dragons.

I put the wand back in my pocket and lean forward. At this altitude, I ought not to hit anything between here at the park. I need speed more than anything right now.

The dragon catches sight of the movement, and turns towards me, belching a thin stream of flame. I pull back on the broomstick and gain more altitude, and the fire goes under me, warming my toes.

"You can run, Lady Ashlyn, but you can't hide," a voice wails. It is C.J. Valentine, because of course it is. The dragon passes under me; its turning radius is wider than mine, which gives me the ghost of a chance. If C.J. can steer at all, she can cut me off based on where she thinks I'm going. She'll turn right, north towards the park, hoping to cut me off. That wide turning radius won't work so well down in the narrow Manhattan streets. High altitude saved me before, so it's time to try low altitude.

I push down on the broomstick, angling to the left of Rockefeller Center. If that's Sixth Avenue, I ought to be able to follow that north to Central Park, no worries. Once I get there, I can cast the spell again and hope that the light leads me to Penny. I swoop down at a height calculated to let me clear double-decker tour buses— assuming this version of New York has them. Apparently, it does, because there's one right below, filled with Viking warriors, shaking their fists at me. *Awesome.*

Dead ahead, there's a long stream of fire—but it's at a right angle to me. I was right; C.J. is trying to cut me off. The dragon is moving west on 57th Street. I slow down long enough to let the dragon's head and the first section of its long, sinuous body pass. Once C.J. appears, riding about halfway down the dragon's back, I send an ice blast in her direction. It knocks her off the dragon, but she still has hold of the lead line. The dragon makes a sharp right turn, and crashes headfirst into the glass windows of a nearby Duane Reade. Perfect. I climb a few more feet, just to get a good look at Central Park to find a decent landing space. The park happens to be on fire, because of course it is.

I climb higher, enough so I can see that it's not an out-of-control wildfire. It's a controlled burn, in the shape of an arrow. The tip of the arrow is on the east side of the park, pointing to a wide meadow somewhere around 77th Street, south of the museum. Could it be a trap? Maybe, but only C.J. Valentine and the Lord of Light know I'm here, and this is the single light in the darkened city. I decide to take a chance. I sweep down from my high altitude and make a hurried landing. I see two stocky forms in the shadows.

"You made it!" Holland says. "I knew you would."

"The Lord of Light sent us," Lincoln says. "Didn't say when you'd be here, though."

"Did he tell you where Penny was?" I ask.

"Over there, an apartment building somewhere east of here. Top floor," Holland says.

"Swanky," Lincoln says.

"Okay," I say. "I think I can find her specifically." I ask my wand again where Penny is, and the copper beam reappears, pointing northeast, and up. "What's the neighborhood like?"

"It's fairly rough, Your Worship," Holland says. "Fear-beasts everywhere. The fire is keeping them away."

"There's a few other creatures out there," Lincoln says. "You had best be wary. This here is a hot LZ, and no mistake."

"Got it. Wait. This is a hot what?"

"Landing zone," Holland says.

"Right. Okay. Thank you, guys. I can take it from here. Do you know how I get Penny back home? Did the Lord of Light say?"

"I think maybe she is home," Lincoln says.

"Maybe so, but this isn't a safe place for either of us. How do we get out of New York, if we need to, in a hurry? And no bobsled runs. Or catapults."

"Let us worry about that," Holland says. "You go and find your sister, and make her as safe as you can."

"Copy that."

Fear-beasts are low-slung, six-legged, panther-like creatures; aggressive and lethal but not too smart. When I started encountering them in my dreams, all I had was a sword. This is not ideal because fear-beasts can leap from outside the radius of your sword, and then land on top of you with their silver-tipped claws and sharp teeth. It is much more efficient to dispatch them with magic. True to their name, fear-beasts become stronger—and more numerous—the more fear that you feel. The way to defeat a large force of fear-beasts is to stay calm, keep your mind clear, and then blast them into oblivion from long-range. (The other alternative is to petrify them, but then you run the risk of tripping over them when you need to maneuver.)

I ignite a tiny ball of fire on the tip of my wand, which lights my way in the darkness. Whenever I see a fear-beast, I flick the wand, sending a fireball in their direction. The good news is that I can hear most of them as they approach; their claws make a distinct clinking sound on the city concrete. (With the city blacked out, it is very quiet on the streets.) I catch two of them waiting to pounce on me as I exit the park, find one hiding behind an abandoned hot dog cart, and incinerate three of them who try to converge on me. I try to block out all thoughts about Penny that aren't related to her location—what I'm feeling about her, what I'm feeling about me. It works. The remaining fear-beasts decide to keep their distance, and the more reckless of them go up in flames as teachable moments for their brethren.

I cast the where's-Penny spell again, and it centers on a penthouse apartment of a fifteen-story brownstone on 84th Street. The entrance is under a friendly green canopy. There are three doormen, all trolls, armed with heavy clubs studded with iron spikes. *I should have kept the broomstick with me*, I think. I wish I knew a spell that would let me levitate up like a soap bubble, and decide it's worth a try. *"Lifebuoy,"* I say, and instantly regret it, as my mouth is filled with a foul taste. I spit out suds. Nasty. I consider trying another spell but I'm afraid that saying *Irish Spring* will create a waterfall in the middle of the Upper East Side. Best not to risk it.

Trolls are resistant to magic, and fond of smashing people who try using magic on them. They are also dumber than paint, so I decide a clever stratagem is in order. I think for a minute, and then trade in my urban-warrior street-fighting outfit (black sweater and jeans over chain mail) for a polyester polo and a pizza box. "Delivery for the penthouse," I tell them. "Ring me in and I'll take it straight up."

"What kind pizza?" the lead troll says. Not that there's much difference between them, they all have the same gray skin and bulging muscles and rotten teeth. The one who is talking is wearing a spiked collar, so that makes him the leader, I guess.

"Pepperoni and green olives, extra cheese." Penny's usual order.

"Green olives no good on pizza."

"What can I tell you. They were out of black olives."

"Pineapple good on pizza. With ham," the second troll says.

"All New York pizza bad. Like Chicago deep dish," the third troll says. He is uglier than the other two, but it's not a contest or anything.

"Well. We're all entitled to our opinions. My opinion is that I would like a nice tip, which I won't get if I stand around here."

"Wait," the first troll says. "How you make pizza in blackout?"

"Coal-fired oven," I say. "Don't need electricity. We still have a landline phone, those work when the power stops."

"Elevator out," the second one says. "You climb stairs?"

"Of course."

The third troll looks at me closely, and I can smell his foul breath. "No like this," he says. "You trying to trick us. You trying to sneak past. Dark Lord said you might."

"I'm sorry, who? The dark what? I'm just delivering a pizza here, guys."

"You remembered pizza," the lead troll says. "You forgot cannoli."

Three things happen at about the same time. I remember—don't ask me how I managed to forget—that Penny is a huge fan of cannoli, and will get it every single time she's eating at anything like an Italian place. Of course, she's also a huge fan of coconut pie, strawberry cheesecake, and peanut butter milkshakes (not to mention mint chocolate chip ice cream, Ritz crackers, and Rice Krispie treats). It's not as though the details of my sister's junk food addiction are all that easy to keep track of.

The second thing is that I drop the pretense of being a humble pizza delivery girl and instantly change my clothes to what I was wearing before, complete with chain mail, with the last-second addition of a crash helmet.

The third thing is that the second troll whacks me in the ribs with his club, and I go flying across 84th Street, impacting on the front steps of the opposite brownstone. The chain mail absorbs a good deal of the impact, and when I take off the crash helmet, it splits in two. The trolls are still standing in front of Penny's building in the moonlit darkness, laughing and pointing.

I do what any self-respecting sorceress worthy of the name would do. I levitate a Hyundai Sonata parked across the street and drop it on their heads. The first one is smart enough to get out of the way, but the other two are knocked down, momentarily pinned under the wreckage. I send a charcoal-gray Honda Accord into the kneecaps of the first troll, smashing him against the wall of the building. He takes out his club and smashes the hood, but he stays immobile long enough that I'm able to throw a parked motorcycle at his head.

The other two manage to push the Hyundai off them and send it cartwheeling down the sidewalk. Since throwing vehicles doesn't seem to do much, I try something smaller—the same spell that works so well on the fear-beasts. I send a miniature fireball in the general direction of the third troll, expecting it to slow his momentum. But luck is on my side. I make a million-to-one shot, and the tiny pinpoint of light somehow runs up his left nostril and explodes inside his skull. I am gratified to see dark black blood gushing from his ears. Either I killed him, or I gave him a serious sinus headache. Either way, there are still two trolls to deal with.

The second troll, enraged by the bloodshed, runs towards me, but being a very stupid troll, doesn't look both ways before crossing the street. He is immediately blindsided by a speeding transit bus, which makes a quick turn, carrying what is left of him uptown.

The dying troll, who had been tottering around blindly, falls with a crash to the sidewalk, leaving a medium-sized crater. The remaining troll extricates himself from all of the vehicles I have tossed at him and throws his club at me. I put up a shield charm that deflects the club before it splits my skull, although I'm not quick enough to keep from being knocked backward into the stairs once again. I get up, my knees wobbly, and the troll picks up another club and crouches in front of the door to Penny's building—a purely defensive posture, designed to test me.

I take a deep breath, which sends knives of pain down both sides of my chest. I figure I might get lucky again with the mini fireball, but the troll idly deflects it with his club.

"What else you got?" he roars.

"Plenty," I say. I draw up my feelings, my fears and anxieties, and all the pain inside me and compress it into a mighty blast of Arctic wind, studded with icicle shards. "*Denali!*" I shout, and send it right in the direction of the troll. It hits him hard, knocking him off his feet, and knocking the doors behind him off their hinges. I cross the street—keeping a sharp eye open for moving vehicles—and try to navigate the ice-covered sidewalk. The icy blast hasn't incapacitated the troll; he shakes himself free of the snow and ice like a dog shedding water. He swings the club at me, and I lose my footing on the treacherous sidewalk. I bounce right back up as the troll tries to kick me in the ribs, and he goes down hard.

"You not very good pizza delivery girl," the troll says. "But you fight okay."

"Thanks," I say. "You're not so bad yourself."

"I work out. Try and eat healthy."

"What now?" I ask. "Can we both walk away from this? You go your way, and I go inside and rescue my sister?"

The troll shakes his misshapen head. "Can't. You kill friends. You no walk away from that."

"My sister is in that building, and she's alone, and she's scared, and you're in my way."

"Doesn't matter. Only one way to settle this."

The troll turns over, leverages himself up, and goes back into his protective crouch.

"Sure you don't need a minute?" I ask.

"Bring it on."

*Okay,* I think. Ice didn't work. Magic missiles didn't work. Throwing around compact automobiles didn't work. He's bigger than me, way tougher than I am, and too dumb to quit.

I bet he's slow.

I take off, running down the sidewalk, betting that I can stay a few steps ahead of the troll, maybe lose him in the traffic. I fly down the empty, darkened street, hoping against hope that I don't run into a pedestrian walking their Rottweiler or a band of Spartan hoplites out on a moonlight stroll. I make it to Park Avenue and make a sharp right, and then another right on 83rd Street. I don't have to look behind me to see that the troll is tracking my movements; he's maybe ten yards behind me, his hobnailed boots making crashing sounds on the pavement. I put on a burst of speed and start gaining on him, hoping against hope that he'll slow down, but it doesn't happen. I was right, he is slow, but he's not wearing down or close to it.

I vault over a Vespa that someone has parked on the sidewalk and make the right turn onto Madison, and hear the satisfying crash of the troll impacting the scooter, hard. I dodge around the lifeless body of the second troll and run into Penny's building.

Where I have fifteen flights of stairs to run up, while being chased by an angry troll, out for revenge. I find the stairwell, rush up to the first landing, and the knives in my chest make a reappearance. I remember that Mary Poppins levitation spell—which I should have used before, come to think of it—but I'm too winded to say the incantation. The troll flings open the stairwell door and sees me, his face black with the effort of running all that way.

"Not fair," he says.

"Life's not fair," I gasp in reply. "*Obstacalus!*"

This spell trips up the troll and makes his ascent up the stairs a good bit harder, but it doesn't make mine any easier. By the time I hit the sixth-floor landing, I am out of breath again, and the troll is making an unholy racket behind me. "*Pennzoilus!*" I shout, and a gusher of crude oil goes down the stairs. The troll makes it five steps up before his feet go out from under him and he crashes back down. He tries again, with similar results, screeching an insult in what I hope is troll-speak. It sounds unbelievably filthy. I cut off the flow of oil and watch, mostly to catch my breath, but partly to see the troll take another tumble.

He is more careful this time, bracing himself against the wall on the left, and hooking the spiked club into the railing on the right. He gingerly climbs up one stair, then two, and then three. He stares at me menacingly.

"Why you no afraid?" he asks.

"No time," I say. "I have to rescue my sister. If there were time to be afraid, I would be."

"You should be," he says, and takes another step, hobnailed boots against concrete steps. They make a spark.

The troll's clothes were already filthy; now they are soaked in the oil that has pooled at the bottom of the landing. The spark catches on the hem of his left pants leg and travels up his calf. He lets out a loud bellow of pain, and then tumbles back for the last time. All the oil around him catches fire, sending foul black smoke up the stairwell. The troll screeches as the flames engulf him.

I climb the stairs without thinking, desperate to get out of the smoke. The troll's screams have stopped by the time I get to the tenth floor, but there are now fire alarms ringing throughout the building. I told the troll that I didn't have much time left to save my sister; now I have that much less to work with and have inadvertently made the danger worse by setting fire to her building. I inhale a lungful of smoke and race up the stairs.

# PAST THE POINT OF RESCUE

**PENNY | NEW YORK CITY | TEN YEARS IN THE FUTURE**

The girl has fallen asleep next to me, her warmth against my body, and I am almost ready to drift off to sleep myself when I hear a loud bang at the front door. I jump to my feet, startled, and the girl starts wailing.

"Sit tight, sweetheart," I say. I run over and check the door, which is still closed but splintered around the deadbolt lock. Another good blow is going to knock it down. The little girl is still keening, but she is at least staying where she is for the moment. I grab the closest thing at hand—a brass carriage clock. When the door flies open, I fling it towards the intruder as hard as I can, and it ricochets off the intruder with a loud *clang*.

"Penny!" a familiar voice says. "Cut it out." As she gets closer, I can tell that it's Ashlyn; she's dressed in a shapeless black sweater and jeans, and she's holding some kind of stick. "Are you okay? I heard screaming."

The girl pops her head up from behind the couch. "Auntie Ashlyn!" she shouts. "Why are you here?"

Ashlyn looks utterly flummoxed, as well she might. "I wanted to make sure everyone was okay," she says. "I came to help, to get you out of here. It's not safe."

"It's just a blackout," I say. "We're fine. Or we were fine, until you broke the door down instead of, you know, knocking, like a normal person."

My sister has the good grace to at least look guilty. "I can fix that," she says, and waves the stick in her hand towards the door, which returns to its hinges. "We need to leave, though. I had to incinerate a troll to get up here. Accidentally, I mean. I don't think I set fire to the entire building, unless we got unlucky. We should still get downstairs."

"Considering the last time you tried to rescue me, you dropped a dragon on my house, I suppose this is about par for the course for you."

"Again, not my fault. We need to go, Penny."

Ashlyn is breathing hard, her hair is askew, and she smells like smoke, but she is coming out of her dream and into mine. "We're going to stay right here," I say. "Everything is fine."

"The building is on fire, Penny," Ashlyn says. "We have to go."

"Is it?" I ask. "Do you hear any fire alarms here? Any smoke detectors going off? Whatever it is that was going on in your dream, that doesn't mean it's going on here. We're perfectly safe."

"The Dark Lord may know that I'm here. If he finds me, then he finds you. I came to rescue you."

"Is that like Voldemort?" the little girl asks.

"Well. No. Not really," Ashlyn explains. "How do you know about Voldemort?"

"Grandpa let me see the movies."

"Of course; I should have known that. Well, the Dark Lord isn't as bad as Voldemort, but he's strong. He's out there somewhere."

"Which is why we're staying here," I say. "Dream your dream and let me dream mine."

Ashlyn looks around the darkened apartment, taking it all in. "This is your dream?" she asks.

"I was surprised, too, but it's not so strange, is it? A husband, a child, a nice apartment. I never thought about dreaming for anything like this before."

"I get it," Ashlyn says. "This is your future. Not a fantasy, not a delusion. Having said that, it can't *be* your future if we don't get out of this building."

I turn away from Ashlyn and towards the girl. "This is what we're going to do," I say. "I need to talk to your Aunt Ashlyn. That means it's time for you to go to bed. Okay?"

"It's still dark and scary, Mommy."

"Aunt Ashlyn is here. She can protect you with her magic wand. The lights will be on by morning."

The girl yawns, and stretches enough that I can scoop her up and carry her to her room. I get her into bed, smooth the covers over her, and touch her hair.

"I know it's scary," I say. "I'll be in the other room, talking to your aunt. When I'm done, I'll come back in here. Mr. Cheetah will keep you company, okay?"

"One question."

"Just one."

"If Aunt Ashlyn is magic, can she make cookies?"

"You don't need to be magic to make cookies. I make cookies all the time, and I'm not magic."

"I mean good cookies."

"You be quiet. I'll be right back."

Ashlyn is standing in my kitchen, leaning against my counter. Her right hand is twitching. Her light hair is matted with sweat, and there are a few rips in her sweater where the chain mail underneath shows through. Her face is pale and lined with tension. It looks like something is chasing her, and whatever it is must be getting closer.

I draw up my reserves of calm. This is not our usual dynamic. Ashlyn has always acted older than she is, more responsible, more mature. This—along with my uncertain health—has always given me free rein to be impulsive and reckless, at least when I can get away with it. Now she's in my apartment, asking me to do something daring and dangerous, and I need to redirect her.

Of course, I think, I'm the older sister now.

"I'm not coming with you," I say. "You have to understand why that is."

"If you stay here," she says, "I can't help you."

"I don't need your help."

"If I'm here, in your dream, I ought to be able to help you. In real life, you're in New York, in the hospital. I can't help you there, but maybe if I rescue you here, that will help you wake up—so you can come home." The last word is almost a whisper, with a sob behind it.

"There's nothing you can do to help me. That's a hard thing for me to say, but it's important. I love you, and I have all the respect in the world for you, and I appreciate what you think you're trying to do, but it isn't necessary and you should stop."

"You could die," she says.

"That won't happen."

"It will happen if you stay here."

"No, it's not. This is my life now. This is what I'm fighting for, and I'm going to keep fighting until I get there for real."

"It's not your life. It's not real."

"Says the girl in the chain mail. I know it's not real now, but I can make it real, one day. I never had anything to look forward to before the transplant. Now I do."

"We can go downstairs. I can get you out of the city."

"What about the girl?" I ask.

"We can leave her here."

"No. That's not going to happen. I am asking you to leave. If you have a battle you need to fight, you need to fight it. Leave me out of it. I'm fighting my own battle, my own way."

Ashlyn, my frustrating, overbearing, obnoxious big sister, starts crying. Not a single brave tear out of the corner of her eye, but sloppy, heartbreaking tears. I hand her a paper towel, wordlessly, and she blows her nose.

"I don't want to lose you," she says. "You're my sister. I need you. I can't..."

"You won't," I say. "Even if I die. You'll never lose me."

"I came here to rescue you. The way you rescued me. If I can't do that..."

"That's just it," I say. "You can't. I know you think you're responsible for me, but I'm responsible for the little girl in the other room who is scared and worried. Even if she isn't real."

"I get that. I do." She blows her nose again. "Look. As long as I know that you're okay."

"You can't know that. *I* don't know that. I want to live, and my doctors are going to try their best, but who knows. There's nothing either of us can do about it. Except maybe one thing."

"Anything. Name it."

"When you were going into surgery, last summer, I was talking to Morton. He said I should pray for you, and I did. No telling if that made a difference or not. I can't explain how else I found you."

"You wanted to find me, like I wanted to find you."

"Maybe that's it. Maybe that's all. If you can't rescue me... maybe there's Someone else who can."

Ashlyn's thin face is red and puffy now. "All right. I'll do what you ask and go. Tell you what. Let me say goodbye to your daughter, okay?"

"That would be nice."

"This is embarrassing, but I don't know what her name is."

I am stricken; I don't know the girl's name, either. I open my mouth, and nothing comes out.

"Wait," Ashlyn says. "I remember now. It's Jennifer."

"Yeah," I say. "That's right."

"Goodnight, Jennifer," Ashlyn says. "I need you to go to sleep for your mommy."

"Where are you going?" she asks, holding Mr. Cheetah tight.

"Back across the river. It's a long way, and I'm not sure how to go, or if I will need to fight my way through. But it will be okay."

"You should go to the Frankenstein room," she says.

Ashlyn looks at me, in utter bewilderment.

"That's just what she calls it," I say. "She means the Frank Lloyd Wright room at the Metropolitan Museum. It was a living room of a house he designed in Minnesota; they brought it to New York. I wrote my thesis about it."

"What do I do when I go there?" Ashlyn asks.

"Walk into the fireplace. Like in *Harry Potter*."

Great, I think. More Harry Potter.

"It's hooked up to the Floo Network?" Ashlyn asks.
Jennifer nods.

"What are you two talking about?" I ask.

"An escape route," Ashlyn says. "I had better get moving. Good night, both of you. Stay safe."

"Night night, Auntie Ashlyn."

"Night night. Is there a fire escape?"

"Right this way."

Ashlyn rushes to the corner of the apartment, opens the fire escape door, and is out on the wrought-iron balcony. "Have Mom and Dad call me as soon as you wake up," she says.

"I will. Ashlyn, please tell me you're not going to burn down the Metropolitan Museum."

"I will... try to avoid doing that. I have to go. You stay safe."

"Pray for me. Pray for both of us."

"I promise. I love you."

"Love you, too."

I stare out the door into the blackened sky, lit by the moonlight and ten thousand candles. I feel the chill of the night air all around me. Then I close the door and head back into my bedroom. Jennifer is there waiting for me.

"I couldn't sleep in my bed," she says.

"I know. It's okay. We'll go to sleep together."

"And we'll wake up together," she says.

"Of course."

"Promise?"

"You're not supposed to make a promise if you don't know you can keep it."

"Mommy, please."

I look at her, caress her golden hair.

"Promise. Super-promise."

I climb into bed, get comfortable, and the girl snuggles in next to me. Before I drift off to sleep, I pray. I pray that I get to keep my promise.

# ESCAPE ROUTE

**ASHLYN | APRIL 5 | NEW YORK CITY, THE REALM OF SUMMERVALE**

The good news is that Penny's building does not appear to be on fire. The bad news is that I descend all of two floors before I start crying again and have to stop.

My rescue mission is a failure, and my sister might die, and there's nothing I can do about it. In all honesty, there wasn't anything I could have done, or that's what I try to tell myself. In her dream, she is alive and safe—and older, and with a little girl who calls me "Auntie Ashlyn," which I was not in any way prepared for. If there's hope, it is that Penny is still alive and wants to survive.

How narrow is that hope?

I had so much to say to Penny, and I didn't say any of it. I said goodbye, and I said that I love her, but there are so many other conversations that we need to have, that I want to have, and I don't know that we'll get to have them, now or ever.

Anyway, I have one more person to rescue, which just so happens to be me. If the little girl is right, I need to get out of here, run two blocks west to the Met, make my way through a largely unfamiliar building in total darkness, to find a room I am not sure even exists, without the Dark Lord knowing I'm even here.

*I love this plan! I'm excited to be a part of it! Let's do it!*

I head down the narrow iron stairs of the fire escape, and make it down to the sixth floor when it happens. I manage to trip over the rail and sail out into the night.

I don't even have time to scream. I pull out my wand, not enough time for an incantation, not enough time for anything in the last few seconds of my life. An invisible hand catches me inches from the hard asphalt of the alley. I hit the ground with a soft and thankfully non-fatal *thump.*

"You okay there?" a drawling voice says from the shadows.

"Never better," I lie.

I look up and see C.J. Valentine, waiting in the alley for me, leaning insolently on her sword.

"You took a hard fall. You do enough of that, eventually you're bound to get yourself hurt."

"You took a worse one not that long ago."

C.J. grins. "Some of us are tougher than others, I expect."

"You don't look so tough without an army of werewolves behind you."

"You want to play it that way, Lady Ashlyn? I still have a lot of furry friends, and they get hungry. They don't care what they eat. Or who."

I hold my wand out straight so she can see it. "All I'm trying to do is get back home. If you have a quarrel with me, then so be it. If you want to get me out of New York, get out of my way."

"I got a quarrel with you," C.J. says. "I aim to settle it."

"You haven't called the Dark Lord in on this, yet. That makes this private business? Am I right?"

"This ain't private business. This here's a swordfight, and these are the rules. You put your wand back in your pocket, careful like, and think up a sword. If you can best me, well and good. If you can't, well, then that's that. Understood?"

"If I win, you help me go home."

"Fair enough, considering that it ain't gonna happen. What do you say, Your Worship? Lady Heartbreak don't like to be kept waiting."

*Be unpredictable*, the Lord of Light said.

"All right," I say. "You've got your swordfight." I make a delicate move with my wand, think up a wordless incarnation, and put the wand back in its pocket in my sword belt.

"What did you just do?" C.J. asks.

"You want to talk," I ask, "or do you want to swordfight?"

I manifest a sword, long and sharp, and raise it in a fencer's salute. C.J. lifts Lady Heartbreak, but nowhere near as high, even with both hands on the longsword's hilt.

I step in and do a quick parry, and the swords clang together with the dull sound of steel on lead. C.J. tries to counter with a quick upthrust, but the point of her sword ducks down instead of up. I parry again, driving her backwards, and she tries an awkward swing in my general direction. I sidestep, and as the momentum of the lead sword carries through the swing, I step back inside C.J.'s radius and smack the flat of my sword against her upper arm. This keeps her going in the same direction; now her back is towards me.

"Had enough?" I ask. "Because I could stab you in the kidneys right now, easy."

C.J. stops her rotation, turns back the other way, and chops out at my left arm. The dull edge of the lead sword bangs ineffectually on my chain mail as I chop at her left knee.

"What in the hell did you do to my sword?" C.J. asks.

"Benefits of a classical education," I say. This is not *exactly* true, but I did manage to learn that the emperor Commodus would only fight in the Roman arena if his opponent's sword was switched with one made of lead. Couldn't resist the quote, though.

C.J. drops her useless sword and tries to punch me in the jaw, but I step backwards and she goes sprawling.

"I can do this all day," I say.

C.J. gets to her feet again, slower this time, takes a step or two back, and then falls backwards into the mud of the alley.

"I win," I say.

"You cheated."

"You didn't say I couldn't cheat, Miss Dark Side. Are you going to help me now, or do I need to keep kicking your butt?"

"It doesn't matter whether I help you or not," she says. "The Dark Lord has a different plan. Maybe you can get past me, but you're not getting past the Dark Lord. There's only two ways out of here," C.J. says. "One is in a body bag, which I would be arranging for you if you had fought fair."

"And the other is that fireplace in the museum."

"Where do you think the Dark Lord is, right this second?" C.J. says. "He knows what you're trying to do. Man, are you in trouble."

"I'm always in trouble. Are you going to help? Or are you going to make me fight this last battle by myself?"

"Help me up. And fix my sword."

"So, you'll help."

C.J. glares at me. "You're a no-good cheat, Lady Ashlyn. That means you're going Dark Side. If that's the case, then I'm proud to be on your team."

I walk over, give her a hand up, and zap her sword back to steel from lead.

"Okay," I say. "Let's ride."

# The Final Battle

**Ashlyn | April 5 | New York City, The Realm of Summervale**

C.J. and I are crouched, hiding behind a deserted taco truck on Fifth Avenue. The steps of the museum across the street are crowded with a small army of animated suits of armor, which are blocking the only way I have of getting off the island.

"You got any ideas, Lady Ashlyn," C.J. says, "best share 'em now."

"Any other way out of here?" I ask.

"You can swim."

"So that's a no, then. What are our assets?"

"Your brains. My steel. And you already made the dumb joke about the holocaust cloak."

I think for a second.

"I wish Nicholas was here," I say. "He'd come up with something."

C.J. giggles, just a little, then literally slaps her knee and starts doing something that I think is technically called chortling, although I've not heard it before from her.

"Simmer down over there, Calamity Jane. What's so funny?"

"Ask yourself. How is it that you come to be here, in New York, in a situation where having Lord Atropos on your side would be most helpful, and yet he ain't here?"

"Because Nicholas needed to convince Jennifer Lamb to leave, in the Garden."

"Right. Who do you think came up with that particular scheme?"

"It was Nicholas's idea, wasn't it?"

"No, silly. Think. Who is incredibly evil, and also owns Madison Square Garden?"

"James Dolan."

"In this world?"

"I'm going out on a limb here and say the Dark Lord. You know. Similar styles and all."

"More than that. Who do you think put Jennifer Lamb there in the first place? Who invited you to come rescue her?"

Realization dawns on me, slow and frigid. "You're saying it was a set-up. All of it."

"Bingo. You're playing checkers. The Dark Lord is playing chess. The queen's sacrifice, and you fell for it. Now his knights are on the prowl, and all that's left on your side of the board is you and me. He's going to checkmate you before you even realize what's going on."

At that moment, we hear a loud rapping from inside the taco truck.

"What is that?" I ask C.J., who is turning visibly red.

"I don't hear nothin'," she says, unconvincingly, over the sound of the continued knocking.

I pull out my wand. "*Alohomora,*" I say, and the side of the taco truck opens enough for me to see Lincoln and Holland peek out.

"How did you guys get in there?" I ask, although I have a good idea.

"Your friend there kidnapped us," Lincoln says.

I look at C.J., who has the grace to appear embarrassed.

"Dark Side," she says. "It ain't just a slogan, you know. You see someone who needs kidnapping, you kidnap them."

"You were going to mention this at some point, right?" I ask.

"We've been in kind of a rush, you know?"

I open the side of the truck wider and help Lincoln and Holland out. "So now we have a couple of more pieces on our side," I say.

"Pawns, you mean."

"That's not very nice," Holland says.

"Next time, work harder to keep from getting kidnapped, and I may say something nice."

"Okay, okay," I say. "We're all working together to figure out how to get past those suits of armor there. Or, if I may say so, under them."

Lincoln considers this. "Could be done. Depends on how much time you have."

"We could start there," Holland says. He is pointing to a manhole a few steps away; it is printed with the words *Secret Entrance to Metropolitan Museum of Art*.

"Ha," I say. "It ought to say *It's a Trap*."

"Still might be easier than a frontal assault," C.J. says. "Less suicidal, ya know."

"Here's what we're going to do," I say. "The unexpected."

"In English, please," C.J asks.

"The Dark Lord is expecting me to make a choice," I say. "Either a frontal assault, in the loudest, most chaotic way that we can, or else we try to sneak in through the sewers. One of the other. What if we do both?"

"We split up," Holland says.

"Right. The three of you take on the knights, while I take the sewer route."

Lincoln drops to one knee. "You have my axe, Lady Ashlyn."

"I wanted to say that," Holland interrupts.

"That's the craziest thing I ever heard," C.J. says. "It won't work. Even if I call in some favors from the werewolves, I'd be lucky to breach their defenses."

"What if I can put the odds in your favor?" I ask. "Bring in some extra forces."

"Still ain't gonna work. The Dark Lord is looking for you; if he doesn't see you in the line of battle, he's going to know you're sneaking in."

"There's a way around that," I say. I take my wand out of my belt.

"Wait a second," C.J. says. "Whatever you have in mind, I don't want any part of it. You understand me, Lady Ashlyn? You try to hex me or poison me, you'll regret it."

"Nothing so awful. *Doppelganger!*" I shout.

In a flash, C.J.'s untamed, flyaway black hair twists into a neat ash-blonde ponytail. Her dark leather armor transforms into a silver cloak of *mithril* links, and her flashing dark eyes become placid blue.

"The hell did you do?" she exclaims, staring down at herself in disgust.

"Camouflage. It might even help you keep the Dark Lord from finding out that you're helping me."

C.J. yanks the end of her new ponytail around where she can see it. "You cannot be serious."

"Like two peas in a pod," Lincoln says.

"This is unacceptable."

"Relax. The glamour wears off in two hours."

"Two hours!"

"More or less."

"So now I look like the most-wanted person in New York for the next two hours, assuming I live that long. Are you messing with me, or do you have an actual plan?"

"Can you summon the werewolves?"

"Looking like this? I hope so. They'll show up, though, one way or another. You going to tell me what you have in mind?"

"Easier to show you."

"What are you waiting for?"

"I thought you might want to bundle up first." I lift the wand, and make a sweeping circle in the air. "*Svalbard!*"

I hear the wind before I feel it, blowing straight down Fifth Avenue on the wings of the hawk. It's a roaring sound, deep-throated, and it takes me a minute to understand that it's more than the wind.

The armored bears of the North are on the prowl, moving down the deserted city street, headed straight for the museum entrance. There are twelve of them, and that may not be enough to win the day, but it will for-sure cause one hell of a distraction. Their white fur is pale in the moonlight, obscured by their crude, clanky plate armor. As they lumber their way down Fifth Avenue, throwing chunks of concrete in their wake as their polished claws dig into to the roadbed, I send a miniature ice storm towards the bodiless knights gathered on the museum steps. As the knights try to turn towards the new threat, some of them slip and fall on the icy steps. The unluckier ones land on their compatriots as the bears tear into their ranks. Lincoln, Holland and C.J. follow in their wake, with C.J. uttering a full-throated wolf howl that sounds incredibly creepy coming from someone who looks exactly like me.

The knights have taken a sharp blow from the bears, but are now regrouping and starting a counterattack. They are facing the wrong way, though, ignoring the werewolves who are starting to gather to the south. The entire battle is going to degenerate into a melee, and I want to get inside the museum before that happens. I told C.J. that I was going through the manhole, but I have no actual intention of doing that. I have another plan, but I need to move fast to make it work.

I point the wand at myself and say, *"Transparent."* My hand disappears right away; the invisibility moving up my arm like a flame traveling up the edge of a newspaper. It takes a few seconds for the rest of my body to vanish. I pocket the wand by feel and cross over Fifth Avenue.

I am trying to circle my way around to the right of the line where the bears are meeting the knights, but the knights are beginning to push them back. The bear closer to me rears up suddenly, raking his claws across the helmet of a determined knight—but gets knocked in the teeth with a morningstar. The bear falls over to one side, and I skitter to get out of his way. I hit the steps at a run, crunching on the ice until my feet slip out from under me. I grab hold of the handrail in time to keep from falling hard. I make my cautious way up until something hard impacts me in the ribs—a helmet thrown backwards from the fray. I don't stop to check to see if there's a head still inside it. This time I hit the stairs, toppling over on my right side, and I scramble up to my feet to keep from being trampled. I make my way up the steps hunched over, with my hands scrabbling against the frozen steps.

When I reach the glass doors at the top of the stairs, I take a quick look back. The werewolves have made their presence felt, acting as the hammer against the anvil of the armored bears. The howls of the wolves are beginning to turn to snarls, as Dark Side reinforcements in the form of Viking warriors are arriving on the scene. C.J. is in the thick of the battle, decapitating an unlucky knight, a battle song at her lips. Holland and Lincoln are hewing away at Viking ankles.

The spectacle of battle is exhilarating, and I am tempted to join the fray and rain down destruction on the enemy forces. My path is forward, and my enemy is inside. I lean against the glass door at the museum entrance, and it opens soundlessly. I dispel my invisibility glamour and step inside.

# INTO THE FIRE

ASHLYN | APRIL 5 | NEW YORK CITY, THE REALM OF SUMMERVALE

The last time I was in the Metropolitan Museum of Art was, I think, a tenth-grade class trip. I remember walking into the building, and it being bright and loud, with teenage voices echoing off the terrazzo floors and vaulted ceilings. Now it is dark, and soundless except for the echo of my boots. There is an octagonal booth in the center of the hall, and a tall woman in a gray dress is sitting patiently inside it.

"Welcome, Lady Ashlyn," she says.

I fire up the end of my wand, just enough to be able to recognize her. "Lachesis," I say. "Well met."

"You have traveled far," she says. "Much farther in the realms of the East than ever I would have feared."

Lachesis is the Measurer, one of the three Fates that guide my life—I've never met Clotho, the Spinner, but of course I know Atropos well in his guise as Nicholas the Talking Rabbit. Lachesis pulled me out of the Hudson when I lost the army that I raised to battle the Dark Lord. She is not someone to be trifled with, or easily overcome.

"Why are you here?" I ask. "To guard me, or guide me?"

"To warn you." She waves a languid hand at the far wall, where the names of donors in a normal museum would be displayed. Here there is one name, THE DARK LORD, carved in stone in four-foot-high letters. "He is the power here, and he is waiting for you."

"Okay. Consider me warned. Do you have, like, a map or something? All I know is I need to find the Frank Lloyd Wright room, and I'm not sure where that's located. Although I'm guessing that's where the Dark Lord is, right?"

"You are correct. My earnest advice for you is to avoid him. Go out into the city. Rejoin the brawl you started outside. Anything you like. Leave this place, and quickly."

"The only way out is through," I explain.

The expression on Lachesis's face curdles. "Linear thinking on your part. Disappointing. You have more options than you think. One way or another, morning will come. You will awaken, no matter what you do."

"I have to look at myself in the mirror. I can't do that if I turn back now."

The Fate tilts her head. "If you seek hope, you must look elsewhere. If you seek justice, that is a lifelong struggle. What do you hope to gain by challenging the Dark Lord?"

"Victory."

"Here? At the heart of his power?"

"This is where the battle must be fought. His power derives from hate and fear. My power must overcome his. There is no substitute for victory."

Lachesis grips the edge of the kiosk, her long fingers turning white from the pressure. "I would not see you destroyed in the process."

"I would not confront the Dark Lord if I feared failure," I say, sounding more confident than I feel.

"Perhaps you know best. You have made it this far already. I have one request of you, if I may."

"And that is?"

"There are many rare and beautiful things in this building. Do try not to destroy it."

"I already promised someone I wouldn't."

Lachesis conjures up a Blue Fairy, which hovers in front of me and then speeds off down a corridor. I nod a quick goodbye to the Fate and follow the fairy, the jingle of my chain mail accompanying me.

The fairy leads me down a long, white corridor, empty except for insets in the walls that house marble busts. It is dark, and I am trying to keep track of the fairy's progress, but I think that one of the busts is my sixth-grade English teacher. I am sure that the one next to it is my high-school field hockey coach. I want to stop and look more closely, but the fairy isn't slowing down. Next is the room where all the medieval armor should be, if it wasn't already outside fighting C.J. and the dwarves and the armored bears.

The fairy makes a sharp right turn, passing by what looks like a temporary installation. *Looks Good Enough to Eat: Highlights from the Ashlyn Revere Instagram Meal Collection.*

"Wait a second," I ask the fairy. "Is this, like, the museum of *me*?"

The fairy hovers in the air, shrugging.

"So maybe there's some kind of weapon here? Or artifact? Something I can use against him. Holy hand grenade, that kind of thing?"

The fairy folds her arms and stares up at the ceiling, tapping her foot in the air.

"Right. Got it."

I follow the fairy through the darkened hallways of the museum. The paintings are dark blotches against the dark walls, but I am almost sure that I see the Arkenstone of Thrain glittering under a glass case. There's a display in a corner that is either *Star Trek* cyber-armor or a stillsuit from *Dune*. Neither of which is going to help me much.

I told Lachesis that I wanted victory over the Dark Lord, but how I will manage that I do not know. The last time we fought, it was anything but one-on-one. It was army-on-army, and I was defeated soundly. But I had been weak at the time, in a coma after a car accident, and I didn't have my new wand, made from the World Ash Tree and a unicorn hair. With the wand, I should be at least a match for the Dark Lord—but I'm never going to overcome him with hate and fear. If I am winning my way out of here, I have to think positive— and be unpredictable.

He's going to expect me to... what?

The fairy comes to a stop by a plaque that says, "Frank Lloyd Wright Room." There isn't a door, but it's dark inside and I can't see anything.

"This is it?" I ask.

The Blue Fairy gives me a disdainful look that could curdle paint.

"Right. Of course it is. Thank you. Wish me luck?"

The fairy rolls her eyes and flies off.

Okay. This is the moment. Him or me. Destiny is calling.

I steady myself and sprint into the darkened room. I point my wand in the general direction of where I think the Dark Lord is and shout an incantation. *"Stupefy!"*

I see the Dark Lord for an instant, sitting in a blocky brown leather armchair, illuminated by the blast of the stunning spell. The next thing I see is a beige carpet, half an inch from my face. Pain radiates around my nose, outward towards the far reaches of my brain and then back again.

"I was going to tell you to watch out for the rug," the Dark Lord says. "You seem to have found it without my help."

The good news, I suppose, is that the Dark Lord hasn't taken advantage of my pratfall to blast me into flinders. The bad news is that I am lying on the floor, embarrassed beyond words, and my wand has skittered halfway across the room for all I know. I work myself up onto my right elbow, and manage to sit up. I feel a warm trickle of blood down my nose.

The Dark Lord snaps his fingers, and the fireplace in the back of the room lights up, bright with orange and purple flames. His suit is rumpled, and his tie is loose around his neck.

"Although I appreciate the comic value of the performance, perhaps we should move on to the main event, as it were. Where is your sister?"

"She's not here," I say. "I asked her. She wouldn't come."

"That was the intent of the mission, though, was it not? You were to travel here, dodging all kinds of dangers, save her from peril, and bring her here. That was the plan as I understood it."

"I did all that. She wouldn't come with me. She felt safer where she was—someplace without troll doormen and animated suits of armor."

"I can't imagine why. Nonetheless, as the rationale for your visit has collapsed, I am at a loss as to why you are still here, and why you made your way to this particular room. This is *her* place, not yours."

I glance around the room, seeing it clearly. The walls are lined with clear glass, inlaid with simple geometric designs. The room is cluttered with period furniture. Everything has a clean, spare design. It looks beautiful, but I've been in a hospital the last six months—pretty much anything looks spectacular compared to that. I can see why Penny—the older Penny, I suppose—likes it so much, but no, this isn't my place. I am not sure where my place is, or what it even looks like, or how I can get there, but I know this isn't it—except for one thing.

"I was told this was the way out," I explain.

"It was, for her. You were supposed to bring her here, and she was supposed to leave this world through the fireplace and return to what, for lack of a better word, we can call *reality*. There would have been a tedious parting scene or some such, some emotional catharsis. I take it that part has already happened."

"Kind of."

"Just as well, from my perspective, but *you* have no need to be here. Surely Miss Valentine should have been able to provide you with an escort back to the Western Marches."

"I wanted to come here," I say. "I heard this was the fastest way home."

"Well, you heard wrong, Lady Ashlyn. The lovely fireplace that you see behind me is a portal out of this world. By which I mean a portal out of this world *entirely*. It would be one thing for your sister to leave. But if you left? All of Summervale would collapse into nothingness. Everything you've built. Everything I've built. All gone beyond recovery. I can't let you go that way, and I wouldn't expect you to want to. That's not why you came, though, is it? You're not looking for the easy way out this time."

"No. I came here to triumph."

The Dark Lord grins. "Oh, well. If it's victory you want, it's over there," he says, hooking a thumb behind his head. "On the table."

The table he is pointing to is long and dark, with a shelf of antique books sitting under the tabletop. On the right, there is a white marble statuette of an angel.

"It's Nike. The winged goddess of victory. It's not actually marble," he says. "It's plaster. The original is in the Louvre; this is just a cheap reproduction."

I give the statuette the once-over. It is not heavy enough so that I can smash it over the Dark Lord's head. I need something else—and spot the end of my wand, sticking out from under the back left corner of the table.

I turn around to face the Dark Lord, my wand snapping back into my hand in one fluid motion. *"Disintegro,"* I shout, and a cone of purple circles spirals towards the Dark Lord. He raises his right hand to block the spell, and for a moment, his hand explodes into a glowing cloud of radiant pixels. The effect is momentary, and the purple circles fade, and his hand goes back to its normal shape.

"Okay. Have to admit it. That was painful." He shakes his hand up and down, as though it has fallen asleep. "It was kind of a nice, warm, tingling sensation at first, but when it all snapped back together, that was not pleasant. What else do you..." But he doesn't finish, because I have thought up another spell that has a chance to work.

*"Defenestra!"* I say, and flick my wand over to the right. The Dark Lord sails through the air for about five

feet, but manages to catch himself and bounces off the fancy windows as though they were a *Star Trek* force field.

"Better," he says. "Not nearly good enough, though, and you've lost the element of surprise. So whatever else you're planning over there, it either isn't going to work, or it's going to damage this very nice room. You still want to keep going?"

"*Minaturio,*" I say, which is—or at least I hope it is—a shrinking spell. He deflects it, and a Prairie Style armchair dwindles down to dollhouse scale.

"Creative," he says. "You're learning, but you can't beat me like that."

"Why not?"

"Because you're not looking for victory," he says. "You're looking for catharsis. You tried to rescue your sister and failed. I'm the next, most convenient target. Beating me, here, in your dream, isn't going to solve anything. You're still going to wake up and be Ashlyn Revere all over again, alone, scarred, and terrified for your sister. Nothing changes that."

"I am changing that."

"You're not changing anything. People don't change. Not deep down. You're still the same—nothing but a scraggly-haired, scar-faced accident victim, and you're never going to get any better."

"That's not true, and you know it. I am getting better every day. I am getting stronger. My speech is getting better. One day—one day *soon*—I will *walk out of that hospital.* You understand me? And you are not stopping me."

"Oh, I'm not stopping you," the Dark Lord says. He is walking closer to me, step by step. "Because there's one way for you to win that victory—my way. You're going to use anger. You're going to use hate. That's what motivates you. When you win that victory, you're going to know that it's *my* victory. Not yours. And that victory will taste like ashes in your mouth."

I feel a hot surge of anger wash over me, but I take a deep breath and let it pass. I want to destroy him for that, for everything. I know this time he isn't lying. It's happened too many times. Every time I've accomplished something, everything I've won, something has happened to ruin it, to poison it. Now I know why. I've been using his weapons, funneling my negative emotions into my goals—and that makes them tainted, makes them bitter. I can't win this battle if I'm doing it out of revenge or hatred. I'm winning this battle for myself. I have one chance to do that.

I point my wand at the Dark Lord and speak a word of command. "*Forzare!*" I don't put everything I have into the spell—I don't channel my rage or my frustration into it. I'm making it easy for him. He puts up an invisible shield, and the force from the spell deflects back to me, knocking me across the room.

Which is what I wanted to happen.

The Dark Lord's counter-spell pushes me backwards, and I land by the fireplace, which is blazing with purple and orange sparks. There is a broad earthenware jar by my left hand, and I take out a pinch of Floo Powder.

"Wait a second," the Dark Lord says. "Ashlyn, you can't be serious. You don't understand what you're doing." There is something in his voice that sounds like panic.

"I know exactly what I'm doing."

"You're ending Summervale. You're ending everything. I don't think you want to do that."

"Then you don't know me very well, then, do you." I throw the powder into the flames, which jump up, orange and purple.

I take one look back and see one last storm rising in the Dark Lord's face. "Home," I shout, and throw myself into the fire.

# A NEW REPUBLIC

### ASHLYN | APRIL 6 | THE WORLD ASH TREE

I open my eyes and see blue sky and white clouds behind a canopy of green leaves, swaying gently in a light breeze.

"That was nicely done," a cultured mid-Atlantic voice says.

I sit up slowly, dizzy from the travel. Nicholas hops into my lap, and I give him a tight squeeze. "I missed you," I whisper.

"I missed you as well."

"Where am I? What happened? The Dark Lord said I would destroy Summervale by using the portal. I thought I had, but this seems to be Summervale. And what are you doing here?"

"The Dark Lord, for once, was telling the truth as he knew it. You have destroyed Summervale. The high towers of New York are no more—as is your castle, and everything else that you have built there."

"The Dark Lord is... what? Gone?"

Nicholas twitches his whiskers. "Gone, yes. For now, anyway. Evil cannot be so easily destroyed. This particular incarnation of evil will not trouble you, but you must be strong and vigilant. Evil can and will return to this land."

"Which land are you talking about?"

"Why, this one. What the Dark Lord did not understand was that your wand contained a splinter of the World Ash Tree. You were able to use that splinter, all unwitting, to create a new world of your own. So, you are here, and I am here, under a new tree. A new beginning."

The new tree is, in fact, much smaller than the World Ash Tree in Summervale. But it has room to grow here. As do I.

"It's beautiful," I say.

"Whether it remains beautiful or not is up to you," Nicholas says. "I know you have much more work to do, but I hope that you continue to look for love and beauty, rather than anger and resentment."

"Wait. What about the dwarves, and C.J.? Does that mean they are... gone?"

"Not necessarily. They represented parts of your personality, you understand. You may encounter them here, or you may not. This is a blank page, Lady Ashlyn. You must write its history. When you return, of course. It will be morning soon."

"Time to wake up."

"Yes," Nicholas says. "That, too, is a victory. One of the thousands of victories ahead of you. They may be small victories, but they add up. Remember that."

"Every little bit counts."

"Indeed, they do, if you make them count. Which you should do."

"Okay, one last question. What about Penny?"

"I know no more than you do," Nicholas says. "If I can make a recommendation?"

"Of course."

"I believe your sister asked you to pray for her."

"I know. I was surprised. I didn't think that she believed in... I don't know what you would call it. A higher power."

"Perhaps she does, perhaps she does not. But it was a wise request, and a kind one. Prayer is a comfort, and speaking professionally, comfort is what you need now. And who knows? Someone may be listening."

"Thank you, Nicholas."

"Thank you for including me in this new world. Which is called?"

"I'm not sure. I will think about it."

"That is acceptable, Lady Ashlyn."

"Maybe we cut out the 'Lady Ashlyn' bit. Maybe this is a republic now."

"As you wish. What do we do next?"

"I'm going to wake up now," I say. "When I come back, we go exploring."

### ASHLYN | APRIL 6 | WEST ORANGE, NEW JERSEY

I open my eyes to ceiling tiles, dark gray in the cold light of dawn. Other than a monitor beeping unobtrusively in the corner, the room is quiet.

"I don't know who You are," I whisper, "but maybe You can hear me anyway. I am doing my best here, just as I am. Like the Dark Lord said, alone, and scarred, and terrified for my sister. I want her to be all right. I need her. I need my family. I need to go home. Anything You can do to help me with that, well, that's what I am asking for."

I am not expecting a response, at least not right away, but that is what I get. My phone chimes, and I pick it up. The text from my dad is four words long, but it rings in my heart like a carillon. *Your sister is awake.*

# Heart's Desire

### Katie | June 14 | New York City, Presbyterian Hospital

"Okay," Katie Wright says. "I hope this is everything you wanted."

"Hand it over," Penny says.

"Starbucks. Mocha latte with hazelnut syrup and a chocolate croissant. Two Sprites and three packages of Ritz crackers with peanut butter. And two protein bars, which you did not ask for, but which you should eat anyway. Will that be enough to tide you over?"

"It's a long ride," she says, "but I think I can manage. Ashlyn says the food is okay there, which means it's terrible. Can't be much worse than here, though."

"You've been eating through your nose tube," Katie says. "Give us a little more credit."

"I had one bagel since I was here, and it was stale."

"If you'd said you wanted a good bagel, I could have gotten you one. Too late now. The van from the rehab hospital should be here any minute, or I would try to accommodate you. I don't usually do catering, you understand."

"Only for special patients?"

"Only for special patients who are taking up valuable hospital real estate."

"That answers that. And thank you. And I'm sorry."

"Sorry for what?"

"For spitting blood all over you. I never got to apologize. I mean, I had a ventilator tube stuck down my throat for a good long time, which made it hard to do that. I'm sorry. I never meant to."

"It's all right," Katie says. She has talked about it to her counselor, who has decided that she experienced a very specific trigger for her PTSD, one that's unlikely to occur again. The counselor prescribed rest and relaxation, and a college friend has a house in the Poconos. She is leaving on Friday, and is weighing an offer from Dr. Milford in dermatology, who is from Scranton and is interested in showing her around.

"I must have freaked you out."

"Yes, you did, and no, I don't want to talk about it anymore. Your ride is here."

Penny is in a wheelchair, and it's not just because of the standard hospital discharge procedure. She has lost a lot of muscle, and her skin is pale. Dr. Cotton has prescribed three weeks in a rehabilitation hospital, and as Penny's older sister is getting treatment there as well, this has lifted her spirits considerably. Katie pushes her over to the van, where an orderly in pale blue scrubs is waiting.

"Thanks again," she says. "For everything. I wouldn't have made it through without you."

"You managed all right," Katie says. "You did good. Like I told you, it's a tough experience, and you had a tougher time than most. Go and get better."

"That's a promise," she says.

The door of the van opens, and a ramp unhinges itself. A nurse, tall and dark in navy scrubs, steps out. "Hey there," she says. "Ready to take a ride?"

"Nneka!" Penny shouts! "Nneka Nneka Nneka! I didn't know you were coming!"

"How are you doing today, Miss Penny? Are they treating you well in the big city?"

"We did our best. I'm Katie Wright, transplant coordinator. I have some paperwork for you."

"That is what hospitals are there for, to keep the paper mills churning," the nurse says. "If I am going to fill all this out, I need a hug first."

Katie takes this to mean that she needs a hug from Penny, who is able to get up a fraction from her chair. "You have been through the mill," she says. "Never mind. We will get you out of that chair, see if we don't. I will take care of the paperwork now."

Katie hands over the sheaf of papers and wheels Penny up the ramp, turning the chair so that it faces forward, and fastens the wheelchair restraints. "Friend of yours?" she asks.

"Nneka has been taking care of Ashlyn—that's my sister—for months now, and keeping me informed."

"That will be nice for you both, I'm sure."

"She's going to be all competitive and weird, trying to get out of there before me."

"Okay. You're all set. Here are your snacks. Are you good?"

"I've got weeks of gossip to catch up on. I am all good."

"I'm glad that you're getting to leave in one piece. Good luck."

"Thanks. For everything." She puts her hand out, then clenches it. "Respect."

Katie completes the fist bump. "Respect."

## PENNY | JUNE 14 | NEW YORK CITY

It turns out that Nneka is a fountain of information, but the way that fountains work is that the intake has to be on par with the output. She spends the entire drive across Manhattan quizzing me on details about my current medical condition and the transplant surgery, most of which I am unfortunately unable to help her with.

"The lungs are fine, at least," I say. "Better than fine. Working as advertised. I had somebody—I mean, I think I had somebody—tell me that they were from an athlete, which is a nice thing. It's not a nice thing for them, of course, but you don't get to pick lungs off the rack."

"The wheelchair," Nneka says. "It is not for show, is it."

"Not one bit. I have a hard time even pushing it. I was flat on my back for two months and that does not do very good things to your muscle tone. I could maybe walk to the bathroom and back, if the bathroom wasn't very far away and you gave me extra time to do it."

The van completes its procession across the city and is now waiting patiently in line to enter the Holland Tunnel.

"This can be fixed, though," Nneka says. "Rehabilitation works wonders. You build up your muscles, you build up your lung capacity. Perhaps you stop drinking so much sugary coffee."

I let out a near-silent growl. The one nice thing—the only nice thing—about cystic fibrosis is that you are expected to eat like a longshoreman; creating all that mucus gives you a hearty pioneer appetite. Morton gave me three different lectures on the topic before he finally decamped back to Philadelphia. I can't eat the way I used to, not anymore, not without getting fat, and I don't have any intention of doing that. I don't have any intention on giving up on Starbucks, either, which means that I get to learn how to work out. It is a sacrifice I am not sure I am up for, but I have all summer to train before going back to school for my senior year.

"So how is Ashlyn doing?" I ask.

Nneka narrows her eyes at me. "What do you actually know?" Nneka, a reliable source of both information and too-much-information, has been quiet the last two months. I have assumed that this was out of courtesy, as I have spent a good part of that unconscious and another good part on a respirator.

"Not much. It's like everyone else has binge-watched a show that you haven't started yet, and you're behind, and you can't talk about it with anyone who's caught up. The last thing I remember is we were talking, right before the surgery, and I was teasing her about her boyfriend." I put special stress on that last word, *boyfriend.*

Nneka lets out a hooting laugh. "That one! Did no one tell you about him? He turned out to be engaged, engaged to this wicked, jealous person who said many horrible and unfair things to your sister."

"Good God. What did Ashlyn do?"

"You would have been proud of her. She walked away. Well, wheeled away. You know what I mean."

That does not sound like Ashlyn, and it worries me. "That's all she did?"

"Well. She said a bad word. Then the young man came back to her, a week later, and tried to make up with her—behind my back, the toad. He tried to apologize. Ashlyn *let him have it.*"

"Okay. That sounds more like my sister. So, did it work? Did he come crawling back?"

"No, and your sister would not have had him back. She is a very sensible person that way. He left the hospital and went back crawling to that wretched woman. Good riddance to them."

"But Ashlyn hasn't made any other... connections with anyone else since then."

"Well. No. She has not, but others have." She lifts her left hand a bit, just enough for me to notice the sparkle.

"Oh. My. God. You're engaged?"

"Believe it or not. Your sister, who is as unlucky as she can be in the romance department, played matchmaker for me and an adorable doctor, who has paid off his student loans and is looking to settle down."

"I am so happy for you."

"Thank you. Thank you so much. I am happy for me, too. I will let you know when we have a date. We are going to Nigeria first, so that he can ask permission to marry me, all of that nonsense."

"That's amazing. But how is Ashlyn doing?"

Nneka bites her lip. "I do not know if they told you this, but your sister had a seizure. Around the same time as your surgery."

"No." I feel the muscles in my neck tighten up. "Nobody told me."

"They did not want to worry you, and you had enough to worry about already. In this seizure, she hit her left hand against the bedrail, and broke several bones. She had to have surgery, over in New Brunswick."

"That can't be good." I have a hard enough time getting through the day with two good hands; how would Ashlyn get by with one?

"She was very upset by this, as you might imagine. And of course, you had a setback right after that. I was worried a good bit, let me tell you, but she pulled through. Alexander—Alexander is Dr. Lindbergh, who is Ashlyn's orthopedist and my fiancée—took the cast off on Monday."

"Does that mean she is almost ready to walk?"

"Yes. She has been walking on the treadmill, with a harness so she does not fall. Her hand should be stable enough to start walking on her own soon, with a walker for stability. She has come a long way, has your sister."

The van makes its way out of the tunnel, into the bright sunshine of a New Jersey morning. I have come a long way, too, and now I am almost home.

We pull off the highway somewhere in Essex County, but I do not know where we are except that there is a strip mall. This is New Jersey, of course there's a strip mall. This one has a TGI Friday's, which makes it seem familiar enough (there's one in Princeton at MarketFair and one at the Somerville Circle). It's early for lunch but I am hungry. We find a van-accessible parking space, and I am somehow not the least bit surprised to see a van identical to ours in the spot across the access aisle.

"This is a setup," I tell Nneka.

"This is a nice surprise for you and your sister. Unless you would rather keep driving, and eat hospital food for lunch."

"No, ma'am. No complaints here."

Nneka opens the door and the orderly pushes my wheelchair up the curb cut and into the building, and Ashlyn is there in her wheelchair, and I have to balance being glad to see her with being cool. I look behind her and there are my parents and my brothers, and my Aunt Stephanie and her husband and kids, and a lot of my high school friends, and they have balloons and signs that say WELCOME HOME.

If I was going to ever be cool in my life, it is not going to happen today. I start crying, and Mom comes over and gives me the biggest hug in the world.

I don't get to see Ashlyn right away, but I know I will have time for that in the hospital. Some of the people here are the older siblings of my friends who are friends with Ashlyn, and she is getting a chance to hang out with them, which is fine. It sounds like she could use the support from what Nneka told me. It's not long before my mom tells everyone to sit down and order, and of course I sit next to Ashlyn, wheelchair to wheelchair.

"G-glad you made it," she says, haltingly.

"Me, too. It was a very scary experience, and I'm glad it's over."

"Home. Soon," she says, as the waiter comes over.

"Yeah. Hey, look, do you know what you want? Point to it on the menu and I can order for you."

"Don't bother," Ashlyn says, then turns to the waiter. "I'm starting with the spinach and artichoke dip, and then the Cobb salad, with unsweetened iced tea to drink." Then she turns and looks at me, with a little half-smile.

"If you don't close your mouth there, Penny," my dad says, "you might swallow a fly."

"You can talk?" I ask. "I mean, for real?"

"Words and everything," Ashlyn says.

"She's been doing very well with her speech therapy," Mom says.

"YOU CAN TALK? WHEN WERE YOU GOING TO TELL ME?"

"Sweetheart, it's hard for anyone to get a word in edgewise when you're around," Dad says. I throw a balled-up napkin at him. Or I try to. It doesn't go very far.

"It started getting better about the time you went in for your s-surgery. I still have problems with some words, but I can manage," Ashlyn says.

"You. You sat there, and let me think that you couldn't string two words together, why? To embarrass me? To make me look silly?"

"No, but it seems to have worked."

I look at Ashlyn, my frustrating, overbearing, obnoxious big sister, and she has a huge grin on her face. The first one I have seen in months.

"I will get you for this," I say, "if it's the last thing I ever do. Next thing, you're going to start walking. Wait. She's not walking yet, is she? I mean, someone would tell me, right?"

"Not yet," Ashlyn says. "Not on my own. A few steps, with a walker, and an orderly at each elbow. I am walking out of there eventually, see if I don't."

"You're going to do it before me, just out of spite," I say.

"No," Ashlyn says. "Not out of spite. Out of love."

**ASHLYN | JUNE 14 | WEST ORANGE, NEW JERSEY**

Penny is in the room next door, but she is worn out from the travel and the party, and goes right to sleep. I go off to occupational therapy, and then to PT. I let them hook up the harness, and step out of the wheelchair and onto the treadmill.

Gretel starts it slowly, as she always does, and I take the first tentative steps. One foot in front of the other. I am getting better at balance, I think. I am finding the rhythm. Gretel turns up the speed to a healthy two miles per hour. I am swinging my arms, not feeling any pain in the left wrist. Tom Petty is blaring in my headphones. I am breathing a little harder now, but not laboring. I glance over to the right, and Nneka is furtively taking a video on her cellphone.

Okay, if I'm on camera, then I should put on a show. I lean forward and set the speed a notch higher. I expect to feel some resistance when I do that, from the harness, but I don't. I don't feel anything. The harness is lying loose against my shoulders.

"It's not tight enough," I tell Gretel.

"It's fine," she says. "Keep going." The typical grimace on her face is gone, replaced by something that absolutely could be an emotion.

I take out the headphones and stare over at Gretel. "Did you unhook the harness?" I ask.

"No," Gretel says. "I reduced the tension on the lift. To zero."

"That means I'm walking again."

"It would seem so, yes."

"On my own."

"That would be the case."

"You were going to tell me this when?"

"You are a smart girl, Ashlyn. You figured it out on your own. Psychology, you understand? You needed to perform without the pressure, especially with your sister here."

"How does it feel?" Nneka asks.

I am walking on my own. It feels... everything. Flowers and puppies and having my sister alive. It is my heart's desire. Or it was my heart's desire until I did it. Now I don't know what that is, but I'll figure that out.

"It feels good," I say.

"Do not sell yourself short, Ashlyn girl," Nneka says. "This is an *accomplishment*. This is something you celebrate."

"It's more than that," I say. "It is a victory." A big one this time.

# JOIE DE VIVRE

ASHLYN | SEPTEMBER 25 | NEW YORK CITY, TEN
YEARS IN THE FUTURE

It is a bright Friday morning, and I step out of the Wall
Street subway station with a song in my heart. I am
young, single, working at my dream job, and by the
way, not that it's important, my first novel is spending
its sixth consecutive week on the *New York Times*
bestseller list. Sunshine spills out of a cloudless blue
sky, lighting up the glass skyscrapers behind the gray
spires of Trinity Church.

"Ashlyn Revere, best-selling novelist," I keep
repeating to myself. It's all I can do not to tell strangers
about it, but this is New York and you don't do that in
New York.

I do not have all that far to go—two blocks north,
then turn right at the twisty red sculpture on the edge
of Zuccotti Park. My office is right across the street. It
is a short walk, but not an easy one most mornings as
the sidewalks are crowded and littered with obstacles.
I am glad for my cane—my favorite cane, the one my
father made for me, carved from ash wood. At my
insistence, he embedded a thin silver wire in a tight
spiral, running the length of the cane. I am perfectly
capable of walking without it, but the car accident I was
in eleven years ago affected my balance and
coordination, both of which are premiums on the New
York City streets. It is not an ideal solution, but it beats
being in a wheelchair all to pieces. Having the cane has
saved me from more than one serious fall. I have not
yet had the chance to foil a street robbery by using it to

trip someone, although doubtless my opportunity will come at some point.

After a quick detour through the local Starbucks, I make my way into my building and up the elevator. The publishing world shut down over August, as it does, and people are starting to realize that we have to start getting some work done so our Christmas books can make it to market. I am halfway through a scathing email to the publicity team when Ian Hornfischer darkens my cubicle.

"Can I see you in my office, please?" he asks.

I like Ian, although he labors under the mistaken premise that publishing companies ought to be profitable. I have tried, very patiently, to explain that my job is to find awesome books and publish them, not to pinch pennies. Ian is a Wharton graduate who doesn't understand anything that's not in a pivot table. He could want to chew me out for approving the travel budget for somebody's three-city book tour; it's probably something petty like that.

"Okay," I say, and gather up my cane.

"It's nothing bad," he says, which makes me worry that it is something very bad, but what that might be I cannot guess. I follow him to his office, which is distressingly free of books. I settle myself into an armchair, holding my cane in a defensive position.

Ian settles himself behind his desk and looks up with a thin smile. I don't say anything; a wise man said that you don't open your mouth until you know what the shot is. This could be anything. It could be that I'm fired. They like to fire people on Fridays. I calculate the value of my advance in my head—the advance that I had been hoping to turn into a down payment on a condo—and figure out how long I could live off it in

New York City. The answer is depressing if not disturbing.

"I wanted," Ian says, "to congratulate you." His voice sounds stiff, like he's been gargling drywall.

"Thank you," I say, which seems safe enough.

"Six weeks on the bestseller list. That's quite an accomplishment."

I give Ian my dimmest possible smile. I know it's quite an accomplishment.

"Of course, it's at another house."

*That's where this is going. Great.* "We have been over this several times," I say. "I understood that I was free to have my agent pitch my book to other houses. HarperCollins made the best offer, and I went with them. If you wanted my book, all you had to do was beat their offer. It is not my fault that the book has been successful, and that HarperCollins is reaping the reward."

"That is... not the issue," Ian says. "I mean, of course, it is, in a way. You're clearly a major talent, and we want to reward talent, in any way we can. If we can't have you as an author, we're lucky to have you as an editor. That is what we're here to talk about."

I make the circular motion with my hand that means *yeah, yeah, go on.*

Ian glowers at me, as though what he is about to say will be physically painful. "We are acquiring a new imprint; a small fantasy publisher that was based out of Boston. Their managing editor took a buyout rather than work for us. They have a small team—two associate editors and a publicist. They'll be working remotely for the time being. We're asking you to take over. You'll still report to me, but you'll have a good degree of autonomy otherwise."

"I think you said the words *managing editor.*"

"I did indeed, and there's a raise that goes along with the title." He slides me a long white envelope. "The details are in there. You can start next Monday if you accept."

"What if I don't?"

"Not a lot of these opportunities come around. The next time somebody else might get the first shot."

"What kind of budget would I be looking at?"

"Limited at first," Ian says. "Room for growth long-term, if you play your cards right. They have a couple of titles in the pipeline that look very promising—that's why we made the acquisition, not because of the quality of the editorial staff. You'll need to bring them along. I know it's a challenge, but I wouldn't have asked you to do it if I didn't think you were ready for it."

Being a managing editor of my own imprint means I will have to learn budgeting. I will have to manage a team—a remote team of people who have worked together for years and who are going to resent me on principle. I'll be stuck with authors and stories that I didn't choose, at least at first. I can do it, though. I've never backed down from a challenge before and I'm not starting now.

"I accept," I say.

Ian looks momentarily nonplussed; I think he expected me to sit here and argue with him about this, but he recovers, gives me a handshake, and walks me back to my cubicle.

"Wait. Do I get an office?"

"I'll talk to HR. I think there's a vacancy two floors up."

"By which you mean two floors away from you."

"We can talk about relocating you to Boston, if you'd like."

I recognize a threat when I hear one. "I'll take the vacancy, if there's a window."

"Okay, okay."

"Overlooking the park."

"Don't push it, Ashlyn."

"They're just *now* making you a managing editor?" Meredith says. "They should have done that years ago. You should be offended, sweetie."

"Stop," I say. "Please stop."

"You've been on the bestseller list for six weeks already. They can't move any faster than that?"

"You are stealing my joy."

"No. No I am not. I am trying to *increase* your joy, which is why I insist that you come to this party tonight."

Meredith is my agent, and my friend, and she thinks she is looking out for me by dragging me to publishing parties. She is wrong. "Can't make it. Already explained why. Quit asking me."

"If you can't think of yourself, and how going to this party might help you, can you think of me? What kind of agent can't get her *New York Times* best-selling author to come to a party? You're making me look bad."

"My sister and her husband are going out to dinner, and they need me to babysit. I agreed. Non-negotiable."

"Is that all it is? I thought this was social anxiety talking."

276

"I do not have social anxiety. Just the regular kind."

"Anyway. Leave it to me. I've already set up an Uber for you."

"I can't afford an Uber."

"I got a sneak peek at your royalties this morning, and I am telling you, as your agent, you can *definitely* afford an Uber."

I think about this for a minute. "You're not telling me that I earned back my advance already."

"That is what I am telling you. By a pretty good factor. Your bad luck that we're early on in the quarter, but you should be getting one hell of a Christmas present. Minus my fifteen percent, of course."

"Your hard-earned fifteen percent."

"Of course. I will see you at six."

"What did you do." Penny says. It's not a question.

"Me? I didn't do anything."

"I get a text that says my six-thirty dinner reservation has been cancelled. Then I get another text, telling me that I have an eight-thirty reservation somewhere else. Somewhere better, somewhere where you normally have to wait six months to get on the waiting list. Tell me that wasn't you."

"I plead innocent."

"How innocent?"

"Somewhat innocent."

"Explanation, please."

"It could be that Meredith is throwing a party, and that she asked me to drop by."

"Meredith changed my dinner reservation for my date night with my husband to accommodate you?"

"That is one interpretation of these events, I suppose. As I said, I am innocent in this matter."

"Somewhat innocent. As compared to your agent, who I assume is wholly guilty, then."

"She's your agent, too," I explain. Penny's book about Frank Lloyd Wright came out last year, published by the University of Chicago Press to excellent reviews. It did not, however, make the *New York Times* bestseller list. I have, so far, refrained from pointing this out to her.

"She was my agent before she was your agent."

"She was my friend before she was your agent. I don't see why this is such a big deal. If you're hungry, have a snack when you get home."

"Enjoy your party, while I explain to Jennifer why her Auntie Ashlyn is late."

"Thank you. I intend to."

Meredith's party is at a rooftop bar overlooking Bryant Park, which means that there aren't any dark corners where I can slink. I have to talk to people, and ask them about what they are doing, and pretend to be enjoying myself. One of the less-fun things about having a traumatic brain injury is that it is not a good idea to drink alcohol, so I am nursing a virgin banana daiquiri and trying to be humble about my recent success. Professional jealousy runs very deep in publishing circles, and you don't ever realize it until you're on the other side of it.

I am having a very interesting technical conversation with a children's book illustrator when Meredith grabs me by the elbow. "Excuse me for a moment, I need to borrow you."

"I have to leave here in about fifteen minutes," I say.

"Won't take that long. I have someone you want to meet."

Meredith propels me towards a tall, rangy man with wavy black hair who is drinking whiskey at the bar. "I found her, Drew," she says. "This is my client, Ashlyn Revere."

"Hello," I say. Would it have been so difficult for Meredith to warn me that she was introducing me to a cute guy? Apparently.

"I've been waiting to meet you," Drew the cute guy says. "I'm a big fan."

He's lying, of course, everyone who says that is lying. You can't read everything everyone publishes, so you fake it. Doesn't even bother me, especially when I'm talking to someone with flashing dark eyes and broad shoulders. "It's always nice to meet a fan," I say. If he's smart, he'll catch the hint of sarcasm, and back off.

"I was wondering where you got the inspiration for the City of the Rivers," he says. "I don't think it's New York, is it? Maybe Pittsburgh?"

"New Orleans," I say. "I went down there years ago, when a friend of mine got married."

"Oh! That makes sense. Never been there, myself, or I would have picked it up right away. The descriptions are mesmerizing."

*The cute guy has read my book. The cute guy liked my book.*

"It's the nice thing about worldbuilding," I say. "You can take the ordinary world and improve on it—or destroy it, depending on what serves the story."

"Drew knows a thing or two about worldbuilding," Meredith says. "You two keep talking; I'm getting another drink."

I get the distinct impression that I may have stepped in it. I am trying to think if I know anyone named Drew and I am coming up blank. "How do you know Meredith?" I ask.

"I met her a few minutes ago, honestly," he says. "I am one of Dawn's clients." Dawn Preston, he means, who runs Meredith's literary agency. Dawn is an agent in her own right, very well established, with lots of important writers as clients, including Andrew Davies, who *oh my God is standing in front of me.*

I will get Meredith for doing this to me if it's the last thing I ever do.

"Can I get you something to drink?" Andrew Davies says. Andrew Davies, who wrote the *Starship Infinity* series and earned two Hugo Awards in the process.

"As much as I would love a drink, it's not a good idea," I say, hoping against hope that I do not have to explain why that is not a good idea.

"Of course. What about dinner? Would that be a good idea?"

*Andrew Davies is asking me out to dinner.* "Yes. No. Wait. Yes to dinner, but no to right now. I have a previous engagement to read a bedtime story to my niece."

"Well, you can't possibly break that commitment. Unfortunately, I have a previous engagement of my own—I'm flying to Los Angeles tomorrow night. I'll be there most of next week, doing some consulting work for Pixar.”

“That sounds impressive,” I say. There is maybe a tiny little surge of jealousy when I say that, but I remember that I am Ashlyn Revere, *New York Times* best-selling author, and I don’t have to feel jealous, even if I’m talking to a two-time Hugo Award winner who has asked me out to dinner.

“Helping out a college friend on some storyboards. It’s still early in the process, and it might not go anywhere. Maybe five years down the road, my name will show up in the credits. Have they talked to you about the film rights for your book?”

“I am told we are in preliminary discussions,” I say, which is accurate, or at least I think so.

“Give it time,” Andrew Davies says. “You’ll get there. You have a cinematic touch, which is important.”

“Thank you. That’s great to hear.”

“I’m serious about dinner, though,” Andrew Davies, multiple Hugo Award winner says. “Dawn can get me your number, right? I’ll call you when I get back.”

“I’m looking forward to it,” I say. I walk towards the door, where Meredith is waiting for me.

“Well? How did it go?”

“What the absolute hell, Meredith? You couldn’t have, you know, prepared me? You couldn’t have said, oh, you know, hey, this party I’m throwing, guess what, *Andrew Davies* is going to be there, I can introduce you, he’s a big fan? And he’s *cute*. What is wrong with you?”

“You recognized him, then! Good. Dawn and I had a bet, and I won. How did it go?”

“He asked me out. I can’t believe it. Andrew. Davies. Asked. Me. Out.”

"So where are you going?"

"I don't know. He's going to California; sometime after he gets back."

"You're not going out with him now?"

"I told you. I'm babysitting."

Meredith sighs theatrically. "We need to work on your priorities. Okay. Go see your niece and read her a Harry Potter book or whatever it is you have planned to warp her mind."

"My father read her Harry Potter already. I think she has it memorized."

"Great. Another generation of fantasy readers, while literary fiction goes all to hell. Go, now, before I start having a moment."

Jennifer opens the door and gives me the biggest hug that she can, hard enough that I grab the doorframe for support. She turns five next month, big enough that I think about whether I can still pick her up and swing her around anymore. I decide against it.

"You're late," she says, wagging an accusing finger at me.

"I was at a party, and I met a cute guy," I say. "I see you're already in your pajamas." They are lavender, with a unicorn on them—in other words, of a piece with the rest of her wardrobe. Jennifer will not wear pink, which has sparked an endless (and highly entertaining, for an outsider) battle of wills with her mother.

"Yes, she's already in her pajamas," Penny says. She is wearing pink, a floral sundress. Her husband is trailing behind her, neat in an anonymous grey blazer.

"She's had her dinner, and is waiting patiently for a story."

"I came prepared for that eventuality." Working in publishing does not have a lot of perks, but I do have access to as many books as anyone could ever want; Jennifer's room is crammed with picture books from her doting aunt.

"Of course. We're leaving, Jen-Jen," and Jennifer gives her parents hugs and kisses.

"When do you think you'll be back?" I ask.

"No idea," Penny says. "As you might remember, our plans got a bit upset. We might take advantage of that. You never know."

"Gotcha."

"Enjoy. And thanks, honestly."

"I got a promotion today. Managing editor. And I met a cute guy."

"You can tell me all about it when we get back. Bye."

"And my book is still on the *New York Times* bestseller list."

"That's nice," Penny says. "See you later."

Jennifer is in bed, already, hugging her stuffed cheetah like a talisman. "What are we reading?" she asks.

"An old book, this time."

"An old book, like Harry Potter?"

"Silly. Harry Potter isn't old."

"It was in the last century. That makes it old."

"You are making me feel old, then. No, this book is even older."

She settles back against her pillow, golden curls shining in the lamplight.

"Chapter One. Down the Rabbit-Hole. Alice was beginning to get very tired of sitting by her sister on the bank, and of having nothing to do: once or twice she had peeped into the book her sister was reading, but it had no pictures or conversations in it, 'and what is the use of a book,' thought Alice, 'without pictures or conversations?'"

"Picture books are the best," Jennifer says. "You should write one."

"Maybe one day. No more interruptions."

"Okay."

"So, she was considering in her own mind (as well as she could, for the hot day made her feel very sleepy and stupid), whether the pleasure of making a daisy-chain would be worth the trouble of getting up and picking the daisies, when suddenly a White Rabbit with pink eyes ran close by her."

"Why is he a White Rabbit?"

"I'm not sure. I have a friend who is a Talking Rabbit, but he's black. Maybe I'll ask him when I see him."

Once Jennifer is for-sure, no-fooling asleep, I walk out of her room and settle in on Penny's good couch. The view is spectacular, although not panoramic. The moon is rising over the serrated ranks of apartment buildings. It is a full moon, luminous in the darkening sky. It has been a triumphant day, filled with joy, with the promise of more to come.

My phone pings, and I fish it out of my purse. It's a text, from an unfamiliar number. "This is Drew, from the party," it reads. "Meredith gave me your number. Are you free for brunch tomorrow?"

I hold my breath, not wanting to respond right away, not wanting to seem too eager or desperate. The three little dots show up in the corner, indicating that another message is coming.

"I hope I'm not moving too fast here, but I was very impressed by your book, and after meeting you in person, I would love to see you again."

"Yes," I text back to him. "Brunch would be lovely. I can't wait."

# About the Author

Curtis Edmonds is a writer and attorney living in central New Jersey. His work has appeared in *McSweeney's Internet Tendency, Untoward Magazine, The Big Jewel, Yankee Pot Roast*, and *National Review Online*. His book reviews appear on the *Bookreporter* website. He has written four novels, *Rain on Your Wedding Day, Wreathed*, and *A Circle of Firelight* and its sequel, *A Circle of Moonlight*. Other works include a flash-fiction collection, *Lies I Have Told*, and a children's picture book, *If My Name Was Amanda*, all published by Scary Hippopotamus Books.

# A Brief Factual Appendix

I don't know if you'll believe this or not, but it happened this way, and as weird as it is, I'm telling it like it happened.

September 21, 2020, a day in the life, six months into the pandemic, seven months and one day after A CIRCLE OF FIRELIGHT was introduced to an indifferent world. I was tired and sore and I made the strategic decision to give *Monday Night Football* a miss and take a hot bath. Once I settled into the water, I picked up my phone and scanned through the usual social media apps, finding a tweet by the inimitable @duchessgoldblatt which said:

*I know you're wondering why Duchess Goldblatt has been quiet lately. If you people would stop writing books I need to read, I'd have more time to talk.*

To which I responded:

*Done and done, Your Grace. Can't make myself get the first chapter to settle.*

You could look it up.

I had gone through three different versions of the first chapter of this book in the prior seven months, and I hadn't liked any of them much. I hadn't decided whether to let Ashlyn run the show, or turn the whole book over to Penny, or to have a balance between them, and how to introduce Jennifer Lamb. Also, I hadn't decided how much of the second book would take place in Summervale, or if any of it could.

This is what happened next, the inexplicable thing, the weird thing. I was sitting alone in the bathtub, and I had a word come unbidden to the surface of my consciousness, and that word was *Christmas*. Understandable enough; at the end of A CIRCLE OF FIRELIGHT, Ashlyn sets herself a goal for being home for Christmas—something that I wouldn't be able to do myself due to the quarantine.

And then another word, which was *embolism*.

Well, as we say where I grew up in Texas, good God Almighty Joe Friday. I have no idea where that came from. You know what? I used the, um, famous search engine you've probably used yourself, and looked it up and *what do you know*, there's a link between cystic fibrosis and gas embolisms, and all sorts of information about symptoms and treatment, and that gave me the structure for the first chapter.

There you go. I can't account for it. I wish I could credit Duchess Goldblatt (author of the amazing BECOMING DUCHESS GOLDBLATT), but I can't, not really. For some reason, the universe dropped those words on me when I was ready to hear them, and it was my luck that they were the right words and that I knew what to do with them.

One of the reasons this book took a long time getting started is that my father died in July 2020, of the coronavirus. I was in New Jersey, he was in Texas, and the restrictions made it so that I couldn't go see him in the hospital—and we didn't have the funeral until that next summer.

I made the executive decision not to address the coronavirus pandemic in this book—you can either pretend that both books take place in a parallel universe where the pandemic didn't happen, or that both books took place well before or well after the pandemic. I don't particularly care. All I know is that the virus is far crueler than anything that happens to my characters, and I decided that I didn't care to address it.

Some technical notes:

The line above originally read "a couple of technical notes," even though there's more than two. I used a program called SmartEdit for revisions, and there is nothing in this world that makes you feel stupider than knowing the exact number of times you use a wordy phrase like "a couple of." I highly recommend it.

A lot of the chapter titles are song titles. "Last Time for Everything" is a Brad Paisley song, so is "When I Get Where I'm Going". "Nothing But the Wheel" is a Patty Loveless song. "Useless Desires" is a Patty Griffin song. They're all about loss, which is part of what this book is about, and I wish it was about something else, but life isn't like that.

The last chapter is named for a sculpture, *Joie de Vivre*, which sits in Zuccotti Park in Lower Manhattan, and which Ashlyn passes on her way to work. (I decided that Ashlyn eventually lives in a studio apartment in Murray Hill.)

I borrowed the discussion about the NCAA men's basketball tournament from the 2010 bracket; all of

Ashlyn's picks would have panned out that year. This was the tournament where Duke beat hometown underdog Butler in the worst finish for any sporting contest since the 1981 NFC Championship game.

I put in the "breadcrumbs"—the dates and locations where the characters are—in this book because there are more characters, and they go different places. I heard several times in A CIRCLE OF FIRELIGHT that there were some readers who took a while to figure out who was speaking. I tried to make that as obvious as possible without beating readers over the had about it, but it did not work as well as I would have hoped. If the breadcrumbs help you, great, if they annoy you, well, sorry about that.

The idea for the catapult to throw Ashlyn and C.J. across the wide Hudson River was inspired by a similar scene in *Winter's Tale*, by the incomparable Mark Helprin.

The idea for having Ashlyn create a whole new world of her own with a splinter of the World Ash Tree came from *Summerland*, by Michael Chabon.

The name of Ashlyn's supervisor is borrowed from the great naval historian James Hornfischer, who sadly perished in June 2020.

If you're stealing stuff, campers, steal from the absolute best.

I never like pointing out that I am an idiot, but I admit a slight blunder. I originally had the sad death of poor Jennifer Lamb (I do hope I don't have to point out the symbolism in the name) take place during the Women's National Invitational Tournament. Because I am a stupid idiot, I assumed that the last round of the women's NIT takes place at Madison Square Garden, because the last round of the men's NIT does. (I got to go see my Baylor Bears play at the Garden in the men's NIT, some twelve years ago.) But that's not the case. The Women's NIT takes place at campus sites—and the St. John's women's team, which you would think would play at the Garden because the men's team does, in fact plays in a smaller gym on campus. I had about sixteen thousand words written at that point, leading up to the scene where Jennifer dies, and I threw up my hands at that point and said, "Fine." So, I changed around the endings of the basketball games and made the executive decision to have Madison Square Garden host an NCAA regional women's tournament, even though (clears throat) I know Madison Square Garden has never done so, and is not likely to ever do so. The alternative would have been to have Jennifer play in the Maggie Dixon tournament, which does take place at the Garden, but that's a preseason tournament which throws off the timeline of the rest of the story.

There is a little bit of basketball in A CIRCLE OF FIRELIGHT, and one reviewer from outside the United States criticized that, saying that the focus on sports made her feel like I was shoving the American flag down her throat. Not going to apologize.

I don't think that you *really* ought to use your novels to advance your personal likes and dislikes but sometimes they find their way into the narrative. I like the orange and fruit punch sports drinks a lot more than I like any of the blue flavors. (I don't actually know whether they use the blue flavor for University of North Carolina sports teams, but it seems reasonable.) Ashlyn and I both like the McDonald's sausage biscuit, although I have had to swear off them. And like Ashlyn's dad, I love Coke Zero and can't stand Diet Pepsi. I was working in Philadelphia when I was writing most of this book, and I can tell you that Penny's WaWa order approximates what I would get if calories weren't an issue. (I had a phone interview with WaWa for a job last year, and didn't get it, and was bitterly disappointed—but I still go there and my only complaint is that they are not Buc-ee's, which, as a Texan, I am obliged to tell you is superior in every way.)

The chapter where Penny and her family go to the famous department-store Thanksgiving parade you may have heard about is named after a line in Abraham Lincoln's Thanksgiving proclamation:

> *I do therefore invite my fellow citizens in every part of the United States, and also those who are at sea and those who are sojourning in foreign lands, to set apart and observe the last Thursday of November next, as a day of Thanksgiving and Praise to our*

*beneficent Father who dwelleth in the Heavens. And I recommend to them that while offering up the ascriptions justly due to Him for such singular deliverances and blessings, they do also, with humble penitence for our national perverseness and disobedience, commend to His tender care all those who have become widows, orphans, mourners or sufferers in the lamentable civil strife in which we are unavoidably engaged, and fervently implore the interposition of the Almighty Hand to heal the wounds of the nation and to restore it as soon as may be consistent with the Divine purposes to the full enjoyment of peace, harmony, tranquility and Union.*

The History Channel website says that this proclamation was written by Secretary of State William Seward, which sounds about right—it's a little flowery for Lincoln. I kind of doubted this when I first read it, but then I remembered that I used to write proclamations for George W. Bush when he was Governor, so I figured that maybe it stood to reason. (This is what's called name-dropping.) I tossed in a couple of (there's that stupid phrase again) Lincoln quotes towards the end, just to balance things out.

One of the things you will encounter in the "writing advice" section of the internet is the idea that you should write every day. This is not wrong as far as it goes. If you are going to be productive—especially if you aren't doing anything else—then yes, you should. If it's a hobby—and I cannot tell you how unhappy it makes me to admit that this is just a hobby for me, and not a particularly lucrative one—then that's less important. In fact, I will go so far to say that taking breaks from your writing can be helpful at times, particularly when you don't know what to do next. That happened at least twice in this process.

The first time was the end of the sequence set in Madison Square Garden. This was the oldest part of the tale; I knew from the outset that Jennifer Lamb would die there, and that Penny would get her lungs, and that Ashlyn would have to travel there to confront her unquiet ghost. But I didn't know how that would end. It took me longer than I would have liked to have realized that, of course, Nicholas would be the key to that scene, that only he could banish the ghost. The problem I had was that I had always envisioned Nicholas making the journey to Penny's dreams to comfort her; all of that had to come out. That required a good bit of rewriting, right at the heart of the story, but it turned out not to be that daunting (which is what everyone says when they go through an ordeal, in order to sound cool and blasé about it).

The second time was the chapter where Ashlyn returns home to an empty house and has a momentary emotional breakdown. I had initially written it where she finds her old field hockey sweatbands and recovers her will to keep fighting, but it didn't seem to fit with how the next couple of chapters would go. (One of my children was the alpha reader for the book as it went along, and one of her comments was "You need to be *nicer* to Ashlyn," and ha ha ha no.) I had the idea that Nneka would go upstairs and retrieve a stuffed animal for Ashlyn, but that seemed unnecessary, not to mention infantilizing and embarrassing. For whatever reason, the ending to that chapter held me up for weeks, and the excuse that I have for it is depression and anxiety, those two thieves. (Nneka's comment in that chapter about not talking away sadness was lifted from the late great Larry McMurtry—I think from SOME CAN WHISTLE.)

Anyway, take breaks when you need to. Your novel will still be there when you're ready to tackle it.

The struggle that Penny has with her double lung transplant was always going to be a part of this story; no way to get around it. The story was informed somewhat by the struggle of Hilary Teachout, wife of *Wall Street Journal* critic Terry Teachout, who died in 2020 after receiving a double lung transplant. I followed Hilary's story on Terry's Twitter feed—which also some years back had directed me to Jack Isenhour's book about George Jones that sparked the writing of my novel, WREATHED. Penny's story has a happier ending, but there are certain (unavoidable) similarities—the long wait for a transplant donor, the false starts, the joy when recovery seems imminent, and the despair when it doesn't. Blessings and prayers for everyone going through the ordeal.

The apartment that Penny has in her dream is, of course, utterly imaginary. The only way that she could afford to live where I have her live is for her to marry a billionaire's scion, something like that. I will counsel readers with superior knowledge of Manhattan real-estate prices to remember that this particular apartment exists in Penny's dream, the same way that Ashlyn's castle exists in hers. Our dreams do not encompass Manhattan real-estate prices; if they did, they would become out-of-control nightmares. This is in part why Penny and her daughter huddle under a Hudson Bay blanket; in your dreams, you can have anything you want and it doesn't cost anything. I would dearly love my own Hudson Bay blanket—in fact, I am looking at one on Amazon right now, and it's seven hundred dollars, and I have seven hundred dollars to spend, and all I have to do is click on "Buy Now." I am sitting here literally paralyzed with fear as to what my late parents, those stalwart stepchildren of the Depression, would have said. "You paid how much? For a blanket? You have blankets in the house already." (In counterpoint, the last carefree conversation I had with my father was about me taking the time to make a cheesecake from scratch. "Why bother?" he said. "You can buy those in the store.")

The board book that Penny reads to her daughter is *Good Night, Gorilla*, by Peggy Rathmann. And, no, I haven't violated anyone's copyright—the book has a minimal number of words; you can tell the story any way you want.

This is difficult for me to write, and there is a good chance that I am going to take this out and you won't read it.

One of the themes in A CIRCLE OF FIRELIGHT is the power of grit and resilience. Ashlyn has a very resilient personality, which is tested mightily in that book and in this one. Resilience is a pillar of what might be called the heroic personality, the ability to absorb shocks and blows and come out on top nevertheless. I believe with Bear Bryant that "the price of victory is high but so are the rewards." To take that one step further, the rewards of victory are high because you are aware of the cost.

At least that's true for most people. I have never gotten to enjoy the rewards of victory in my life, not once.

Let me give you an example. Right before I was writing A CIRCLE OF FIRELIGHT, I went back to school—I completed my master's degree work at Rutgers in December 2017. For whatever reason, Rutgers doesn't have December graduation for the master's program I was in, so the actual ceremony didn't take place until the following May. I sort of didn't want to go—I was semi-unemployed at that time, and a little touchy about it. (I would not get an actual job until September 2018, and it was with a small social services agency operating out of a strip mall—which, let me tell you, is not what I went to grad school to do.) But I went anyway, and my wife and daughters were there, and we were going to a fancy restaurant afterwards. It ought to have been a perfectly fine day.

Again, for whatever reason, Rutgers doesn't give out *magna cum laude* or *summa cum laude* awards for graduate work. (Grade inflation, I think.) What you do get, if you graduate with a 4.0, is a gold cord to wear over your shoulders in graduation. They had the graduation in the RAC—the Rutgers basketball arena—and you had to go down to the arena floor, over to the left of the student section, and they had a table set up where they were handing out the gold cords. I went over to pick up mine, because I had a 4.0, and I had earned it.

"Your name isn't on the list," they said.

I am sitting here at my desk right now, looking at my diploma up on the wall, and every time I see it, I think about that, and the way that I felt. I was angry. I was Samuel L. Jackson mushroom-cloud levels of angry. I handled it in a mature, reasonable, level-headed way. I brought up my transcript on my cell phone, showed it to them, proved to them that I had earned that stupid, ridiculous-looking cord. And they gave it to me, although begrudgingly, with obvious sourness and hurt feelings on their part. This was three-plus years ago, and I am still mad about it, and the force of that emotion all but negated the feeling of accomplishment that I ought to have experienced after completing a year and a half of hard work on my part. Graduating was a victory, but I never got to enjoy it. And in thinking about that, I realized that I was dumping a lot of my psychological problems on Ashlyn.

This is... well, it isn't nice, but it's understandable. This is what writers do, sometimes. We create these characters, and they look back at us, and sometimes—like poor Katie Wright—we see our own faces looking back.

My guess, my absolute best guess, is that this is my last novel. I certainly *could* write another novel, but I don't feel driven to do that, but I figure that four novels should be plenty for anyone who, admittedly, isn't selling that much in the way of novels. I doubt that it is the last *book*, but my next projects are pulling me in different directions. I may feel differently in ten years, who knows. I may come across a project I can't turn down. I have a completed baseball novel that I could brush up, and a completed road-trip novel, both of which are safely in a Dropbox subdirectory, and would take a mort of work to get either of them ready even for self-publication.

My advice to anyone who wants to write a novel is this: it's easier than you think. At least the writing is. The process of getting published through the traditional means is utterly brutal; don't walk through that door unless you feel you need to (and duck right out again if you have to). It's a meaningful accomplishment, one that you can take to your grave, and if you do it right, you'll touch people you don't even know. You might as well try. As Lyle Lovett, the sage of Southeast Texas, once said (paraphrased to avoid copyright issues); you have to at least try, because what would you be if you didn't at least try?

I at least tried. Maybe I didn't get very far. I can look on my shelf, and see my books, and that sparks joy on some days, and maybe you don't need much more than that.

I am just adding this to the print version, because I figure if you are reading this on a Kindle, you probably don't care a great deal about typography. (Maybe you do! I care a great deal about typography, and I use the Kindle phone app a lot, but that is more about me getting older and not being able to read small print as well as I once could.)

Okay. The text of the book is Georgia 12, like a boss. The headings and the chapter titles are in Medusa Gothic, which was created by a guy named Dennis Ludlow and is very sharp—it was *perfect* for the book cover, and (since I had to pay for it) I decided to use it throughout. (If you have an older version of A CIRCLE OF FIRELIGHT, it uses a cool font called Charlemagne, but I switched the newer version over to Medusa Gothic.)

The dinkuses—those are the little glyphs between chapter segments; there's one at the top of this page—are ideograms, specifically Japanese *kanji*—the one for this book means *moon*, and it's circled, because the name of this book is A CIRCLE OF MOONLIGHT. Get it? Get it? Anyway, yeah. That's about it for typography.

Curtis Edmonds
October 2021
Duckthwacket House, New Jersey

www.ingramcontent.com/pod-product-compliance
Lightning Source LLC
Chambersburg PA
CBHW071413200726
48294CB00002B/384